Big Bucks

A Small Town Murder Mystery

Kirsten Weiss

MISTERIO PRESS

About Big Bucks

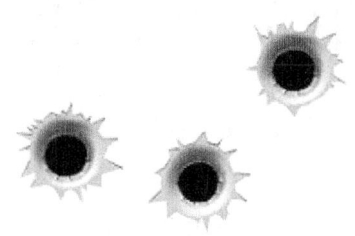

Another Small Town. Another Big Murder.

I'm Alice, a thirty-something ex-bodyguard, and DNA tests are the Devil. My brother Charlie took one, and it turns out he's only my half-brother. Our parents aren't around to explain things, but Charlie tracked down his real father, in the fancy-pants spa town the hill over. Charlie's father is loaded. Or he was until someone killed him.

Now Charlie, high off helping me solve a murder last month, has decided he's going to find his father's killer. I'm not sure if it's pride, or delusion, or… No, that's not fair. Charlie cares. This hurt him. Bad. I'm going to have to solve this murder—and fast—before his rich new relatives eat him alive.

Big Bucks is the third book in the Big Murder Mystery series. If you like laugh-out-loud mysteries, relationships with heart, and stories about figuring out where you belong, you'll love *Big Bucks*. Buy the book and start the quirky cozy mystery today.

Murder mystery game in the back of the book!

Contents

Copyright	VII
Chapter One	1
Chapter Two	16
Chapter Three	26
Chapter Four	33
Chapter Five	43
Chapter Six	53
Chapter Seven	63
Chapter Eight	70
Chapter Nine	80
Chapter Ten	89
Chapter Eleven	96
Chapter Twelve	109
Chapter Thirteen	117
Chapter Fourteen	127
Chapter Fifteen	135
Chapter Sixteen	142
Chapter Seventeen	148

Chapter Eighteen	157
Chapter Nineteen	165
Chapter Twenty	172
Chapter Twenty-One	179
Chapter Twenty-Two	189
Chapter Twenty-Three	198
Chapter Twenty-Four	207
Chapter Twenty-Five	216
Chapter Twenty-Six	223
Chapter Twenty-Seven	232
Chapter Twenty-Eight	239
Chapter Twenty-Nine	245
Chapter Thirty	251
Chapter Thirty-One	258
A Hot Springs Murder RPG	264
More Kirsten Weiss	294
Get Kirsten's Mobile App	298
About the Author	299
Connect with Kirsten	300

Copyright

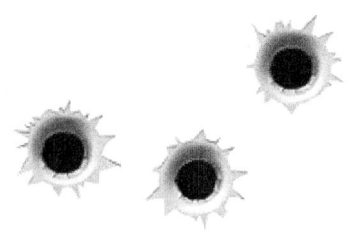

THIS BOOK IS A work of fiction. Names, characters and incidents are either the product of the author's imagination or are used fictitiously. Any resemblance to actual persons, living or dead, is entirely coincidental.

Copyright ©2022 Kirsten Weiss. All rights reserved, including the right to reproduce this book, or portions thereof, in any form. No part of this text may be reproduced, transmitted, downloaded, decompiled, reverse engineered, or stored in or introduced into any information storage and retrieval system, in any form or by any means, whether electronic or mechanical without the express written permission of the author. The scanning, uploading, and distribution of this book via the Internet or via any other means without permission of the publisher is illegal and punishable by law. Please purchase only authorized electronic editions, and do not participate in or encourage electronic piracy of copyrighted materials.

The publisher does not have any control over and does not assume any responsibility for author or third-party websites and their content.

Visit the author website to sign up for updates on upcoming books and fun, free stuff: KirstenWeiss.com

misterio press / print edition July, 2022

ISBN-13: 978-1-944767-83-9

Chapter One

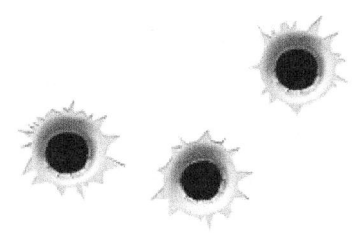

Some people enjoy a challenge. Me? I'm thrilled with easy when I can get it—which isn't often. So invading a wooded estate with no guards or cameras seemed like a day at the spa. Just without the massages, cucumber water, and saunas. I really missed those.

And because the big house was so secluded, the odds of a neighbor reporting me were low. It was unlikely anyone would spot me on the thick hillside. But I'd taken care to wear white to blend in with the patches of December snow between the pines. I was happy with easy, but I also liked to play it smart.

The effortlessness of the surveillance gig should have been a clue that things were fated to go sideways. But if the universe has been sending me warning messages, they'd been going to spam.

A breeze rustled the pines, dropping clods of snow to the earth. Kneeling, I peered through my camera on its tripod. Cold seeped through the knees of my white jeans.

The mansion had massive arched windows at the back. They gave me a clear view of a wide, marble stairway leading to the ground floor living area as well as of most of the second floor. It was a nice place if you liked oversized mausoleums.

A woman slumped in a wheelchair at the top of the steps. Her white hair hung lank and unbrushed down her back.

"Dammit." Mrs. Stanton had been sitting there over thirty minutes. I worked to tamp down my anger. This was a job. I needed to stay cool because hot emotions rarely led to good decisions. And this neglect would be going in my report. But it was hard to watch.

I'd been watching her for days now, and she was starting to feel like a friend. Not that I'm in the habit of stalking my actual friends. And I *still* didn't have any video to prove elder abuse, aside from this stretch of neglect.

I double-checked the camera was recording then shifted to look through my second camera, also on a tripod. I scanned the rooms in the upper stories.

A thirty-something brunette, Mrs. Stanton's niece, Irene, sat at Mrs. Stanton's dressing table. Irene tried on a pair of jewel-studded earrings. She turned her head this way and that, admiring, and fluffed her long hair.

I snapped photos, my heart solidifying to something cold and hard. But the niece didn't put the jewelry in her pockets. She carefully returned them to their box, rose, and strolled from her aunt's bedroom.

"Take your sweet time, why don't you?" I muttered.

I shivered and glanced up. The sun was already low over the Sierras. Soon it would be gone, and the temperature would drop. I tightened my ivory jacket and flipped up the faux-fur collar. My breath steamed the air.

The niece reappeared at the top of the stairs, and I grunted. "Finally." *Give the old lady a break and some conversation.*

She grasped the wheelchair's handles, bent, and said something to Mrs. Stanton. I stilled, unease spiraling in my gut. Mrs. Stanton turned to her. The older woman's eyes widened, her face contorting. Irene shoved her wheelchair down the stairs.

The wheelchair jounced, tilted. Mrs. Stanton tumbled from the chair.

Swearing, I jolted to my feet, knocking over the nearest camera, and bulleted across the lawn, clear of patches of snow. I was reacting, not thinking. This was never a good state for a personal protection specialist. And it's not like this was the first time I'd witnessed violence. But it had still startled the hell out of me.

I raced up the flagstone steps and across a broad patio toward the French windows. They'd be locked. They always were. But I didn't slow.

The wheelchair had plummeted to the bottom of the stairs and lay on its side. Incredibly, the old lady clung to one of the bannisters near the top.

The niece walked slowly down the two steps to her and knelt, then stood. She raised a foot over the old woman's hand.

I cursed, raised my elbows in front of my face as both cover and battering ram, and jumped through the glass doors. Elbows were some of the hardest parts on a body. They were great for fighting at close quarters and for crashing through windows.

At least in theory. I'd never actually done it before.

The glass shattered into harmless pebbles, and the broken panes clawed at my skin. I landed, and my boots slipped on the safety glass. Windmilling my arms like a cartoon coyote, I skidded across the floor. By some miracle, I didn't land on my butt. I charged up the stairs.

The niece's eyes grew large as silver dollars. She gaped. "Get out! Get out!"

I jammed my palm heel into her chest. The force of it knocked her onto her butt. Dismissing the niece, I knelt beside Mrs. Stanton.

The niece scrambled to her feet. She tore up the steps and down the hallway. Her shoes clack-clacked on the marble floor. "I'm calling the police. Help! Police!"

That was Irene's idea of calling the cops? I shook my head. "I'm Alice Sommerland," I told Mrs. Stanton. "I work for a private investigator." And I wasn't happy that my last three assignments had been catastrophically exciting.

Don't get me wrong. You didn't get into surveillance if you weren't looking for a certain level of intrigue. But my past surveillance work hadn't been quite so action oriented. I was closing in on forty, and this seemed the wrong time of life to be getting *more* physical.

"Can you put your arm around my neck?" I asked.

"I think so." Her voice quavered. Though in fairness, mine hadn't been perfectly steady either. Her eyes were wide and frightened, and her fear made me angrier.

"Don't worry. I've got you." I was pleased to note the tremor had gone from my voice. *Cool and professional.*

I helped her down the marble stairs. She was light as the proverbially bird. And though I'm a beanpole—nearly six feet tall and lean muscled—it was still slow going. I didn't want to injure her more than she'd already been hurt. At the bottom, I righted her wheelchair. I helped her inside it, giving the downstairs a better look.

The end tables were bare, and there were no chairs or carpets in the wide room. I was willing to bet the niece had sold them off. A breeze from outside flowed through the smashed French door. I pulled the throw blanket from the back of the wheelchair and put it around her shoulders.

I dialed my current employer, Fitch Rhodes, PI. Just to be clear, I was *not* a PI—just a down-on-her-luck contractor who was very good at surveillance.

"Anything?" he asked, brisk.

I took Mrs. Stanton's hand. It trembled in mine. "Attempted murder," I said. "The cops are on their way. Ah, and they might arrest me. The niece got the call in first." You always want to be the first party to call the cops. The first person to talk is always more believable.

Fitch seemed to know this rule too because he swore long and colorfully. "I'll call and report." He hung up.

"You have glass in your hair," Mrs. Stanton said.

I reached up and pulled my blond ponytail forward. It glittered. I shook it experimentally. Tiny chunks of glass pinged to the marble floor.

"She moved my Motherwell," she said.

I glanced at her, startled, and she pointed. "I've been staring at that blank spot on the wall for thirty minutes. She moved it."

"You had a Francis Motherwell?"

"I would hardly have said she moved it if I didn't have one," she said dryly. "She's always moving my things. You know Motherwell?"

"I took some art history courses in college." And a Motherwell would go for a pretty penny. Mrs. Stanton would be lucky if it was still in the house.

"I've called the police," her niece yelled from somewhere upstairs.

"Piss off," Mrs. Stanton hollered back.

I blinked. So, that was unexpected.

"See? See what I have to deal with?" Irene shouted. "She's crazy."

"On occasion my husband employed salty language for emphasis," Mrs. Stanton confided. "I do hope you're not offended."

"Ah. No." I sat on the stairs beside her. "I occasionally enjoy some emphasis myself."

She laughed quietly and buried her head in her hands. "Oh, goodness. This isn't funny at all. I do believe I'm a bit hysterical."

"You've got reason to be." I paused. "Your friend, Mr. Harrington, was worried about you."

"Is that who sent you?" Mrs. Stanton raised her head. "Franklin. Such a dear. But I haven't seen him for..." She rubbed her wrinkled brow. "He used to come for tea every Wednesday. I don't know why he stopped."

"Your niece told him you were too ill for visitors."

She sat up straighter. "But I'm not." Twin spots of pink rose to her wrinkled cheeks. "Aside from this." She motioned toward her legs. "But that's not—" She crumpled forward, her head in her hands. "That girl really tried to kill me, didn't she?" she whispered.

"She won't try it again." I reached out to comfort her, then withdrew my hand, uncertain. Comforting shaken survivors hadn't been part of my old career. I wasn't sure what the procedure was. I cleared my throat. "She's..." The words died on my lips.

A metal dog on spindly legs minced through the broken door and across the glass. I froze, ice rippling down my spine. I'd never seen anything like it. But having grown up on a diet of *Terminator* movies, I was prepared for us not to be friends.

The robot dog's head panned right and left. Its glowing blue eyes stopped to fix on me. My temperature dropped several more degrees.

"Mrs. Stanton," I said, without moving my lips. "I'm guessing that's not normal."

"No," she said shakily.

And then I registered the letters in white on its dark-blue back: TTHSPD. The Town of Hot Springs Police Department had a robodog. I rolled my eyes. Of course they did.

Two police officers in crisp navy stepped carefully through the shattered French window. Their guns were drawn and aimed at the floor.

I forced my breathing to slow. Cops were human and made mistakes like anyone else. And I wouldn't like it much if they made a mistake with me. I kept my free hand on my knee where they could see it.

"We got a call about a disturbance," the taller cop said. He looked to be in his early forties, just a few years older than me. And though most men looked good in uniforms, his was particularly effective. I had it on good authority that the Hot Springs PD had—I kid not—its own tailor.

"My niece tried to kill me," Mrs. Stanton said in a shaky voice.

"I'm not her niece," I said quickly. "She's upstairs." Probably making off with the jewelry.

"Who are you?" the other cop asked. His hair was reddish beneath his hat.

"Alice Sommerland. I'm a contract worker for a private investigator from Reno, name of Fitch Rhodes. I've been surveilling the niece due to suspected abuse."

"You're from Reno?" he asked.

I *wish*. "No, I'm from Nowhere."

The two men glanced at each other, their expressions growing warier. "Nowhere," one said flatly.

"Relax, will you?" I said. "Just because our town hall has a fifty-foot lawn flamingo is no reason to get difficult." Nowhere's collection of record-breaking big things was the envy of... nowhere. "Hot Springs is special all on its own."

"It's The *Town* of Hot Springs," the redheaded cop said.

I snorted. "Whatever."

"We're opening a miniature museum next year," the taller one said.

I swore. I'm a reasonable person, but that was a direct slap at Nowhere's big things. I wondered if our temporary mayor knew. "And what's with the robot?"

"It's a police dog," the tall one said.

I crossed my arms. "Don't get me wrong, but if that's a police dog, you're doing something seriously wrong. I mean, look at it. It barely comes up to my knee."

Things got weird after that. The cops managed to be super polite while treating me like I was radioactive. The niece tried to claim I was a criminal, which I'd pretty much expected. But between Mrs. Stanton's testimony and my video, which had kept recording, we cleared up that lie quick enough.

An hour later, the first faint stars had appeared in the sky. I stood outside Mrs. Stanton's front gate. The ambulance's taillights faded in the distance. Mrs. Stanton would be okay. Fitch had called Mr. Harrington, and he'd meet her at the hospital.

Outside the mansion's imposing front steps, the police guided a cuffed Irene into a black and white. Bending over, I pulled the band out of my hair and shook it out. More glass pattered to the ground.

I sighed. My new life of low-paid odd jobs in a town called Nowhere stretched before me, and it didn't look half bad. It looked *mostly* bad.

Someday, I was going to reclaim my old career in the personal protection industry. I had to. But I hadn't been arrested, and no one had died, so I'd call this day a win.

The phone rang in my jacket pocket. I answered without looking. "Whatever you said did the trick," I said. "The cops have the niece in custody."

"What niece?" my brother Charlie asked. "Where are you? I'm at the theater and you're not here."

I tugged on my ear. *Whoops.* Was I supposed to be at Nowhere's dinner theater? I didn't remember agreeing to that. "I'm on a job."

"Cool. You're a detective again? Where?"

"I'm not a detective. It's surveillance." I winced guiltily. "And I'm in Hot Springs."

"It's The *Town* of Hot Springs. They get really tense when you just call it Hot Springs. And why didn't you tell me you're there?"

I grimaced. I'd been trying to give my brother space as he got to know his new family. He'd recently discovered our dad wasn't his biological father. His real father was the head of a tech company and lived in a mansion here, in Hot Springs.

I'd gone with Charlie for their first meeting. After the initial shock and suspicion (and a private investigator), Adan Levann had stepped up. The tech gazillionaire had embraced my brother—literally and metaphorically. They'd gotten on so well, Charlie had moved out of his treehouse and into Adan's home.

I admit, I wasn't too happy about him moving to Hot Springs. But I was trying to be a supportive adult. It wasn't as easy as I'd have liked. "I'm on my way home now," I said. "Want to grab dinner?"

"No, no. You stay there. Adan said he wants to meet you. I mean, he met you once, but that was a weird time. He wants to get to know you. And he thinks he can help you with your PR problem."

My heart jumped. Could he? Then I got ahold of myself. I didn't want any favors from strangers. Okay, I wanted them, I just didn't want to pay the inevitable price. "It's fine. I don't need help."

"Yeah, yeah. Can you meet me at the house? I'll be there in thirty minutes."

I started to say no then stopped myself. This was important to Charlie. And if Adan and his kids were part of Charlie's family now, I needed to get with the program. "Sure. Thirty minutes."

We said our goodbyes and hung up. I returned through the gates and found a cop. She gave me permission to leave with my equipment. They kept the memory cards from my cameras as evidence though. I'd expected that too, but it annoyed me anyway.

I collected my cameras, packed them in my black Jeep Commander. Clipboard braced against the steering wheel, I wrote a brief report on the form I kept for such a purpose. Then I drove to Charlie's new home.

When I said Charlie had been living in a treehouse, I hadn't been speaking figuratively. He'd been crashing in an actual treehouse in an actual tree. I can only imagine what the private investigator his bio-dad had hired had thought of that.

Since the weather had turned, I was glad Charlie had found less drafty and squirrel-free digs. But the Levann mansion had a San Quentin atmosphere.

At the gate, I pressed a button and announced my arrival to the butler. Yes, Charlie's new father had an honest-to-goodness butler. His dulcet voice informed me I was expected, and the gates buzzed and swung open. Glancing at the modern security camera above the gate, I took my foot off the brake.

I drove down the winding, gravel road and parked beside a blue Tesla in the circular driveway. The sun had sunk behind the western hills. Pinpricks of stars dotted the sky above the gothic manor's gabled roofline.

I shook my head and climbed the brick steps to the front door. It sprang open before I could ring the bell.

"Hey!" Charlie emerged and gave me a hug. My brother was as tall as me (five-ten), and just as blond. His hair was not as long as mine, but it was past his ears to his chin. He finger combed it behind his ear and grinned. "You rocked the timing," he said. "I just got here." The butler, Shelley, stood behind him looking haughty in his gray business suit and perfect blond hair.

I glanced down at Charlie's navy blazer. He was wearing it over navy board shorts, but that wasn't what raised my eyebrows. The jacket had a yachting emblem over the breast. "Seriously?" I asked. "A yachting jacket?"

He patted the gold embroidered logo. "Cool, huh? It's from Adan's club."

"A yacht club in Nevada? Sure. Why not. Aside from the fact that the state's landlocked."

"The club's in California. The place is awesome. There are all sorts of, you know, yachts and stuff. He took me there last week. We flew in his private plane and everything. You're really going to like him." Charlie ushered me, my feet dragging, inside the high-ceilinged foyer.

Adult. I'm a mature adult and this is all good. Black and white marble tiles. An elegant and useless round table in the center, its vase overflowing with freshly cut flowers. Twin curving staircases, carpeted in crimson, ascended to the second floor.

"May I take your jacket, ma'am?" Shelley asked.

"Um, sure. Thanks." I began to shrug free. He whisked behind me and helped me out of my thick jacket.

"Thanks," I said again, feeling awkward. In my job, I'd been around a lot of wealthy people, but I'd rarely been treated like one. It felt weird. Unnatural. Or maybe it was just Shelley.

The butler was six-one and with lean muscles that were built for speed and power. I didn't like letting people get that physically close unless I trusted them. And I didn't trust Shelley.

"Would you like a comb, madam?" he asked.

My eyes narrowed. My hair wasn't that messy.

"There seems to be some glass in your hair," he said.

"It's fine." What was it that was so familiar about the man? I really hoped I hadn't spotted him in a mug book.

"Hey, Shelley, where's Adan?" Charlie asked in a half-whisper.

"I believe you'll find him upstairs in his room."

"Thanks. Come on." My brother climbed the stairs, and I trailed behind. "You need to see my room. It's got its own fireplace and everything."

"That's great," I said gloomily. *Adult. Supportive.* I forced a smile.

"Uh, why is there glass in your hair?"

"I jumped through a window."

"Okay..." He scratched his beard. "Uh, why? I mean, no offense, but I'm usually the one who goes through windows."

That's what *he* thought. "It seemed like a good idea at the time. How's the rest of Adan's family adjusting?" I asked, changing the subject.

His nose crinkled. "They just need to get used to me. Holli's been super cool though."

"Adan's new wife?"

"She's not that new. I mean, they've been married three years. And don't worry about all this." Charlie motioned toward the top of the wide stairs. "I know it's not really my vibe. But this is only temporary, until I find a full-time job."

"Full-time? Are you going to give up your work at the theater?"

"No way. The theater's my family." He colored. "I mean, you're my family too. And so is Adan and—"

"It's okay. I get it." Life had been a lot simpler before genetic testing had become a fun way to pass the time.

"But Adan had this amazing idea," he said. "He thinks I can sell my murder mystery games outside the theater. We're developing a game set in The Town of Hot Springs. Adan's got a contact at the Chamber of Commerce that can help promote it. The murder sites are going to be connected to actual locations in one of The Town of Hot Springs tourist brochures. Cool, right?"

It would have sounded a lot cooler if he'd stop saying *The Town of Hot Springs*. But selling the game outside the theater wasn't a bad idea.

"It's a good opportunity," I admitted. And I was impressed Adan was helping my brother with something Charlie loved. It might have been easier to give him a nothing job at Adan's company.

"What was this job you had in The Town of Hot Springs?" Charlie asked.

"An elder abuse case."

"Whoa." He stopped at the top of the stairs, the skin between his blue eyes puckering. "What kind of person would do that? I mean, I know it goes on, but that's terrible."

"Not anymore. I got the woman on video trying to harm the victim. The police have her in custody now."

"*Did* she hurt her?" he asked.

A cold lump formed in my chest. "Not badly." But the knowledge that to her niece, Mrs. Stanton was only money, only a means to an end, only a thing to be rid of... That hurt would take longer to heal than the bruises.

We walked down a long hallway, its thick carpet absorbing the sound of our footsteps. The lump in my chest turned to something else. Adan was the man who could have blown up my parents' marriage. I wasn't sure I wanted to sit down for a friendly chat.

And yet I had so many questions. I just wasn't sure I wanted the answers. The hallway seemed to grow narrower, the thick carpet higher, the air thicker. But I was an adult, and this meeting meant something to my brother.

Charlie stopped in front of a wood-paneled double door. "Are you ready for this?"

"I'm on the edge of my nonexistent seat."

He lowered his chin, tilting his head.

I laughed a little. "I'm ready." I grasped his hands. "I'm happy for you. Really. It's just a lot to adjust to."

"I know. But it's not going to change me."

Wouldn't it? How could it *not* affect him? "No, of course not," I said quickly.

"Okay." He drew a deep breath. "Ready? Ta-dah!" He swung open the door on a darkened room.

I frowned into the shadowy space.

He looked inside. "Oh. Energy saving lights." My brother stepped inside and flicked on the switch. He made a sweeping gesture with one arm. "Ta-dah!"

I gaped. An older version of my blond brother lay face down on the carpet, blood trickling from behind his ear. Adan Levann.

Chapter Two

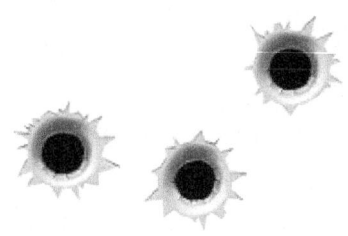

SHOCKED, I SWAYED, THEN hurried to kneel beside the fallen man. I took his pulse. There was none. His eyes were blank and open and dead, dead, dead. His longish blond hair, threaded with silver, spilled out upon the thick, golden carpet.

Charlie's birth father. Good God. I swiveled on one knee to face my brother.

He gripped the doorframe. His entire body sagged, his jaw hanging open. "That's... Is he okay?"

We'd lost our father—the man who'd raised us—five years ago. I hadn't been here when the accident had happened. It had taken me two days to get home from my assignment in Uzbekistan. Two days when Charlie had been on his own. When I'd finally arrived, I'd found a dazed wreck, Charlie's hair lank and uncombed, clothing stained and smelling.

And now this sudden, awful death, obviously murder. "Charlie." I could barely get his name out. My chest ached. "I'm so sorry. He's gone."

My brother's legs folded, and he sat cross-legged inside the door. "No."

Swallowing, I pushed away the horror and mentally recorded the details of the bedroom scene. Though he was a good thirty years older, Adan bore a startling resemblance to my brother. Today they were even dressed alike in identical Navy suit jackets. But Adan wore khaki slacks instead of shorts.

A small, iron figurine of a dog lay beside the fallen man on the thick carpet. Blood stained one of its metal paws.

Though the light was on, the bedroom still seemed strangely dark. Belatedly I realized it was because its walls were near-black. The unlit fireplace seemed to fade into them. The four-poster bed was a study in shadows. And Adan was dead. I couldn't help him. But I could help my brother.

"I'm sorry," I repeated. I crawled across the thick carpet to him and sat beside him, slung my arm over his shoulders. His muscles were stiff beneath the fine fabric of his navy blazer. Beside my boot, a matching thread snaked across the sand-colored carpet. "We'll get through this," I said.

He scraped a hand through his hair. "But... he was alive." His voice cracked. "I was just getting to know him. I barely knew him at all. He was alive."

Lifting one hip, I pulled my cellphone free. "I need to call the police." I glanced at the time. *Five-ten.*

"Someone killed him," he said.

"It looks that way," I said levelly.

"But... Why would someone kill him?"

My brother wasn't asking for an answer. He knew I didn't have one. This was shock speaking, and I looked away, blinking. He was still trying, and failing, to process his father's death. And I didn't know how to help him. I'd done a rotten job of it when our father had died. Why were physical crises so much easier to manage than emotional ones?

I called nine-one-one. The extremely polite dispatcher agreed to send emergency assistance tout suite.

Her tone turned frostier when I gave her my name. But I guessed the Hot Springs PD had a small dispatch department. The dispatcher could have been the same woman who'd taken Fitch's call earlier.

I hung up and pocketed the phone. "We should go downstairs and wait for the police."

"Right," Charlie said, unmoving. "Right."

"I see you found Mr. Levann," a man said from behind us, and Charlie and I both twitched. I scrambled to standing.

The butler, Shelley, stood in the hallway, his blond head cocked, his gray suit immaculate, his broad shoulders tight. I'd no idea how long he'd been standing there. Judging by his smooth expression, I guessed it had been for more than a moment. But his face wasn't entirely smooth. Something sparked in his eyes. I thought it might be anger.

"I just got off the phone with the police," I said. "They should be here soon."

"In that case," he said stiffly, "I'll inform the family tea will be served in the drawing room." The butler strode away, his footfalls silent in the long hallway.

Well, damn. I liked men who were cool in a crisis, but this was chilly to the point of unsettling.

I helped Charlie stand, closed the bedroom door, and realized I might have messed up any fingerprints. Grimacing, I shook my head. I still hadn't gotten a handle on this private detective business.

On the other hand, I still wasn't a PI. I was surveillance. And personal protection. But mainly surveillance now. I think Fitch might have filled out some paperwork on me for the state. But that was his business. And I was letting my mind rehash trivialities rather than focusing on my brother.

"Where's the drawing room?" I asked.

Charlie swallowed. "Oh. Right. It's downstairs. This way."

I followed him down the stairs and toward the back of the house. We passed several open doorways until we reached a drawing room straight out of a BBC special. The walls were covered in red silk and paintings in gilt frames. Holly and white twinkle lights swagged the carved, white marble fireplace. It was an idyllic holiday tableau if you ignored the body upstairs.

Picture windows overlooked the rear of the property. A waning moon illuminated the scene—a wide lawn cascading toward pine-covered hills. I wondered about the security at the rear. There'd been a camera at the front gate, but I hadn't seen any on the exterior of the mansion.

Charlie dropped onto a striped couch. "I'm glad you're here. I mean, I'm sorry you have to deal with this too, but I'm glad you're here."

I sat beside him. "Me too. About being glad, I mean." I'd only met his other family once before. They'd been about as welcoming as a school of piranhas. There was no way I was leaving him alone with them under these circumstances.

A young woman in gray cashmere sweats, her cropped green hair rumpled as if she'd just gotten out of bed, slouched into the room. She stopped just inside the doorway, her round face pale, her eyes wide behind her glasses. "I saw him. It's real. He's dead."

This was Adan's youngest, his daughter Adalina. She was plump and five-foot-two. The green hair gave her the look of an elf who took her Christmas cookies seriously.

I frowned. "You saw him?"

Charlie leapt to his feet. "Addy, I'm so sorry." He lifted his hands up and let them fall.

"Unless you killed him, I don't see what you have to be sorry about." She adjusted her thick glasses and peered at him. "You didn't kill him, did you?"

Charlie took a step back, bumping into the couch. "No. Of course not."

"You saw your father?" I repeated.

"When Shelley told me... I had to..." As if her strings had been cut, she dropped onto a red-and-gold striped Edwardian chair. Adalina met my gaze. "And you're here, too."

"Yes," I said. "I'm very sorry for your loss."

A man strode into the drawing room and scowled. "Is this some joke?" Her brother, Arystarch, was tall and lean with dark hair. He wore a paint-stained smock over his black turtleneck and black woolen slacks. His long fingers were colored with paint as well. I still wasn't sure how to pronounce his name. I planned to get around this with judicious use of pronouns. Lots of pronouns.

"I don't know Charlie well," Adalina said tiredly. "But I don't think Shelley would be in on a joke that tasteless."

Arystarch tilted sideways, and he grasped the back of the couch we sat on. His knuckles whitened. "Then he's dead? He's really dead?"

"I've seen him." His sister blinked rapidly and looked away. "He's upstairs."

He shook his head. "But that's—" A feminine shriek echoed through the house.

Adalina rolled her eyes. "It's Holli. Quick, lock the doors, Charlie."

"But we can't..." My brother leaned closer to me. "We can't lock her out," he whispered. "She's his wife."

Adalina snorted. "Right."

A petite brunette in her twenties burst through the tall, white doors. "He's dead? Adan can't be dead." Her curves strained against her ivory minidress. The dress had gold zippers in odd places. They could have been décor or necessity. Maybe she'd needed all those zips to squeeze into the thing.

Holli burst into tears. She threw herself at Arystarch, gripping him in a desperate hug.

He stood stiff, his arms limp at his sides. "There, there," he said tonelessly.

The butler wheeled in a tea cart, and suddenly the room felt small, crowded. I wanted to run. Charlie and I didn't belong here. The knees of my white jeans were stained with damp and dirt from squatting on that hillside. My Henley was a little too short. I didn't belong here.

But Charlie did belong. Or at least he had, for a time.

"Thank God." Adalina heaved herself from the chair. She went to examine the goodies. The tea cart had been piled with scones and Christmas cookies, tiny sandwiches and tea. Those I understood. The blue canisters with soft plastic cups on their ends baffled me.

She grabbed a canister, put the end over her face, and inhaled, her chest swelling. *Oxygen.* It was all the rage in Hot Springs—not because of the altitude or ill health, because it was trendy. And expensive.

Charlie cleared his throat. "So, have you all been here all afternoon?" He had a mulish, determined look on his face that worried me.

I shot him a sharp look. I do occasional work for a PI, but not too long ago, my brother had thought *he* could be a detective. The universe of things that could go wrong if he got involved now was vast and deadly.

Adalina turned and removed the oxygen canister from her face. "What part of work-from-home don't you understand?" She flushed. "Of course I was here."

I folded my arms. Her reaction had been unreasonably defensive. Or she was just devastated by her father's death and reacting badly. That *wouldn't* be so unreasonable, but she didn't look all that devastated. Sad and shocked, yes. Devastated, no.

"When's the last time you saw your father?" Charlie's jaw set.

My mouth tightened. My little brother *was* playing detective.

"Around three," she said. "He came into my office to ask if I'd seen Barney. I hadn't." She returned the canister to her face and inhaled.

"Barney?" I plucked a canister from the cart and studied the blue label. Oxygen from the Swiss Alps. *Unbelievable.* Though if Charlie kept interrogating his step-siblings, I might need a hit of the stuff too.

"His dog," she said.

"What kind of dog is he?" I asked, trying to derail the murder questions.

Adalina's brows furrowed over the blue plastic. "What kind do you think?" she mumbled.

I returned the cannister to the cart and sat back on the striped couch. Was I supposed to know? Did Adan have a passion for a certain breed? I glanced at my brother, but he shook his head.

"He's really dead." Holli sobbed.

"When—uh—when was the last time you saw him?" Charlie asked her, his blue eyes hard, and I stepped on his foot.

She released Arystarch. Her step-son took a hasty step backward and smoothed the front of his smock. Remarkably, none of the paint had transferred to Holli's ivory dress.

"It was just this morning." She sniffed. "I went shopping and got back about an hour ago. I went to his study, but he wasn't there, or in our bedroom. I didn't think— I didn't know— I just thought he was somewhere else, not... dead." She wiped her reddened eyes.

"What about you, Ary?" Charlie asked.

He arched a brow. "Why? Are you trying to determine time of death?"

"I'd like to know that too," his sister said, removing the oxygen from her face. "I think we all should know what happened and when, don't you?"

"Of course," he said. "But— I think it was three-thirty." He jerked his head toward the picture windows. "He came to my studio looking for his dog. I also hadn't seen it."

I shifted, uneasy. Where *was* the dog? "Should we go look for him?"

The two siblings stared at me. "Why?" Arystarch asked.

"Maybe the dog's in trouble," I said. I'd recently and unwillingly become a dog owner. My dog, Fredo, wasn't one of those grateful rescues who loves you forever and unconditionally. He was a holy terror. But still. I didn't like the idea of any dog in distress.

"Who cares?" Arystarch shrugged.

I jerked down the hem of my thick Henley. The hell with this. Why was I asking permission? I strode toward the door. "I'll go look for him."

"I'll help," Charlie said.

A ruggedly handsome man walked through the door. Blocking my passage, he smiled politely. He had a boxer's nose, a blunt haircut, and an excellent suit—Gucci was my guess. I'd met him before under less-than-ideal circumstances, and my heart pounded. He pulled the double doors shut behind him, and I took an awkward step backward.

"I see everyone's here," the newcomer said. "I hope you haven't been discussing the case with each other much. I'm Detective Guthrie from The Town of Hot Springs Police Department." He turned to me, and he sucked in breath. "You've got to be kidding me. You?"

He remembered me? I waggled my fingers. "Hi again." I hadn't thought I'd made that much of an impression. *Go figure.* But I also couldn't square Guthrie's haircut with the amount of money required to afford those threads. Add that to the list of things that confounded me.

"Why have you got glass in your hair?" the detective asked.

"I went through a window at the Stanton house."

"That was—?" He closed his eyes and exhaled heavily. "Of course that was you. I'm going to have to separate you all." The detective's dark-eyed gaze held mine. "You'll be interviewed individually."

Arystarch poured himself a cup of tea. "I call the drawing room."

"I was here first. That's not—" His sister flushed and clapped the oxygen to her face.

"Where do you want us?" I asked before anyone else who wasn't me could say something stupid.

"Into the hallway please," Guthrie said. "The police officers will escort you to different rooms, where you'll be interviewed."

"Fine." Head high, I strode past him, banged my shin, and tripped over another police robo-dog. It turned its head and wagged its metal tail. A red light on the camera atop its head blinked. Muttering an embarrassed curse, I pulled my dignity about me and straightened. How was I expected to avoid low objects if they were *moving*?

The tall doors burst open. An elegant platinum blond in her late fifties strode into the drawing room. She wore a dark-blue St. John suit I found myself envying. Her slim hands clenched on the matching purse.

A uniformed officer trailed after her. "Madam. Ma'am. I'm sorry. Please wait," he bleated.

The woman stopped short and sucked in her breath, and my stomach twisted. Adan's ex-wife, Gina Levann. She'd kept her husband's name. And yeah, I guess I *had* been doing some investigating into Charlie's new family. But I was unofficially in training to a PI, so I'd had a legitimate reason to snoop.

Gina gave my brother a hard stare. "You," she said. "You did it. You killed him."

Chapter Three

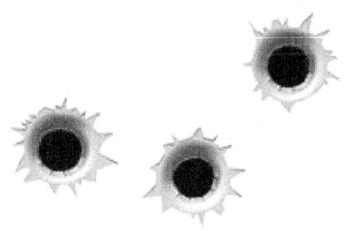

My fists clenched. Gina had no right to accuse my brother. "No," I said. "He didn't."

She pivoted to look at me. The older woman's expression turned to something else. Distaste. "And the sister, too."

Charlie raised his index finger, his eyes widening in panic. "Oh. Oh. Alibi. I have an alibi. And so does Alice."

"I'm afraid he does." Shelley appeared in the drawing room doorway behind Gina.

"Mr. Sommerland was gone all afternoon," the butler continued. "He arrived at the manse just before Ms. Sommerland." *Manse?* I studied him more closely.

The detective cleared his throat. "Yes, well if you'd just step into the hall—"

"So the question is who had the opportunity?" Charlie jammed up the sleeves of his yacht club jacket. "Who was here at the house between, say, three and when Alice and I discovered the body around five?"

"Five-ten," I said.

The new Mrs. Levann, Holli, raised her hand timidly. "I was here."

"Yes," the detective said, "but—"

"This is ridiculous," Arystarch snarled and jerked his head toward Charlie. "Get him out of here. He wasn't here, he doesn't know anything. The man's a fool. He's not a part of this, and he's not family."

My hands fisted. Mourning or not, Ary had gone too far.

"I'm sort of family," Charlie said.

"Sorry, Charlie," Adalina said. "You're not."

"Of course he's not," Gina touched her pale blond hair. "But he had the most motive to kill Adan."

"He did not," I said loudly—too loudly for the genteel drawing room judging by everyone's reaction.

On the couch, Holli gasped. Ary's mouth pursed. He dragged his palms down the front of his smock. Adalina's thick brows drew downward, and she took another gulp of the oxygen.

The detective blew out his breath, his gaze flicking toward the ceiling. "Oh?"

So *now* Guthrie was okay with us talking in a group? He must have given up on trying to control the situation and was now trying to make the best of it. At least we had that in common.

"Money," the older woman said. "He came here for money, and he got it. Don't think I didn't notice that new Tesla in the drive. *And* his sister is a known murderer." Gina frowned at her daughter. "And must you? You look ridiculous with that thing clapped to your face. And that hair..." She trailed off mournfully.

Adalina drew in a long, defiant breath.

I frowned. The Tesla outside was Charlie's? Then my stomach barreled downward when I realized the rest of what she'd said.

I was no killer. But I knew what she was referring to. A few months ago, I'd been acting as countersurveillance for Toomas Koppel, blackmailer and all-around dirt bag. He'd snuck off with my car and driven it into a tomato truck.

For reasons I won't go into, I became the face of that disaster. The memory still burned, largely because no one would let me forget it.

"I'm only borrowing the Tesla," Charlie said. "Adan said it would get me here faster than the bus. I mean, yeah, it's in my name. But it's not really *mine*."

The detective recoiled slightly. "You were taking the bus?"

I rolled my eyes. The bus to Hot Springs existed to bring in worker bees from Nowhere and the other nearby towns. I was willing to bet Guthrie would never set foot in any conveyance so lowbrow. Though in fairness, I couldn't stand the slow pace of public transportation either.

"Yeah," Charlie said. "The schedule's the pits. The bus gets to Hot Springs in the early morning and leaves at seven at night. And Alice didn't kill that Koppel guy. It was an accident. Just ask the FBI."

"Convenient accident," Guthrie said.

My jaw hardened. It hadn't been convenient for me. Especially since the story still bubbled into the news every now and again like a stinking mud volcano.

"Do you see?" The older woman gestured helplessly toward Charlie.

"I think I do," the detective said.

"That's not fair." Holli crossed her legs. "Charlie was just trying to get to know his father. He's got a right to bring his sister to the house."

The first Mrs. Levann's nostrils flared. "I don't need to hear from you about rights. You're only a replacement. You came through the company and into his bed just like—"

"So," I said brightly, pointing toward the doors with my thumb. "Into the hallway?"

"But where were you from three PM to five?" Charlie asked the older woman.

"That's none of your business young man," Gina said.

"I would like to know," the detective said.

Gina slipped her clutch beneath one arm. "I was at home," she said. "Reading."

"Like, what?" Charlie said, sidling closer to her. "A mystery novel or something?"

"Please." She rolled her eyes. "I was reading about the lives of the Stoics, if you must know."

"Which one?" I asked, interested. The Stoics were my favorite philosophers.

"Marcus Aurelius," she snapped.

Hm. Maybe she had, maybe she hadn't been reading. Marcus Aurelius was stoicism 101.

"So Arystarch was painting in his studio," Charlie said. "And Adalina was working in her office, and Holli was…"

"Trying on clothing in our bedroom," Holli said.

We were inside a hellish nursey rhyme. *The maid was in the garden, eating bread and honey. The king was in the parlor, counting out his money. Or was the queen in the garden? Whatever.*

"Which leaves Shelley," Charlie said.

Shelley arched a brow. "The butler did it? Really?"

"I'm not saying you did it." Charlie pinked beneath his beard. "I'm just curious about, you know, where you were."

"I was in my office. I'm not only a butler you know. I manage the grounds."

"Is there anyone else on the grounds at present?" the detective asked.

Shelley studied the parquet floor. "No. The gardeners come on Wednesday. The cleaning service works in the mornings and are gone by noon."

"And the cooking staff?" the detective asked.

The butler looked up. "There is none. Mr. Levann was an amateur chef. He believed his children should learn the skill as well."

"I noticed a security camera at the gate but none on the front door," I said.

"Mr. Levann liked his privacy." Shelley shot Adalina a look. "After *someone* demonstrated how easy it was to hack into security systems, he decided to only maintain a camera at the gate. The Town of Hot Springs is sufficiently low crime."

"At least it was," Charlie muttered, and the detective scowled. "Hey," my brother said, "that means someone could have come from the back or the sides to get into the house, right?"

"Of course," Arystarch said. "An intruder makes the most sense."

"Did Adan have any enemies?" Charlie asked.

"Aside from you?" Adan's ex-wife said. "No."

Adalina snorted. She clapped the oxygen to her face.

"You disagree?" I asked her.

She lowered the canister, and her face contorted. "My father was rich, and he was powerful. Of course he had enemies."

"Anyone specifically?" I asked.

"No."

Holli raised her hand again. "I think—"

"Oh, shut up." Arystarch whirled on her. "You haven't done any thinking since grammar school."

"That's not fair," Charlie said.

Holli's lashes fluttered. "Maybe I should talk to the detective alone."

"Yes," Guthrie said. "Thank you. Mrs. Levann..." The detective shot an embarrassed glance at Gina. "Er, Mrs. *Holli* Levann, this way." He motioned her toward the door.

Holli rose and glanced over her shoulder. She walked into the hallway, her hips swinging.

"Now," he said, "please, if the rest of you would follow suit?"

Grumbling, the others rose and walked into the hallway.

Charlie and I followed and were separated by the cops. I was a little surprised Guthrie didn't interview me himself. I wasn't sure if I should be insulted or relieved I hadn't gotten the white-glove treatment.

The uniformed officer who questioned me asked the usual questions. But the really interesting reveals had all happened in the drawing room. It had been like a scene from an Agatha Christie novel.

At least my brother had an alibi. But it was obvious he wasn't going to leave this murder alone. Family was the most important thing in his life. He hadn't had his biological father long, and he'd gotten hold of himself after his initial shock.

But I could see through his actor's mask. Adan's death had hit him hard.

My throat hardened. If he needed to deal with it by playing detective, I was going to have his back.

Though I was less worried about him getting arrested for interfering than putting himself crossways of a killer. The murderer was most likely part of Adan's family. Even the non-homicidal members would eat Charlie alive.

The cops finally said I could leave. I practically speedwalked to the front door and stepped outside.

A dozen glowing blue eyes stared up at me from the darkness. I sucked in a breath and stepped backward, then laughed shakily. More robodogs. The Hot Springs PD had gone a little overboard with their robot budget.

I edged forward. They stepped forward as well. The dogs lowered their heads, menacing.

I swallowed. "Nice doggies."

Chapter Four

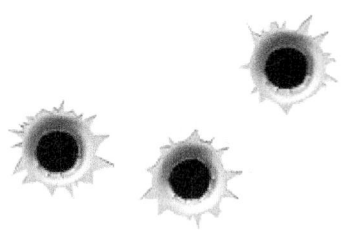

I HAVE THIS THEORY. When you see something on TV or a movie screen, your conscious mind knows it isn't real. But your subconscious believes it *is* real. So the ideas and images stick in your memory as if they'd been real experiences. This is a long way of saying I really wished I hadn't watched all those *Terminator* movies.

The metal dogs lowered their heads. Their glowing blue eyes seemed to flare. I hoped it was the better to record me with, and not to target me for an attack.

The door opened behind me. Charlie emerged from the mansion to stand beside me beneath the portico. "Oh, hey." He switched on a flashlight on his key fob and scanned the dogs with his beam. "Darn, no Barney."

I felt the muscles between my shoulder blades relaxing. If Charlie wasn't freaked out by the dogs, there probably wasn't any reason for me to be.

"Hold on," I said, "Barney's a robodog?" That made Arystarch's reaction when it had gone missing a lot less awful. But I still wasn't prepared to forgive him for the way he'd treated my brother. I'm shamefully good at grudge-holding.

"Oh yeah," Charlie said. "Didn't I tell you? Adan's company makes them. Just about everyone in town's got one."

"For security?"

"No, as pets. They can record video if you set them to, so the cops use them to take statements and stuff. And I think to go into situations to see what's up before people do. But they were designed as pets." He scratched his beard. "Weird that Barney's not around."

My pulse quickened. *The dogs could record...* Had Barney seen something he wasn't supposed to? *Weird indeed.* "There's got to be a way to track Barney," I said. "I can track my phone. I can't believe they invented a robot dog that couldn't be found with an app or something."

"Sure, but it's probably linked to an app on Adan's phone." His face fell.

"We're going to get through this," I said in a quiet voice. I grasped his shoulder.

"Adan was a good guy. I guess I just wish I'd had more time to get to know him." His head lowered, his expression bleak. Suddenly, we were kids again, and Charlie was coming home without his shoes. They'd been taken by three eight-year-old bullies.

Heat flushed from my chest to the top of my head. Anger wouldn't help the situation now. It certainly hadn't then. But someone had taken a life, and they'd taken my brother's chance to know that life. My muscles tightened. "We'll figure this out."

"I know we will. You're great at this stuff."

I grimaced. Charlie had an exaggerated view of my capabilities when it came to crime solving.

He coughed. "He believed you were innocent, you know. About that whole Koppel thing."

I smiled bitterly. If that was true, Adan had more than just genetics in common with my brother. They'd also shared a certain trusting naïveté. I *was* innocent, but no one in their right mind believed it.

Headlights swept the driveway. I raised my hand and squinted against the light.

A charcoal Jaguar stopped behind my Jeep, and a tall, lean man in a dark suit stepped from the car. He approached us, his footsteps crunching on the gravel. The man stopped short of the brick step. "Charlie, right?"

"Yeah," my brother said. In a lower tone, he said to me, "This is Adan's business partner, Jameel Rich."

"Right," he said. "And you are?"

"Alice. Alice Sommerland."

His expression shifted, grew guarded. "The bodyguard."

I sucked in my cheeks. *Surveillance specialist.* "Yeah."

"Gina called me. Is she here?"

"She's inside," I said.

We stepped aside, and Jameel walked past, his movements stiff. Though he tried not to show it, I could tell he was watching us from the corners of his eyes.

"Um, I'm not sure if I should stay here tonight," Charlie said. "It feels weird."

And I didn't want my brother anywhere near the murder mansion. "You can crash at my place if you want."

"You sure?"

The Christmas sweater I'd just finished knitting for him was tucked away in a drawer where he wouldn't see. "I'm sure."

His shoulders dropped. "Thanks." He hopped off the step and headed for the Tesla, paused. He turned to me. "Uh, with everything that's going on, maybe I should..."

"We can take my car."

We drove down the mountain highway and up the road to Nowhere. It was after ten at this point, and most of the lights were off in the small town's shop windows. Unlike glamorous Hot Springs, Nowhere rolled up its sidewalks at night.

"Look," Charlie said, "I know the Tesla's a little ridiculous—"

"I'm not judging." The car was between Charlie and his bio-Dad. Or at least it had been.

"I told him I didn't want it, but he'd already put it in my name and everything."

"Well," I said, grudging. "I respect Adan for buying American."

"It *is* the best built car in America today."

Odd shadows loomed on Main Street. The giant coffee pot in the Sagebrush Café's parking lot, the huge metal mushrooms in the park, the world's biggest lawn flamingo at City Hall. Spotlights highlighted the dying lawn and patches of dirty snow.

I pulled into the lot behind the old brick theater, and Charlie looked around. "Your Jeep's big enough to sleep in. Maybe I could—"

"Don't even think about it." I love my brother. But I didn't want him turning my new car into his home away from home. It'd make it too easy for him not to find a real place to live.

He stepped from the car and stared up at the two-story brick theater. "Have you seen the ghost yet?"

"There's no ghost," I said irritably. "The bathroom's just drafty." Maybe I was getting too comfortable with my crummy living quarters too.

Dog breath and a menacing growl woke me the next morning. I cracked a cautious eyelid. Fredo, the world's ugliest dog, sat on my chest and panted. Sammie, the world's blackest cat, made alarming noises beside my right ear.

I sat up hastily. Charlie snored on my couch, one bare leg slung over its back, his blankets rumpled.

I fed the animals, hooked a leash onto Fredo, and dragged him outside for a walk. We strode down Main Street until Fredo plopped down in front of the world's biggest corkscrew, wound with unlit twinkle lights. The dog scratched behind one ear. his bulging eyes rolling. He yawned, his crooked fangs sticking out every which way.

I yawned involuntarily in response. The little gray dog smirked. "You're a laugh a minute."

I tugged him onward to the Sagebrush Café. Ignoring the giant blue coffeepot in the parking lot, I brought the dog around to the back patio. I unhooked the latch in the gate, and we walked through the six-foot-high redwood fence and into the patio filled with blow-up holiday characters. A snowman. A Santa. A reindeer.

At a table, I ordered two coffees and one of their massive cinnamon rolls to go. The metal chair was freezing, and the nearby gas lamp wasn't putting out much heat. But I didn't want to bring Fredo inside. I scrolled through my phone, looking for news on the murder.

A shadow fell across my table. "Is it true?" a woman asked. I looked up.

Mrs. Malone stood leaning on her cane. "Well?" she asked impatiently. The old lady was bundled in a thick black coat the color of her dyed hair, and a red scarf and gloves. She must have gotten a dye job recently, because her white roots today were only a quarter-inch thick.

Gert Magimountain, our temporary mayor, trailed behind her. His arms were piled high with bags and boxes. On his head, his glasses glittered above the mound of shopping. Tufts of the gnome-like man's white hair danced above his balding scalp.

I don't know where she'd managed to get Christmas shopping in at this hour. But the storeowners were probably too terrified to turn her and Gert away. I rose and pulled out a chair. "Hi, Mrs. Malone. Hi, Mr. Mayor. Have a seat."

Gert preened. He was enjoying being a big fish in our small pond—maybe a little too much.

"No thank you," she said. "It's freezing out here. I heard Charlie's father was murdered."

And Mrs. Malone, true-crime aficionado and town gossip, wanted the goods. I shrugged half-heartedly. "It's true," I said, resigned to feeding her murder habit. I sat back down.

"Good heavens." She pressed her gloved hand to her chest. "How's Charlie doing?"

My heart defrosted a little. "It was a shock."

"And I heard you're working for Hot Springs," Gert snapped. "They're building a miniature museum. We've got to stop it."

"I'm not," I said. "There's no way to stop it. And where'd you hear that?"

"Never mind where," he said. "As long as you remember you work for Nowhere."

"No," I said. "I don't. That implies Nowhere is compensating me for my services, and it's not."

"Oh, we're not, are we?" he asked. "What about your discount rent at the theater?"

"That's from Mrs. Malone, not Nowhere," I said, indignant.

"And I've got your marker." His spectacles glittered.

I shifted, uneasy. Gert and I had a somewhat twisted history. Suffice it to say, he'd tried to kill me on multiple occasions. Also suffice it to say, he'd failed. To make up for it, he'd made a promise to some very bad men he'd make sure I toed an invisible line.

"Who found the body?" Mrs. Malone asked brightly.

Oh, why not tell her? She'd find out soon enough, and it would make her Christmas. She fancied herself an amateur sleuth, though her "detecting" seemed to consist of ordering me to do the work for her. "Charlie and I did. But Charlie's not a suspect. He came to the house straight from Nowhere, and I met him at the door. We went upstairs together. Charlie wanted to show me his room, and we found Adan Levann inside."

"What was he doing in Charlie's room?"

I set my cellphone on the black wire table. "That's a good question."

"Charlie showed me a photo of the two of them," she said. "They looked remarkably alike. Could it have been a case of mistaken identity?"

I bit my lip, my appetite evaporating. If it was mistaken identity, someone wanted my little brother dead. "I'll be watching him."

"What else can you tell me?" she asked.

"Adan appeared to have been bludgeoned with the bronze figurine of a dog."

"Back of the head?"

"Exactly."

She rubbed her chin. "We can't discount the mistaken identity idea then," she said. "But we don't have enough evidence to reach any conclusions. You'll have to return to the house and find more. I suppose Charlie can get you inside?"

I nodded, then wondered why I was agreeing with her. I didn't work for Mrs. Malone. Though I had a bad feeling that was about to change.

"Who was there when he was killed?" she asked. I went over the suspects and time of death. Mrs. Malone snorted. "Everyone could have been lying to you. His kids might have been in on it together and lied about seeing him." She nodded. "Report back to me when you have more information." The old lady stomped into the café, narrowly avoiding the waitress carrying a bag and my coffees in a carrier.

"We'll talk more about that museum," Gert said and followed her out.

Not if I had anything to say about it. Shaking my head, I pulled out my wallet. I was starting to see some benefits to the murder occurring in Hot Springs. The odds of Mrs. Malone physically entangling herself in the investigation was a lot lower with the murder out of town. She'd gotten herself hurt the last time she'd played detective. I didn't think my heart could take it again.

"Like a bad penny, she keeps turning up." Fitch dropped into the chair across from me and grinned. In spite of the cold, he only wore a faded blue t-shirt and jeans. I'd suspect he was showing off his well-muscled arms, but he wasn't that vain.

My stomach fluttered betrayingly. Fitch was, to put it mildly, easy on the eyes. He was over six feet tall with broad shoulders, dark hair and green eyes. But I'd pretty much give anyone a second look who's taller than me. And just to be clear, my heart wasn't beating a little faster because I had a crush on my boss. That would be clichéd and gross. He wasn't really my boss. I was a contract employee.

"You're in my territory now," I said. "You're the one who keeps turning up." Beside my chair, Fredo growled an agreement.

The waitress set my things on the table, and I handed her a tenner. "I'll be back with your change," she said.

I smiled briefly. "Keep it."

"Thanks." She returned inside the café.

"Nice work with Mrs. Stanton," Fitch said, settling back against the chair.

A proud, weightless feeling spread through me. *Sheesh.* How desperate was I for praise these days? "We both got lucky," I said modestly.

"Mr. Harrington was so pleased, he's given us a bonus."

"Us?"

He shrugged. "You were the one who saved the damsel in distress. It's only fair if I split it."

True. But I'd worked for other guys who wouldn't have bothered to share. "Thanks."

"I've got a new case, if you're going to be around."

I shot him a sharp look. He knew my old career was still in a deep freeze. Charlie's father may have believed I hadn't been involved in Koppel's death, but the rest of the world didn't. I wasn't going anywhere.

"I might have some time," I said indifferently. "What's the job?"

"It pays well, but you're not going to like it." He shifted, his shoulder muscles moving interestingly beneath his t-shirt.

I pried the lid off my coffee. "Why not?"

"It's in Hot Springs. As in The Town of."

Perfect. It would give me an excuse to nose around the town and maybe around Charlie's new relatives. But I couldn't let him think I was too eager. I took a sip. "That's a little inconvenient."

"I know, but the pay will make up for it, and it shouldn't take long."

I exhaled slowly. "Well... I guess... Okay, I'll do it," I said, feigning reluctance.

He slumped in the chair and smiled. "You will? I thought you hated that place. The only way I got you to take the last job there was because of the elder abuse angle."

Dammit. I hadn't argued long enough. I lifted one shoulder, dropped it. "I may as well. Hot Springs is starting to grow on me. If it's that important, I'll take the case."

"It is important, but you haven't heard what it is yet."

"Okay. What is it? Cheating spouse?"

He crossed his legs at the ankles. "No."

Fredo sat up and looked interested.

"Worse than a cheating spouse?" I asked. "What is it?" That it was something unpleasant didn't surprise me. You don't hire a PI when life is going well.

"I need you to find a dog."

Chapter Five

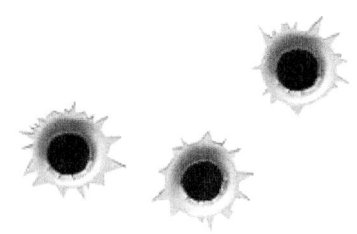

I narrowed my eyes. "A dog?" He was sending me after lost dogs now? I was supposed to be putting the past behind me, moving forward with my life. Dog catcher felt about a million miles away from a step up in my career.

Worse, instead of burning with righteous fury, my thoughts kept turning to Fitch. And not Fitch as boss, Fitch as a man, before I'd started doing odd jobs for him. I remembered the pressure of his muscular arms around me, the feel of his mouth on mine.

It was aggravating.

"Don't give me that look," Fitch said. A waitress carrying a loaded tray brushed past him on the patio.

"What look?"

"The I'm-too-good-for-this look. Your feelings are written all over your face."

I released my grip on the metal chair's arms. *Good thing they weren't.* "Trust me, you've got no idea what I'm feeling right now."

"You're a dog lover," he said. "I figured this would be perfect for you."

I glanced down at Fredo. He panted up at me, like he knew I'd just stepped in something bad.

"Fredo hates me," I said. "And so does the cat." I'd sort of inherited both, and they'd united in an unholy alliance against me. Fredo still needed me for food, so he could only push things so far. Sammie the cat was another story. "Hold on, do you mean Barney?"

"Who?" The skin around Fitch's eyes crinkled.

"Is it a robot dog?"

He blinked. "How'd you know?"

"Charlie's murdered bio-dad makes them."

His emerald eyes widened. "Back up. Murdered?"

"He was killed yesterday afternoon," I said, confused. "That's not what the case is about?"

"No. I had no idea anyone was murdered. I'm sorry. What happened?"

"Unclear. It looked like a blow to the head."

"Looked like?" His tanned brow wrinkled. "You were there?"

"Charlie and I found the body."

"What is it with you and bodies?"

"I'll have to consult my astrological chart."

"Damn." He plucked the other coffee from the carrier, uncapped it and took a sip.

"Hey!"

"I'll get you another one," he said absently.

"You'd better," I growled. "If it's not Barney, what's the case?"

"Who's Barney?"

"Adan's robo dog that's gone missing." I took a sip of the java. If the Sagebrush had any fault, it wasn't their coffee. "It might be nothing or—"

"It might be something." His lips pursed. "When did it disappear?"

"Some time yesterday," I said and rolled the cup between my palms. The warmth in my hands was delicious.

He shook his head. "Then it's probably not connected to this case. The dog we're looking for vanished three days ago."

"Stolen?"

He shrugged, and the v of his collar edged sideways for a better view of his chest. "One would assume. They go for over fifty grand."

I whistled. "That's an expensive toy."

Fitch leaned forward in his chair and opened the base of the nearby heat lamp. He turned up the gas flame. "It's not a toy for Selina March. She's got MS. She uses the dog for balance and to help her stand." He sat back in his chair.

"Like a real service dog."

"Yeah, but with less personality. Tell me more about Levann's murder."

I ran him through it, then ran him through it again. He nodded thoughtfully, taking notes in a small pad he'd pulled from his back pocket and with a pen he'd cadged off the waitress.

"Why can't Mrs. March track the dog?" I asked. "There's got to be some way to do that electronically."

"It's Ms. March, and she tried, but for some reason it's not working."

"Same story with Barney. Must be a design defect. Maybe I should visit the company, ask around," I said, keeping it casual.

He lowered his head and stared. "That's not surveillance."

"Neither is chasing after a missing robot dog." I squinted at him. He'd been very careful to keep my gigs to surveillance only. What was up?

"I'm glad to see you're ready to step up." He grinned. "You're now officially a trainee investigator."

"But I'm still a contractor," I said quickly. I had a real career to get back to. Someday, when the world forgot I was the protection specialist that had let Toomas Koppel get killed. It had to happen eventually. And yes, I may have been engaging in magical thinking, but I needed something to work toward.

"Right," he said. "Contract trainee. But you only ask the company about the dogs, got it?"

I crossed my fingers under the table. "Got it."

He stood, his chair scraping across the concrete. "I'll email you Selina's contact info and case file. She's expecting you tomorrow at three."

I saluted with two fingers. "Three o'clock."

He hesitated, as if he were going to say something, then shook his head and left.

I stared at his empty coffee cup. "Son of a—" I ordered another.

The next morning, I showed my ID to the burly guard at the ROVER security gate. He compared me to my photo, and I smiled.

He frowned and handed my license back to me. "You look familiar."

"I get that a lot. It's my wholesome, all-American good looks. So am I in?" I smoothed the lapel of my long, navy coat. Hot Springs was giving me all sorts of opportunities to wear my professional outfits—in this case, a navy blazer with some stretch in it, matching slacks, and a white blouse.

"You're in," he said, expressionless. But I couldn't expect everyone to appreciate my sense of humor. "Drive to building D," he continued, "on the south side. Someone will be waiting for you in the lobby."

"Thanks."

The gate swung open, and I pulled into the lot. The low white buildings were industrial the way the Google complex is—sleek and clean and modern. If it also contained free candy dispensers, things might be looking up. I found building D, beside a creek lined with bare-branched trees.

Fresh snow dusted the western mountains, though we hadn't gotten any last night in Nowhere. Neither had this complex, just outside Carson City. The temperature was brittle and cold, and I could feel the tips of my toes going numb. Not anything as glamorous as frostbite. Chilblains. A revolting, Victorian-era condition that turned my toes red and itchy every winter.

My breath steamed the air as I strode to the blue-glass entrance. The glass doors opened automatically. I hurried inside, rubbing my bare hands together and regretting my choice not to wear gloves. At least my fingers weren't chilblains-prone too.

No one stood behind the high security desk, and I looked around. The lobby was decorated for the holidays in silver and red. Bathrooms on the right. A wide staircase up to the second floor in the center. An elevator on the left. Faux wood-tile floor. A few potted trees strung with silver Christmas ornaments stood about looking elegant and aloof.

A robot dog emerged from behind the desk. Its leg gears wheezed.

"Oh," I said. "Hi. Are you security?" It tilted its mercury head. "I'm Alice Sommerland," I continued, feeling foolish talking to a dog. And not even a real dog. "Here to see Jameel Rich."

The dog walked toward me, its feet clicking on the tile floor. It moved unnaturally, its right front leg working in exact time with its left rear leg.

The dog stopped about an inch from my thigh. I took an involuntary step back. It jerked forward, ramming me, its tail wagging.

"Careful," I said and rubbed my thigh. That was going to leave a mark. The robot may have been better looking than my mutt, but it was creeping me out. "Jameel Rich," I said more loudly. "Alice—"

The dog leapt, front paws extended. The weight of it sent me staggering.

"Cut it out." I tried to shove it away, but it was heavier than a real dog its size.

There's nothing more sociopathic and unstoppable than artificial intelligence. A sudden vision of robo dogs patrolling the streets flashed into my brain. I didn't like it. "Down!"

But the robot dog paid about as much attention to me as my own dog did, which is to say, not at all. It hunched for another playful leap.

My insides tensed. If it actually did knock me to the ground, I wasn't sure what would happen. But I'd learned the hard way not to let people do that to me. I figured the rule applied to robo-dogs too. I just wasn't sure what to do about it. It was a valuable piece of equipment, and I had no idea how to turn it off.

I bolted for the ladies' room, slamming the door behind me and bracing it with my shoulder. The dog thudded into it. The door gave an inch, my boot slipping on the floor tile. I swore again.

The dog banged against the door again, and the wood seemed to shiver. "Hey!" I shouted, fumbling my phone from the pocket of my blazer. The phone clattered to the tile floor. "A little help, please!"

There was a third bang, and the door bounced painfully off my shoulder. I clenched my jaw and forced the door shut. I could hide in one of the stalls, but it was too easy to imagine the dog crawling beneath the door and getting inside.

"Hello!" I yelled again. "Call off the dog!"

"Ms. Sommerland?" a man asked from the other side of the door.

I cracked it open and peered out. Jameel, in a black business suit and armband stood looking elegant and perplexed. "Is there a problem?"

"Your dog chased me in here."

He lifted a brow. "Chased you?" He glanced at the dog. It sat beside a Ficus tree and cocked its head.

My neck stiffened. "It jumped on me," I said, more loudly than I'd intended.

"Our dogs don't jump on people unless they've been programmed to do so. This one hasn't. It's a greeter."

Cautiously, I stepped from the bathroom. "It practically knocked the door in."

He shook his head. "It's not programmed for that."

"Then how do you explain these marks?" I gestured roughly at the scarred indentations on the wooden door.

"I don't know. How do you explain them?"

"I just told you..." I exhaled slowly, trying to lower my blood pressure. "The dog did it."

"I'll check its logs," he said doubtfully. "My office is this way."

Remembering I was here as a contract trainee investigator, I forced a smile. I should be building rapport, not biting his head off. "Thanks for seeing me this morning. I'm sure this is a difficult time."

"It is." Jameel pivoted and climbed the steps to a long, white hallway. I followed him inside a spacious, corner office with a view of the snowcapped mountains. He motioned me toward a comfy leather chair and sat behind a wide desk with a glossy wooden top.

Jameel tapped on the computer keyboard. He frowned at his wide computer screen and shook his head. "The logs record your initial interaction with the dog—"

I removed my coat and sat, draping it over my knees. "Initial interaction?"

"Identifying yourself and asking to see me."

"And then?"

"And then the dog went to the door and stared into the parking lot."

My jaw tightened. I *hate* modern technology. "That's not what happened."

"You can watch the video, if you like." He turned the screen to face me.

It showed the parking lot through the blue glass windows. The angle was low. Dog level. So either Jameel was gaslighting me or someone had tampered with the dog.

My lips flattened. "Could that video have been altered?"

"Altered?" He laughed shortly. "Hardly."

I smothered my annoyance. "One of your clients, Ms. Selina March, has lost her dog. She's tried tracking it the usual way, and it's not working."

"Then she's probably doing something wrong."

"Barney, Adan's dog, has also gone missing," I said stiffly.

"Are you sure?"

I opened my mouth to object, then realized I didn't know if Barney had been found since I'd been at the house on Monday. I should have come better prepared. "Is there an alternate way to track one of your dogs?"

"No. If Ms. March is having trouble, she should call our help desk."

"According to her case file, she has."

"Hm..." He tapped the computer. "I'm not seeing that record here."

Six months ago I'd had to call the IRS. They'd kept me on hold for three hours before a live human being had picked up. And he'd given me the runaround. This meeting—including the robo-dog attack—was only mildly less aggravating.

"These dogs," I said. "Why did you and Adan decide to build them?"

He swiveled his leather chair to face me. "Adan thought they'd be fun and there would be a market. Humanoid robots can seem a little threatening, but dogs are man's best friend. And he was right. We used The Town of Hot Springs as a test market, and we can barely keep up with production."

"I noticed the Hot Springs police has some."

"They've got about a dozen. But Adan wanted them primarily for personal use. Like for your client, Ms. March. She has MS, I believe?" I nodded. "That was Adan's dream," he continued. "That technology could be used to make people's lives better. And make them more fun."

"And your dream?"

He smiled faintly. "Crass profit, I'm afraid."

"We all like that. I understand Adalina works for the firm?"

He shifted in his chair. "Yes, she's brilliant. Her work here caused some friction with her mother, but there's no better place for Adalina than Rover."

"Why friction?"

He grimaced. "Gina felt the company broke up their marriage. Rover was an obsession for Adan. I'm afraid she saw Adalina's interest as a betrayal."

"So Adalina inherited Adan's genius for tech."

"Well, she and her brother were adopted, but yes."

"Adopted? I didn't realize." And then Adan's biological son had strolled into their lives... Had that made Charlie more or less of an emotional threat to the family?

"Right," Adalina said from the open door. "I'm not Adan's real daughter. Is that what you wanted to hear?"

Chapter Six

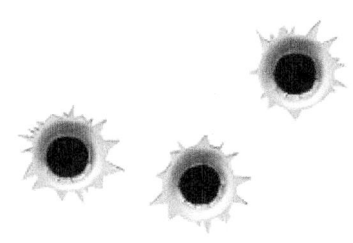

Jameel rose slowly from behind his sleek desk. His brows pinched together. "Adalina. That's not what I meant at all. You must know that."

She strode into the room in a shapeless red cashmere sweatsuit that clashed with her green hair. Adalina dropped into the leather chair beside me. "Real or not, Adan left his shares in the business to Ary and me. We're all partners now."

"And with your technical skills," Jameel said, "you bring much to the table." He hesitated. "I'm surprised Ary is interested in the business though." She'd pronounced his name *airy*. About time I knew how to pronounce it.

"He's not." She pressed a blue oxygen canister to her face and inhaled. "As long as the bank deposits keep rolling in, he'll be happy," she said, her voice muffled by the plastic mask.

Jameel sighed. "There's a lot you both need to know." His gaze flicked to me. "But perhaps this isn't the best time."

"Maybe Adalina can help me with my question about the dogs," I said.

She lowered the blue canister. "Oh?"

"A client has lost her robo dog and can't find it through the usual methods," I said.

Her mouth twisted. "That seems to be going around."

Jameel leaned forward and braced his elbows on the desk. "What do you mean?" he asked sharply.

She examined her chipped nails. "We can't find Barney either and believe me, I've tried." She looked up through her thick lashes. "I hope you didn't miss a bug in the programming."

"There's nothing wrong with the programming," he said sharply.

"And yet," she said, "two dogs have dropped off the proverbial radar. If it happens to others..." She shrugged.

"I'll look into it," he said, his brown eyes narrowing. "So perhaps this isn't a job for a private investigator after all. It sounds like an internal matter."

Adalina swiveled in her chair to study me. "You're a PI now? I thought you were a disgraced bodyguard?"

"I do contract work for a PI," I said stiffly.

"Career 2.0?" she asked.

"No." My heart sank. I loved surveillance. I loved my old career. The travel. The people. The laundry service. But what if this *was* my new life? Forever?

"Female bodyguard turned detective—it makes a good story." She rose. "Want a break? I was thinking of going to the Sky High Café."

Why not? It looked like I'd reached a dead-end here. And Adalina wouldn't have made the invitation if she hadn't wanted to talk about something. "Sure. If you learn anything about Ms. March's dog," I said to Jameel, "will you let me know?"

"I'll let her know," he corrected.

My gaze flicked to the ceiling tiles. That would have to be good enough. I nodded and followed Adalina into the parking lot.

"Meet me at the Café. It's in Hot Springs. You know it," she tossed over her shoulder. She stepped inside a silver Tesla and zipped from the parking lot.

Thoughtful, I drove more slowly into Hot Springs. Snow glittered off the rooftops, on the pines, and in little slopes between the stone-covered buildings and the paving-stone walks.

I frowned. The snow was pristine, as if it had fallen recently. But we hadn't gotten any in Nowhere. Did they have special cleaners for the snow? In this town, nothing would surprise me.

Adalina must be one of those lucky people when it came to parking. She pulled into a spot on the street near the café. I had to drive another six blocks to an overpriced parking garage.

I walked back toward the coffee shop and bent to touch a thick fleck of snow. It was... oddly slippery and didn't melt in my hand. It was cold, but so was the sidewalk.

"Alice?" a muffled feminine voice cried. A snowman waddled toward me. A red backpack was strapped to its back, connected to what looked like a leaf blower. "It *is* you," she said.

"Lilyanna?" Lilyanna Gomez was a Nowhere native. Like my brother, she had a "portfolio career" of odd jobs. I wasn't surprised one had taken her to Hot Springs.

"What are you doing here?" she asked.

"Meeting someone for coffee. And you're... working, I see?"

"I'm snow patrol." She lifted the end of the blower.

I squinted at a six-inch drift of snow against the nearby building. "Are you making this stuff?"

"Yeah. It's a commute to get here, but it pays well. And the costume's great."

"Uh, huh." I nodded. Lilyanna believed she'd been abducted by aliens—a mystery that was above my paygrade. Whatever had happened, it had left her with severe anxiety. Only weighted blankets and heavy costumes seemed to alleviate the stress.

"Is, ah, Charlie around?" she asked.

"Not that I know of."

A tanned blonde in a ski parka and furry boots strolled past walking a robo dog. Lilyanna waved at her. The woman ignored us both and sipped from a plastic bottle of water.

"I'd better get moving," I said. "See you back in Nowhere?"

"Sure. I get off just before five," she said cheerfully.

"Want a ride home?" I asked.

Her round white shoulders sagged with relief. "That would be great. Could I meet you here?"

"Sure thing. I'll see you then." I continued on to the café.

Adalina had already claimed a table outside beneath a heat lamp. She zipped her lined leather jacket up higher. "You made it."

"I had to park in the garage." I scraped back a chair and sat across from her.

She studied me, her fingers laced over her rounded stomach. "So you're chasing down missing dogs now?"

"I understand it's an expensive piece of equipment." I brushed back my hair.

Her face contorted. She leaned forward. "*Equipment* is all they are. Real dogs are dying in shelters and being experimented on by sick scientists, and the rich buy electronic toys as substitutes."

"It doesn't seem like much of a substitute," I said. A waiter strode behind Adalina's chair.

"They're easier to care for." Adalina sat back in the patio chair. "No food or vet bills."

"I can't imagine they have much personality though."

She sighed. "You'd be surprised. Wait 'til they start mounting guns on their backs. Then they'll have real personality." A trio of robo police dogs marched past on the sidewalk in blue jackets.

I shivered and pulled my coat collar up higher. "Tell me about Barney."

"The latest version. With personality. Adan was so proud. As AI went, they were limited, but as dogs..." She shrugged.

"Do you know when your father's dog went missing?"

"I know Adan was looking for him Monday afternoon."

I eyed her. I'd never called my parents by their first names. Not even when speaking of them in the third person. But different strokes. "And the dogs act as recording devices?" I asked.

"They can." She plucked at a thread on her jacket sleeve. "They're constantly picking up sound and visual. How long they retain that for is up to the owner."

"Did Adan's?"

"He had everything going on that dog. It was his show model. Why?"

"Just curious. Why do you think you can't find it?"

"I—"

"Your Himalayan Fresh." A waiter wheeled a white plastic contraption with large canisters attached to our table. He unhooked an oxygen mask and handed it to Adalina. "Is there anything else I can get for you?"

An oxygen bar. We were sitting outside, in the fresh mountain air, at an oxygen bar. They'd damned well better serve java. "I'd like a cup of coffee please," I said. "Black."

The waiter nodded and walked inside. At least this place had something aside from air. But if I'd just paid ten bucks for a coffee, I was putting it on my expense report.

"It's like Barney's just off the radar," Adalina said. "Or just… off." She pressed the clear mask over her nose and mouth.

"I assume the dogs run on batteries. How long do they last?"

She mumbled a response.

"What?" I asked.

She removed the mask. "Ninety-six hours before they need to recharge. They go to the recharging station on their own when their power gets below ten percent."

"Could someone have turned Barney off?"

"Yes, though it would be easier to return it to its factory settings." An odd expression crossed her face.

I lightly bit the inside of my cheek. "It's easier to reset a Rover than turn it off?"

"The hard off switch is difficult to get to," she said. "It's beneath the right ear. You need a paperclip to jam in the hole to turn it off, and then to hold it for eight seconds. Though you could do it electronically through the app on Adan's phone. You think the missing dog is connected to Adan's death, don't you?"

"Is it strange that it went missing?"

"That's not an answer."

"It sort of is."

She took another hit of the oxygen. "Yes, it was strange. And it's stranger that it happened the day he was murdered. So it probably wasn't a coincidence."

"But it could have been."

"It could have been," she agreed.

"Especially since another customer's robo dog went missing two days before the murder."

"Rover," she corrected. "We call them Rovers." Her voice rose. "So why are you really here?"

"I'm really looking for a dog."

"And Toomas Koppel was really killed by a tomato truck," she said flatly.

I blew out my breath. *That again.* "He really was."

I killed more time in Hot Springs and felt sorry for myself. I—a simple, good-hearted surveillance specialist—was going to be haunted by the Toomas Koppel incident for the rest of my life. No one wanted to let it go.

Eventually, the FBI had admitted that I hadn't been responsible for personally guarding Koppel. I'd just been the sucker whose car he'd stolen. But by that point, the conspiracy theory—that I'd been in on a hit—had been set.

His death and the speculation surrounding it had been front page news. The follow-up stories had been buried. And I couldn't fight the narrative. Story trumped reality every time.

Doleful, I stared in the windows of a men's clothing store. It was a good bet I couldn't afford anything in it for Charlie, but I walked inside anyway. I found a blue hiking jacket that matched the color of Charlie's eyes. The price tag was ridiculous.

I bought it anyway, shoved it in the back of my Jeep, and drove to Selina's. The house was Greek-revival style and fake-snow free. The lawn was green and lush and rolled on for acres until vanishing into the tree line.

I flipped up the collar of my thick jacket, walked up the brick steps, and rang the bell. It gonged inside the house.

After a few moments, the door opened. A slender woman with hip-length brown hair looked out. Her eyes were big and brown and serious. She looked to be in her mid-thirties and leaned on a hiking stick.

"You must be Alice Sommerland," she said.

"Yes. Selina March?"

She nodded. "Come inside."

Selina walked slowly, awkwardly. I followed a few feet behind. She led me into a Bohemian-style living room with a wooden floor, bare of rugs. The colorful throws and potted ferns were somehow shocking in the architecturally formal room.

A Christmas tree stood before the wide, paned windows. A fire crackled merrily in the white-marble fireplace. Holly and red candles lined the mantle.

"Sit anywhere," Selina said. Her walking stick skidded from beneath her, and she staggered. She gasped. "Dammit."

I moved to grab her arm, but she glared at me, and I stepped back. She steadied herself.

I waited until she found a chair, then I sat opposite her. A low coffee table covered in magazines and scented candles stood between us.

"So you're missing a dog," I said.

Her smile was taut. "Rover. And if you're wondering why I've got nothing better to do than hire a private detective to track it down, well..." She gestured toward the walking stick. "I guess that's partly true. I write part-time, but I get brain fogs..." She turned her head toward the windows. "Mainly I was mad because I got the brush-off from Rover. The company, not the dog."

"I've read your case file, so I know the basics, but would you mind going over it with me again?"

"Sure. Would you like some coffee or tea?"

"No, thanks."

She nodded. "Oh, and here's a photo." She pushed her cell phone across the coffee table toward me.

I picked it up and glanced at the screen. She stood smiling beside the Rover. It was identical to the others I'd seen, save for the gray foam pad on its back. The pad looked like one you might sit on at a sports stadium but fitted to the robo dog.

"I first noticed it behaving oddly on Friday night," she said.

"How so?" I handed the phone to her across the coffee table.

"It was slow to respond to my commands. And sometimes it did just the opposite. I said "come," and it went. It was still new. I thought maybe it hadn't gotten used to my voice commands, though it had been doing well before."

"And then it disappeared on Saturday?"

"I went out to get the mail, and it came with me. And then it ran off. I called to it, but it didn't come. I tried to control it through the app. No dice. I thought maybe a hacker had stolen it—the Rovers are quite valuable. Then Fitch came out and looked around, and he couldn't find anything."

I crossed my arms over my chest. Fitch had just run over here to search for a dog? I was starting to get the feeling she hadn't found him in the Yellow Pages. "How do you two know each other?"

She smiled. "We've been friends for years. He's a great guy."

My insides grew heavy. He was that, I thought, rueful. And their relationship was none of my business. "I've talked to the people at Rover—"

"You could get through? It took me ages to get customer support."

"I talked to one of the owners actually, Jameel Rich. He said he'd look into it from the tech side."

She pursed her lips. "I'm impressed. They wouldn't give me the time of day. Do you mind if I ask... How'd you do it?"

"A slight family connection. But let's see how he follows up. In the meantime, mind if I take a look around outside?"

"Not at all. If it helps, Rover ran toward the woods." She pointed at the far-off tree line.

I rose, and she struggled to standing.

"I can see myself out," I said.

She collapsed back in the sofa. "I'm sure you can."

Chapter Seven

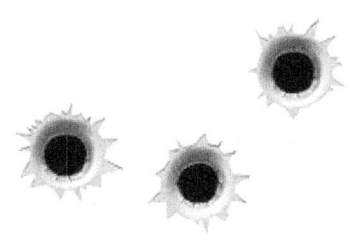

I STROLLED ACROSS SELINA'S wooden patio and tried to look like I knew what I was doing. It seemed like a good metaphor for my life. But the reality was, surveillance and tracking were two different skill sets. I was no tracker.

But I was here and getting paid for my time. I put on a show of studying the floor. The porch had been decorated for the holidays with white twinkle lights and miniature Christmas trees. I descended the steps onto the lawn.

Here, I did have luck. It turned out robo-paws were hard on lawns. I found a set of not-quite-doggy tracks and followed them. They made a straight line into the stand of pines at the end of Selina's property.

Which was exactly where she'd told me the Rover had gone. No doubt Fitch had already followed these tracks.

I continued through the pines to a low, rail fence. The Rover looked like it had crawled beneath it. Since the other side of the fence was someone else's property, I didn't climb over. I didn't need Fitch bailing me out for trespassing. I'd call the property owner later and ask for permission to snoop.

"Mercury's in retrograde, and I'm chasing a dog." I wandered along the fence's perimeter not really expecting to find anything. So I was surprised when I spotted a flurry of Rover prints. They churned the soft earth, mashing the pine needles deep. Amazed my diligence had paid off, I took a picture with my phone.

The tracks led back toward Selina's house. And when I say tracks, I mean more than one dog. Again—I'm not a super tracker. But either several Rovers had gone in that direction, or one Rover was doubling back over and over and over.

Maybe Selina's dog was on some sort of broken software loop? I liked that solution because it meant I might actually find the robo-dog. Feeling more optimistic, I followed the tracks through the pines.

I returned to the tree line. The tracks turned at a hard right angle, staying just inside the pines. *Weird.* I frowned, squatting to examine them. It was almost as if the dogs were keeping to the cover of the trees.

A branch cracked behind me. Slowly, I rose, turned.

Half a dozen Rovers stood, metal tails wagging, beneath the trees. One had a thick gray pad on its back. *Selina's Rover.*

"Hey, guys."

Their tails stopped wagging. In unison, they cocked their heads.

Great. I swallowed. I'd found Selina's dog, but now what? I didn't have a paperclip to turn it off with. I rummaged in my pocket and found a ballpoint pen. Its nib was a little thicker than a paperclip, but it might work. I took the pen apart, pocketing all but the ballpoint tip.

"Here boy." I stepped toward the dogs.

GRRRRRRR... Their tails stopped wagging.

I froze. They were growling. Why were they growling? I rubbed my arms and looked around the forest. Why would someone program a Rover to growl?

"Rover, sit," I said in a commanding voice that Fredo always ignored.

The dogs stepped closer. My pulse skittered. This was just silly. The worst they could do was bump into me and video me while doing it. But something about those silent metal dogs raised the hairs on the back of my neck. "Sit," I said, less commandingly.

As one, the Rovers bounded toward me.

I turned and ran and cursed myself for doing it. After all, what could they really—?

Something clamped down hard on my heel. I yelped, jerking free. Rovers *could* do more than record things.

A leaning pine loomed in front of me. Without slowing, I scrambled up its angled trunk. A dog lunged, tearing off my shoe. I crawled higher. When I figured I was out of reach, I looked down, panting.

The dogs prowled beneath me. One leapt at my shoe-free foot. I jerked it upward and wobbled on the branch. Grabbing frantically for a higher branch, I steadied myself. I exhaled slowly. At least the dogs weren't climbers. I seemed to be safe.

But I was in a tree and missing a shoe. And my foot hurt. I reached down to rub it and nearly fell off again.

"Or, I'll just wait here." I clasped the tree trunk and settled in. After all, the dogs would have to leave sooner or later.

Two hours later, they hadn't left, and I was deeply annoyed. Darkness had fallen. I was still in the damn tree. My heel was swollen, and other parts I won't mention weren't happy about the situation either.

I stopped playing solitaire on my phone, bit the bullet, and called Fitch.

"What have you got?" he said.

I forced cheer into my voice. "The good news is, I've found Selina's Rover."

"Whoa. That was fast. How?"

"It chased me up a tree." My face heated.

He laughed. "Good one."

My spine bent, my toes curling up. *This*. This was why I'd waited so long to call him. "And he's got friends," I continued.

"Wait, you're not kidding?"

"No. And they may not have teeth, but they can bite."

"Are you okay?" he asked, his voice laced with concern.

"One got my shoe." It lay at the base of the pine. True, it wasn't a new shoe. But *you* try finding an attractive but comfortable size ten. I wanted it back. "I thought they'd lose interest, but they're still here."

"How many dogs are we talking about?"

"Six. I've got photos." I'd had plenty of time for nature and technical photography. I texted him a picture of the dogs staring up at me, their blue eyes unblinking. Those eyes were even creepier in the dark than in the daylight.

"That's Selina's all right," he said, voice grim.

"I'm sending you my GPS location, but I'm still on Selina's property. And..."

The dogs turned their heads. Moving as one, they trotted into the darkness.

"And they're leaving," I finished. Was it a trick?

"So you're no longer treed."

"I guess not," I said slowly. "Stay on the line."

I shimmied down the tree, stepped on a pinecone with my bare foot, and choked on a swear word. Hopping on one foot, I found my shoe and squeezed it on. It was a little tighter around the heel than usual, but it was wearable.

"They haven't returned yet," I said. "I'm going to head back to my Jeep."

"I'll let Selina know. And stay on the line until you get to your car."

"Thanks," I said, pathetically relieved he wasn't abandoning me. Not that there was a lot he could do if they returned aside from wishing me a poignant farewell.

I hobbled across the darkened lawn and to my Jeep. Once I was inside, Fitch hung up, presumably to call Selina. I drove into Hot Springs to collect Lilyanna.

She was waiting where she'd said and still in her snowman costume. It took some maneuvering to get Lilyanna into my car, but I didn't bother to suggest she take off the head. If this was what being kidnapped by UFOs did to a person, count me out.

"Whew. Thanks." She closed the door. "Did you get everything done you needed?"

"Eh. There were a few hiccups. I'll finish up later." And next time out, I was bringing a paperclip and a taser.

We drove to Nowhere, Lilyanna chatting animatedly about life as a part-time snowman. Since my refrigerator was empty, we stopped at the Sagebrush Café for a bite.

The usual trio of old-timers plus our temporary mayor, Gert, sat beneath a metallic red garland at the counter. The mayor shot me a speculative look, and I hurriedly looked away. Gert had a nasty habit of expecting favors from me. Just because he'd failed to kill me, it didn't mean I owed him.

Christmas carols played over the diner's sound system and grease crackled in the kitchen. The place smelled of burgers, fries, and baking sugar. Charlie sat with an unfamiliar man in a sky-blue booth.

My brother waved. "Alice, Lilyanna. Over here."

The man twisted in his seat. He was mid-fifties, with thinning gray hair. His gut strained against his navy business suit.

I sat beside the stranger. Lilyanna squeezed in beside Charlie. She removed her snowman's head, setting it on the checkerboard floor beside the table.

"This is my sister Alice." Charlie motioned toward me. "And my, uh, friend Lilyanna." His cheeks darkened. "Guys, this is Adan's lawyer, John O'Reilly."

"Hi," I said, wary. Lesson one from my divorce? Lawyers were not my friends.

"Are you certain you want to continue this conversation here?" the lawyer asked.

"Oh, yeah," Charlie said. "I don't have any secrets from them." He met my gaze. "John was telling me about Adan's will."

"Really?" I asked, surprised. "I'd assumed Charlie wouldn't be in it. No offense." But my brother and Adan hadn't known each other all that long.

"He's not." The lawyer turned his half-empty mug on the table. "The thing is, last week, Adan called me to his office for a meeting. He asked me to draw up a new will that would include Charlie. Unfortunately, he never got a chance to sign it."

My jaw set. *How convenient.*

Charlie shrugged. "It's fine. I wasn't in it for the money."

"So Charlie's out, and yet you're here." I studied the lawyer.

He shifted uncomfortably in the booth. "I can't ignore Adan's wishes. He expected to sign the new will yesterday, Tuesday."

"Have you told the police this?" I asked.

"That's hardly the point," the lawyer said. "The point is your brother has a strong case for challenging the current will."

"I told him I didn't want to," Charlie said.

"And you're offering your services?" I asked the man.

"No. But I was more than Adan's lawyer. I was his friend. He told me his wishes. I can't ignore them. I'd be happy to recommend someone to represent you."

Charlie shook his head. "It doesn't feel right."

"It might not feel right," he said tartly, "but your father wanted it. Do you really want to ignore one of his last wishes?"

Charlie's brow wrinkled. "Uh..."

"He'll think about it," I said.

"Good." The lawyer made to leave, and I scooted from the booth. He slid from it and stood. "Adan's estate is significant. If you're worried about being fair to his other children, don't be. There's plenty for everyone."

But I wondered if his new wife and other kids felt the same.

Chapter Eight

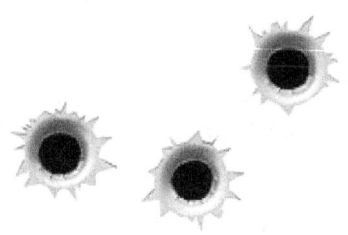

"I'm telling you, the Rovers have gone feral. I have proof." I pulled out my phone, opened one of the photos I'd taken, and handed it across the desk to Detective Guthrie.

He raised a brow. "Okay. Those are Rovers. So?" I'd never seen such a well-dressed cop. The guy's suit was—I kid you not—Armani. I'd seen enough of them on the job to recognize the brand. Granted, even the shlumpiest guy looked good in Armani, and Detective Guthrie was far from shlumpy. The muscular outlines of his shoulders strained against the fine fabric. But how much did Hot Springs cops get paid?

"So," I said, "look at the angle. I'm in a tree."

"Why am I not surprised?"

"They chased me up there!" I folded my arms and glared. Hot Springs was the worst. It was the worst when I was a kid growing up in Nowhere. The town had gotten, if possible, even more supercilious and snooty since then. Especially their PD.

He handed me my phone and glanced at the police robo-dog in the corner of his spacious office. "They look like they're just standing around."

"What?" I snarled. "You want an action shot?"

"You seem upset," the police detective murmured in a humor-the-crazy-lady tone. Rising, he walked to the fancy coffee maker in his office. The windows looked out on the western mountains. "Would you like some tea? Coffee? Chai?"

"I'm not upset," I snapped. "You wanted to meet with me. I'm meeting with you. And now you don't seem to believe I was treed by six Rovers. And I'll have a chai." Since I was here, it seemed wasteful not to.

"Mr. Rich has assured us something like that would never happen." He fiddled with the machine, set a mug beneath it, and a froth of steaming liquid poured into the cup. Returning to the desk, he handed me the chai.

I studied the Hot Springs logo on the ceramic cup. "I know. He denied it to me too, but I'm telling you it happened. Did you ever find Adan's missing dog?"

"No. Mr. Rich says it most likely lost battery power." He sat against his polished desk, his stance emphasizing his thighs, and damn Armani for making me look. A good suit on a man is as entrancing as a magic spell.

I got a grip on myself. "But he still should be able to track it. And aren't the dogs programmed to return to charge when they're about to lose power?"

The metal dog in the corner swiveled its head to look at me. I made a face at it.

"Yes," Guthrie said, "but something may have prevented it." He carried himself with an irritating degree of confidence. I blamed that on the suit too.

"Or someone?" I asked.

The detective arched an urbane brow. It was as finely groomed as the rest of him.

"If you think my story is bogus," I said, "why are we talking?" I sipped the chai. *Damn.* It was really good.

"Mr. Rich would appreciate it if you didn't spread rumors about Rovers running wild around town."

I gaped. "This is why you dragged me in here? I'm bad for his business? What, are you his enforcer now?"

"No, no, no. And I didn't drag you. I invited you and you accepted. However, I would hate to see you sued for slander."

"Two Rovers have gone missing," I said flatly. "Something's wrong."

"And the Rover Corporation will take care of it. Ms. March has agreed to let their customer service team handle the problem. She's received a replacement Rover and is no longer in need of your services."

I deflated. She hadn't told me that. "Okay then." I stood, gripping the warm mug. "We done?"

The door to his office burst open and slammed against the wall. A shortish, stoutish seventy-something woman in navy Valentino glared at him. Her hair was an unnatural black. "Is it true? A murder in the Town of Hot Springs? I *insist* you tell me what's going on."

Leaning on a cane, she stomped into the room and sat in the chair I'd just vacated. A book fell out of her purse. Glancing at the black and red cover, I bent and retrieved it. It was true crime. I handed her the book and studied her too-black hair.

Detective Guthrie sighed. "We're done."

"Okay," I said uncertainly. The newcomer reminded me of... someone. But... I shook myself. *Weird*. I walked through the door.

"Wait," Guthrie said. "That's my—"

I shut the door behind me and strode into the cubicle area. I was still new to all this private investigating business. But even I could tell I was getting the bum rush. I looked down. I was still holding Guthrie's mug. They probably gave them out to everyone though. Shrugging, I hurried with it from the station.

A guy I'd guarded once had explained something called regulatory capture to me. It occurred when the companies end up controlling their regulators. The local cops were in no position to regulate Rover, Inc. But this had the same vibe.

It was irritating. On the marble steps, I took another sip of chai. How did something this good come out of a cop shop? "It's just not right."

I returned to my Jeep outside the stately police department and drummed my fingers on the wheel. So Jameel had sicced the cops on me. That deserved a response.

I phoned him. And I wasn't terribly surprised when he accepted my call.

"Ms. Sommerland?"

"Mr. Rich. I just spoke with a Hot Springs detective."

"*Town* of Hot Springs."

I rolled my eyes. "Whatever. He said you might sue me for slander if I kept asking about the missing dogs."

He sputtered. "That's... That's a customer service issue now. We've provided Ms. March with a new dog, and the matter is settled."

"Six dogs attacked me yesterday. Which makes me think at least four more dogs have gone missing, not including Adan's. And given their price tag, the owners must have contacted your company about them. Have you given them new dogs too?"

"That's an internal matter."

I rubbed my brow. "What would make the Rovers run off on their own?"

"Nothing. I don't know what you thought you saw, but it didn't happen. And if you pursue this matter, you'll be hearing from our corporate attorneys." He hung up.

I made a face. The denials could have been corporate CYA, or they could have been something else. The burning question was, could the runaway Rovers be connected to Adan's murder?

Two Rovers minced down the steps of the police station. Their heads swiveled toward my car. Uneasy, I started the Jeep and drove off.

I'd confronted Jameel because the veiled threats from Guthrie had felt like a bluff. Also, they'd made me mad. But there was another person in this equation—Fitch. I was technically working for him, and my actions would impact his business. I tugged my collar. Maybe I should have kept my mouth shut.

I returned to Nowhere and my theater apartment. If I'd been living in New York, renting a place above a theater would have been hipster cool. In Nowhere... not so much. But the rent was cheap.

Letting myself in through the old theater's rear entrance, I climbed the steps to the landing. Furtive scrabbing sounded from behind my apartment's closed door.

I hesitated, then unlocked it and nudged it open. Snarling, Fredo hurled himself at me. But the small gray dog's tail was wagging. That's the nice thing about dogs. They're always happy to see you, even when they're trying to rip you limb from limb.

Sammie the theater cat lay coiled on my bed. He cracked an eyelid and closed it again, indifferent.

I took Fredo for a walk up and down Main Street. Fredo was particularly fond of the four-story flamingo in front of Town Hall. He took his time sniffing around the dormant grass.

Gert emerged from Town Hall's tall doors. The mayor's shirt sleeves were rolled up, exposing bony elbows. A gust of wind caught his white hair, tangling it in a dandelion fluff. "I thought that was you. Get in here."

"No. You can't make me." I shouted and tugged Fredo away. He growled and leaned into his collar.

"We need to talk about that miniature museum," he shouted.

"No, we don't." What did he expect *me* to do about it?

"You're a part of this. It's your duty to—"

"I'm not listening." I raced back to the theater, Fredo nipping at my heels. Locking the theater door behind me, I climbed the stairs to my tiny apartment. I called Fitch.

"If it isn't my favorite spy," he rumbled, and my treacherous heart quivered.

"Surveillance specialist," I said, not one to take a compliment lying down. I shifted the blue-checked curtains and glanced out the window. If Gert was following me, I couldn't see him.

"My favorite spy with surveillance gadgets. How'd it go with the cops?"

I let the curtains drop. "They told me to back off or get sued for slander. Selina's got a new dog and all's well."

"Yeah," he said, "she told me that too."

"To drop the case?" I asked, surprised.

"She's got a new dog, so I'm calling this a win. Selina doesn't really need us anymore. It was always more a customer service than a detective problem."

And yet, Fitch had taken the job. I shoved that question aside. "I called Jameel Rich. He denied the dogs could have gone off on their own."

"You—" He groaned. "Of course you did. Why leave well enough alone when you can poke the bear?"

"I like to be thorough." I braced an elbow on my boxing dummy's shoulder.

"Thoroughly a pain in my..." his voice faded.

I straightened off the dummy. "Don't leave me in suspense. It's bad manners."

"Hm? Oh. What did Jameel say?"

"He said if I bothered him again, I'd hear from his attorneys. The problem is—"

"Charlie."

"Yeah," I said heavily.

"You want to keep nosing around, but if I got sued, you'd feel bad."

I grimaced. Was I that transparent? "Yeah."

"Meet me in my office in an hour." He hung up.

I futzed around my tiny apartment for thirty minutes, then stepped into the hallway and locked my door. Turning, I bumped into Charlie on the landing.

"Hey," he said. "Good, I caught you. Are you going somewhere?"

"Reno."

"Cool, I'll come with you."

Inside my apartment, Fredo barked energetically. It was a good thing I was the only person who lived in the building.

I glanced at my watch. "Ah, it's work." And I couldn't bring my little brother along.

"You're going to see Fitch? Even better. I want to hire him."

I love my brother. He's got a huge heart. But he's terminally broke. Also, what was I? Chopped liver? What had happened to him thinking I was an amazing investigator?

Plus, I didn't want to get Fitch involved. If Fitch was involved, he'd start telling me what to do. "No offense, but how are you going to hire a PI?"

He folded his arms. "I've got money."

"How?" I asked, my eyes narrowing.

"Adan gave me a sort of… allowance."

A *what*? "Aren't you a little—"

"Old for that, I know." His face flushed beneath his beard. "But he seemed so happy. I didn't spend any of it. It's all sitting in my bank account. But now he's dead, murdered, and well, it seems like a good thing to spend it on."

Yeah. It did. But I didn't like the idea of hiring Fitch, though I couldn't say exactly why. I just knew it was more than pride.

"All right," I said reluctantly. "You can come." Fitch would have to turn him down anyway. It had to be a conflict of interest or something. It certainly would have been in the protection business. But by asking, Charlie would feel like he'd done something, and I could keep doing what I'd been doing. Win-win.

Fitch's office was not in the best part of Reno. Rhodes Investigations was in a five-story building held together by spit and graffiti. We took the elevator to the third floor. I rapped on the pebbled glass window in the door. When there was no answer, we strolled inside the reception area.

Fitch hasn't had a receptionist as long as I've known him. So it was no surprise the room was empty. We walked to his inner office door, and I knocked again.

"Alice? Come in." He shouted, and we walked inside. Standing beside his battered wooden desk, Fitch shoved the phone into the rear pocket of jeans. He wore a green golf shirt that brought out his eyes, and I had no doubt he knew it. "Hey, Charlie. I'm sorry about Adan. How're you doing?"

"I want to hire you," my brother said.

Fitch cocked a brow and glanced at me. I shook my head. *Just say no.*

"I got money," Charlie continued. "From Adan."

"Is this future money or current money?" Fitch's forehead wrinkled.

"It's in my bank account," he said. "Adan deposited it last month. It's mine."

I crossed my arms and waited for the inevitable rejection.

"Then you're in luck," Fitch said. "I happen to be in between clients."

My arms dropped to my sides. "What? I mean, good, but isn't that a conflict of interest or something?"

"Why?" Fitch walked around his desk and sat in the executive chair behind it. "*I'm* not inheriting Levann's money."

"Because... I work for you. Charlie's my brother."

"This isn't personal protection," he said, "where a wrong move could cost a life. It's investigating." The PI's lips curled.

"Besides, I just got off the phone with the *Town* of Hot Springs PD. They weren't happy you bothered the Rover execs." To Charlie, he said, "It seems your sister needs more training in people skills."

"No kidding," Charlie said. "Did I tell you about the time she attacked me with a cane?"

"I didn't attack you," I said. "It was an arm control hold." But I winced. Jameel hadn't wasted any time complaining.

"You can get some practice in with Charlie's case." Fitch rested his feet on the desk.

"Hold on," I said. "Who says I'm available?" I was going to do it regardless, but I didn't want to seem easy.

"You available?" Fitch asked.

"I'll have to check my schedule."

"She's available," Charlie said. "She's just playing hard to get. She always does this. It's super annoying. But she'll do it."

What? That was a foul and dishonest misrepresentation of my character.

Fitch shrugged. "The customer's always right," he said. "Looks like we're stuck with you." His feet dropped to the floor. The PI opened his desk drawer and pulled out a stack of paperwork. He stood. "I'll just need you to sign some papers, Charlie."

"Cool." Charlie grabbed the papers. "This is going to be great. The three of us working together."

Fitch stilled, the hand with the papers raised above the wooden desk. "Three of us?"

"You, me and Alice," Charlie said.

I grinned. Fitch was going to *love* working with my brother. "After all," I said innocently. "The customer's always right."

Chapter Nine

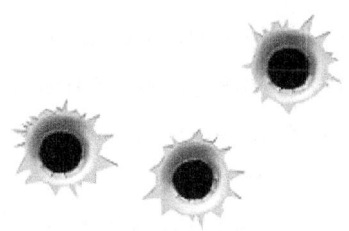

"Three law enforcement..." Charlie squinched up his face. "Private law enforcement officers, working together." He dropped into one of Fitch's faux-leather office chairs. Pale light streamed through the mini-blinds and formed prison bar stripes across my brother's face. He squinted and shifted his chair.

I shook my head. *Here we go.*

"Law enforcement?" Fitch inclined his head.

"Yeah," my brother said brightly. "I just took the security guard job for the cannery. Didn't I tell you?"

"No," I said. "That's great, Charlie." He'd been resisting the job because it was too "nailed down." A part of me I didn't like much understood that. My personal protection career hadn't been *nailed down* either.

"Yeah," my brother said, "Adan convinced me to take it."

A part of me I liked even less hardened. "Adan?" I'd been telling my brother for months to take the job and *Adan* had convinced him?

Charlie's blue eyes sobered. "He was a really good guy."

And I was a jerk for getting insecure. The important thing was Charlie was getting steady work, taking responsibility.

Fitch walked around the desk and clapped his shoulder. "We'll do what we can to figure out who killed your father."

"Okay." Charlie edged forward in his chair. "So here's what I'm thinking. I can get us all into the house."

"How?" Fitch asked.

"It's easy," he said. "I left a bunch of my things there. I'll tell them you're helping me move."

I nodded. The family would be so thrilled to see Charlie gone, they might even volunteer to help. Scratch that. They'd volunteer Shelley to help.

"You sure you want to do that?" Fitch asked.

"Why not?" my brother said.

"If you stay in the house," he said, "it's a claim, isn't it?"

"A claim?" Charlie shook his head. "You mean like challenging the will? I don't know. I mean, I know what the lawyer said, but it doesn't feel right."

"What did the lawyer say?" Fitch asked sharply.

"Adan planned to change his will to include Charlie," I explained.

"Don't standard wills usually include all children, known or unknown?" Fitch asked.

I shrugged. "Even if they do, including Charlie explicitly would make things easier. The lawyer suggested he challenge the will, so... I'm not sure what the exact situation is." And I should have found out. But I'd been so stunned by current events I hadn't been thinking. I scrubbed a hand over my face. I needed to be less stunned and more proactive.

"On the positive side," Fitch said, "Charlie loses a motive for murder. And everyone else mentioned in that will gains one."

Yeah. And the bad news was they were all living at that house.

The next day was cold and bright. Or at least, it was cold and bright after sunrise. I got a good look at pre-sunrise when Fredo woke me at five by jumping on my chest.

I repaid him by taking him for a jog, which the dog hated as much as I did. I'm not sure whose eyes were rolling more by the time we made it back to my apartment.

I showered and changed. Charlie, in khaki slacks and a navy paranormal museum sweatshirt, arrived at the theater at ten. We drove to Hot Springs in my Jeep. Fitch was waiting outside the gate in his blue Ford Explorer.

I pressed the intercom, and after a moment, the butler's voice issued from it. "Yes?"

My brother leaned across me. "Hey, Shelley, it's Charlie. I've come to get my things out of my room." The gate buzzed and swung open in response.

We drove through the gates and up the drive. Charlie's Tesla had vanished, and I wondered how they'd moved it. Had Adan kept an electronic key? And if so, who had it now?

We climbed the brick steps. The door opened the moment we reached the landing.

Shelley, in his butler's uniform, drew it wide. "Good morning, Mr. Sommerland. Mr. Levann is having breakfast in the dining room." The way he said it, it sounded like a warning.

"Oh, cool," Charlie said. "You remember my sister, Alice. And this is my friend Fitch. He's going to help with the move."

Shelley arched a brow. "Indeed?"

Fitch flexed a bicep. "I'm just here for the heavy lifting." He wore a plain white t-shirt and jeans as a moving uniform that made me acutely aware of his physique. I really needed to get over this or stop working for Fitch.

"I doubt you'll be too troubled," the butler replied obliquely.

Charlie rubbed his hands together. "We'll just, er, go upstairs then. Unless... We can go in, can't we?"

"The police said they were done with that room," Shelley said.

"Great," Charlie said. "I mean, okay."

"Yes, sir." Shelley nodded.

My eyes narrowed. He was playing the butler role to the hilt. Presumably that's what he was paid for, but the act seemed off.

We followed Charlie up the stairs, down the carpeted hall, and to his room. The first time I'd been inside, I hadn't been paying as much attention to it as maybe I should have. Discovering Adan's corpse had thrown me off my observation game. I scanned the bedroom now.

It was bigger than my entire apartment. The walls were painted near-black, the color broken only by the dark, wood trim. French doors led onto a wide balcony.

A sleigh bed with an expensive looking black and brown coverlet stood in one corner. A portrait of a man in old-fashioned military dress hung above it. A sitting area filled with antique furniture stood beside the black marble fireplace.

"Nice," Fitch said.

"My stuff's in the closet," Charlie said.

"Where did you find the body?" the PI asked, then shook his head and knelt in an easy, fluid motion. "Never mind. I see." He squinted at the stains that discolored the sand-colored carpet.

"It looked like he'd been hit with one of those fireplace dogs." My brother nodded toward the fireplace.

Fitch rose and walked to it. For lack of anything better to do, I trailed after him. The PI picked up an andiron—a twin to the dog that had been used on Adan. He swung it experimentally. "That would do it. But what was Adan doing in your room?"

"No idea," Charlie said.

"Did he think you were home?" he asked.

"I don't know." My brother jammed his hands into the pockets of his khaki slacks. "I called him and told him I was bringing Alice by."

I goggled at him. "Wait, you spoke to him earlier that day? Why didn't you tell me?"

"Sorry. Didn't I mention that before?"

"No," I said, annoyed. "What time was this?" My own brother had been holding out on me, and I hadn't known it. It didn't say much for my intuition.

He pulled out his phone and checked. "Three-twenty-two," he said triumphantly.

"That narrows the time of death," I said. "What did he say to you?"

"He said he had something for me, and he'd see me when we got here."

"Did he say what he had for you?" I asked.

"No. He sounded excited about it though."

Fitch wandered around the bedroom. "And you didn't see anything unusual here?"

"No, but I was looking at..." Charlie swallowed, and my own throat seemed to harden. "I guess I just wasn't noticing things."

"That's understandable," Fitch said. "It was a bad situation. Do you see anything now that doesn't belong?"

Charlie followed him around the spacious room. He straightened. "There's— Never mind. That's not new."

I tested the French doors, and they opened onto a balcony. It ran along this side of the house. I leaned out. More French doors hinted at other rooms. "Did you keep these doors unlocked?"

Charlie rubbed the top of his head. "Um, I don't remember. I didn't go out there much. It's been kind of cold."

Fitch joined me on the balcony. He checked the other doors. They were locked. "Other bedrooms?" he asked.

"Yeah," my brother said. "And there's a sort of living room too. They called it something else though."

"The solar?" Fitch asked.

"Yeah," he said. "That's it."

I raised my brows. *The solar?* I wouldn't have been able to pull that word out of my mental dictionary. "I'm going to snoop around."

"Good idea," Fitch said. "I'll keep looking around here."

I wandered back into the long hallway. If I were lord of the manor, where would my bedroom be? Somewhere with a view of the mountains, I figured. I walked down the hallway, pressing my ear to doors, and knocking gently and opening them when I heard nothing.

Where was the rest of the family? Granted, this was a house made to get lost in. But I'd thought I'd have run into someone by now.

I went through my listen, knock and open routine for the sixth time and opened the door to a bedroom the size of the Nowhere dinner theater. It had been decorated in gold and black, and the four-poster bed was curtained.

Picture windows overlooked the Sierras. Irresistibly drawn, I walked past the bed to the glass. A wide expanse of lawn rolled toward a small stone hut. A neat line of pines ran behind it. And behind them, the land folded upward into the hills.

"What are you doing in here?" Arystarch said, and I jumped. He wore a painter's smock over his black slacks and turtleneck. I wasn't sure if the black was his mourning costume or if he just always wore it.

"Sorry. I got a little lost, and then I saw this view."

"This was my father's room." His saturnine face drew into a scowl. His hands balled into fists.

"Sorry," I repeated, contrite. "I was wondering where everyone was."

"Adalina's at work. God knows where that gold digger Holli is. Off spending Adan's money before the tap is cut off, no doubt."

Oh, *this* was interesting. "Will it get cut off?"

He lifted one shoulder, dropped it. "I don't know, but I'm sure she does. She plays the dim bulb, but she's sharper than she looks."

"Is she?"

"She came up through the ranks at Rover. That's how the two met. And she wasn't his secretary. She was an engineer, like Gina."

"Maybe I should talk to her about what's going on with the robo-dogs."

"What's going—?" He shook his head. "No, never mind. I was never a part of that business."

"Has Adan's dog turned up?" I asked.

"No idea." His brown eyes sparked with irritation.

"When's the last time you saw it?"

He nodded toward the window. "Out there, with Holli. They were walking toward the woods."

"Not to that little hut?" I pointed at a charmingly ramshackle hut with a moss-covered shingle roof.

He snorted. "Hardly. The hot spring's been closed all year. It's gone off."

"There's a hot spring in there?"

"It's an acid spring now. Stinks to high heaven and is broiling hot. Adan was looking at repairing it somehow, but it's a natural spring. I don't think he ever figured it out."

"When was this? When you saw the dog and Holli, I mean."

His gaze flicked upward. "The afternoon Adan died. I saw them from my studio."

"Right," I said, "you've got a view of the mountains too. Did they come back together as well?"

"How should I know? I was working, not watching for them. What are you doing here anyway?"

"Charlie's moving out. My friend and I are helping him."

"About ti—" His lean face darkened. "Your brother had better not be taking anything that doesn't belong to him."

I stiffened. "Hold on. Charlie's not—" I said to his departing back. Cursing, I hurried after him, then stopped. Charlie could handle himself. And this just might be the diversion I needed.

Chapter Ten

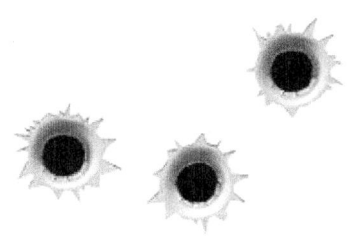

I stopped admiring the view and got to snooping—I mean investigating. Unfortunately, Adan seemed to have been one of those people who kept business out of the bedroom. I didn't find a single suspicious object in the drawers or underneath the four-poster bed.

So I returned to the carpeted halls and to trying doors, while Arystarch's shouts echoed through the house.

When trying random doors proved unsuccessful, I trotted downstairs and explored that level. Finally, I hit paydirt when I opened the door to Adan's home office.

I trotted across the Persian rug and to his polished wood desk. It overlooked a wide lawn and the mountains beyond. His datebook lay open upon it. Hurriedly, I pulled out my phone and took a picture of the pages. I reached to turn to the prior week.

Someone coughed behind me. Pressing my phone to my ear, I turned. Shelley stood in the doorway. "May I help you with something?" he asked.

"I was just looking for a good signal." I motioned to the windows on the other side of the desk. "Quite a view. It's a wonder Adan got any work done here." Or that the chair was positioned with its back to the door. But he'd probably had no reason to think someone was out to get him.

The butler tilted his head and paused. On the fireplace mantle, a golden clock beneath a glass dome ticked. "He did most of his work at the Rover office," he finally said.

I pocketed my phone. "Adan must have been an interesting man to work for."

"Indeed."

I tried again. "Do you think he had any idea that he was in danger?"

"I wouldn't know."

I had a hard time believing that, and I lowered my head to study the butler. In fact, I had a hard time believing anything he said, and I couldn't put my finger on why. His blond head had not a hair out of place, and his chiseled face was still as marble. His suit was immaculate, the creases blade sharp. His blue-eyed gaze glittered, and I was pretty sure it was with amusement. Likely at my expense.

"Really?" I said. "I'd imagine you'd know pretty much everything going on around here."

"If I had known a murder was about to be committed, I assure you, I would have informed the authorities."

"Of course. I didn't mean it that way. It's just—"

He arched a brow. "The unseen, unheard servants hear and see everything?"

I leaned against the wooden desk. "You mean life isn't like *Downton Abbey*?" I asked. "Bummer." His mouth quirked.

"Actually," I continued, "I'd have thought there'd be more servants in a house this size."

"Mr. Levann was uncomfortable with having people who weren't family in the house. He preferred a limited staff."

"And Mrs. Levann?"

"I am unaware of her opinion on the matter."

Something thudded upstairs, and we glanced at the ceiling. The crystal chandelier jingled.

"It appears Mr. Sommerland may be in need of your assistance," the butler said.

"You're probably right." I hesitated. "The family was quick with their alibis. Were they all where they'd said they were when Mr. Levann was killed?"

"I find that highly unlikely." He took a step back and pulled the door wider.

Unable to ignore a hint that pointed, I strolled into the hallway. He followed me into the high-ceilinged foyer. Fitch, a knapsack slung over one broad shoulder, walked slowly down the curving stairs.

"Let me help you with that." I reached for the bag. Shelley remained at the bottom of the stairs, watching.

"It's okay, I got it." Fitch rolled his eyes toward the ceiling. "It's all he's got," he hissed.

My brother did tend to travel lightly through life. I never thought the trait would be so inconvenient. I jogged up the stairs to Charlie's room.

Inside, Arystarch stood beside the black marble fireplace looking thunderous. Sunlight streamed through the French windows but failed to make any inroads against the black walls and deep colors.

Charlie was making a business of studying the inside of an empty closet. Regretfully, he closed the black, louvered doors. "Looks like this one's clean."

"Have you checked under the bed?" Arystarch snarled.

"Good idea," my brother said. "I'm always losing things there."

I joined Arystarch. He cut a wary glance at me. Charlie lifted the coverlet and stretched beneath the sleigh bed.

I considered questioning Arystarch from an oblique angle, couldn't think of one, mentally shrugged, and just asked. "Was your father worried or concerned about anything?"

He snorted. "Just the opposite."

"What do you mean?"

He nodded to Charlie, whose bare legs flailed from beneath bed. "When the golden boy arrived, dear old Dad seemed to take it as a sign now was the time for his second childhood. He was careless as the proverbial lark. I don't think he spent more than a few hours in the office since your brother turned up."

"How did Jameel take that?"

He crossed his arms over his paint-stained smock. "How do you think?" His mouth thinned with displeasure.

"Honestly, I have no idea."

"Jameel was initially unhappy, then realized with Adan out of the way, he could run the business the way he wanted."

"And how did he want it?" I braced one elbow on the mantel. On the hearth, the remaining dog andiron grinned up at me.

"His way." A muscle flicked in his jaw.

"Did the two butt heads in the past?"

"Good lord," Arystarch said sardonically, "you think you're an amateur detective."

"Personal protection," I said automatically. Everything that came out of this guy's mouth seemed sneering. I wanted to knock the smirk off his face. But he'd just lost his father, gained a surprise step-brother, and I needed info.

"That career's smashed on the rocks though, isn't it?" His smile was frosty. "Yes, I know all about Toomas Koppel. Adan looked into your background too."

Heat flared at the front of my skull. "And he shared what he found with you?"

His face contorted and smoothed just as quickly. He looked toward the French doors to the patio. "Of course."

Ha. Adan *hadn't* shared. From Arystarch's reaction, I guessed Adan had rarely shared when it came to business. At least, not with his adopted son. So how and what had Arystarch found out?

"Found it!" Charlie pulled his head from beneath the bed and raised a brass coin triumphantly.

Arystarch made a face. "That cheap trash?"

Charlie clambered to his feet. "I dunno. I think it's kind of cool."

"What is it?" I asked.

"One of Adan's momento mori's," Arystarch said. "He gave them to everyone."

"Remember you will die?" I asked.

"But Adan didn't think he would really die," Arystarch said. "It was never real to him, just a philosophical thing."

"It's from the Stoics." Charlie ambled to the fireplace. "The idea is to remember you could die any moment, so you live your best life today."

"And was Adan living his best life?" I asked.

"Who knows? Who cares? He's dead now." Arystarch strode to the door and kicked it wider. "And now, if you're done here...?"

"Oh," Charlie said. "Yeah. Thanks." He shot me a look.

I gave a slight shake of my head and grimaced. Our expedition had been a bust. Defeated, we left the bedroom and walked down the red-carpeted stairs. Arystarch trailed at our heels.

Fitch climbed toward us. "What else can I grab?"

"Nothing," Arystarch said.

Charlie stopped at the bottom of the curving set of stairs and turned to Arystarch. "I just wanted to say—"

"You think of me as a brother?" He jammed his fists into the pockets of his smock and hunched his shoulders. "We're not."

My fists clenched. Did he always have to be such a creep?

"No." Charlie shook his head. "Adan was really cool. He created things. He built this amazing life." My brother motioned around the foyer. "I'm sorry I didn't get to know him better, and I'm sorry for your loss."

Arystarch folded his arms. "Just get out."

I gripped Charlie's shoulder. What Arystarch didn't get, because he was a selfish jerk, was that my brother meant every word. "Let's go," I said in a low voice.

We returned to my Jeep. Arystarch followed us outside and glowered at us from beneath the portico.

"Any luck?" Fitch asked me.

I shook my head. "Just a photo of Adan's planner pages for the week."

"Send it to me." His forehead creased. "I'm surprised the police didn't take that."

"They probably have some high-tech portable scanner," I said, sarcastic.

"They probably do," Fitch said. "I'll meet you back at the Sagebrush for a debrief." He strode to his Explorer.

Charlie turned the oversized coin between his fingers. "Adan did live his best life though. He said when I came, everything changed for him." He swallowed. "You don't thi nk... You don't think it's my fault someone killed him?"

"No," I said. "You aren't responsible for what happened." He slipped the coin into the pocket of his khaki slacks. "I mean it," I said more firmly. "You're not." And I was going to prove it to him, beginner detective or no.

Charlie and I got into my car. Fitch followed us to the iron gates. They were in the process of swinging open for a blue Mercedes. The luxury car stopped. Holli, in a fitted, camel-colored coat and matching hat, stepped from it and hurried to my door. I rolled down the window.

"Oh, hi!" she said. "What are you doing here?"

"We were just getting Charlie's things," I glanced in the side mirror. Fitch rolled down his window and stuck his head out.

She blinked. "You're moving out?"

"It didn't seem right to stay," Charlie said.

"But you can't," she cried. "Turn your car around right now. We need to talk."

Chapter Eleven

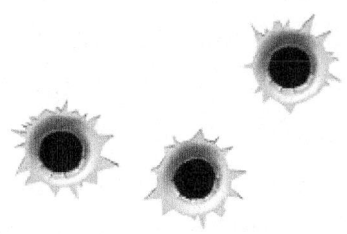

Whenever someone says we *need to talk*, you know it's not going to be good. I'm pretty sure it's a rule. And if it's not, it should be. I glanced at my brother in the seat beside mine.

"Uh... talk? At the house?" Charlie leaned across me, slipped, and his elbow struck the Jeep's horn. It blared, short and sharp, shattering the late morning quiet.

An irritated stellar jay shot from a nearby pine carrying its brunch in its beak. Wincing, Holli stepped away from my open window.

Charlie straightened off me with an apologetic look. "Um... Okay." He tugged down the lapels of his yacht jacket.

I sighed and signaled for Fitch to back up behind me. We turned our cars and followed Holli's Mercedes back down the gravel drive.

Fitch stepped from his SUV and opened Holli's car door. She held out her hand. He took it, helping her from the car.

"Wow," Charlie said. "That's a real power move."

Yeah. It was. Not that I was jealous or anything. That would just be dumb. I shrugged. "If you say so." We got out of my Jeep and joined Holli and Fitch on the mansion's front steps.

"—kind of you to help a friend," Holli was saying, basking in the glow of the PI's aw-shucks smile. She slowly unbuttoned her flared coat, and I managed not to roll my eyes.

Fitch rubbed the back of his neck. "It's the least I can do." His emerald eyes gleamed, tigerish.

"Come inside and have tea," she said. "I know it's early, but in Germany, people have tea all day. Of course, they don't actually drink *tea*. But the point stands." Holli flounced into the mansion. She handed a waiting Shelley her coat and hat, revealing a fitted baby doll t-shirt and jeans. Across her chest in red letters, the t-shirt read: I ♥ Rover.

I found myself liking her more for her casual outfit. The tee looked better on her than designer wear—more honest, less pretentious. But we tend to like people like us, and jeans and a tee were my go-to when I wasn't working. I didn't think the casual-wear was a ploy to win us over though. It looked natural on Holli.

We followed her into the drawing room. The holly on the mantel glowed with twinkle lights. Portraits of people long dead smiled knowingly down at us from the red-silk-covered walls.

Holli motioned us into chairs and dropped onto the red-and-gold striped settee. She pulled off her red leather driving gloves. "Shelley will be here in a minute to take our orders. Just you watch. He knows everything that goes on in this house."

He'd also seen us come in, but that didn't mean she was wrong. I got the feeling the butler knew a lot more than he was saying.

Shelley appeared in the high doorway. "Mrs. Levann. Tea for four?"

"Yes, please." She nodded, and he backed from the room.

"Told you," she said and shuddered theatrically. "It's not even teatime, but it's like he can read my mind or something, or hear..." She lowered her voice. "This is why I find it hard to believe he doesn't know anything about who killed my husband."

"You think the butler did it?" Charlie leaned forward in the fragile-looking chair and braced his elbows on his bare knees.

"Someone in this house is a killer," she whispered. "And I think... I think I may be next."

Fitch frowned. He leaned forward, forearms loose on his thighs.

"You think you're in danger?" I said and grimaced. It had been a stupid question. Of course she was worried. Her husband had been murdered. How could she not wonder if she was next? "Has something specific happened?" I asked, trying to redeem myself.

"No," she said slowly. "Not exactly. But it stands to reason, doesn't it? If someone killed Adan for his inheritance, I'm the next logical person to go. Half the estate belongs to me now."

"But if you die, wouldn't the money go to your heirs?" Fitch asked.

She rested her feet on the coffee table and crossed her ankles, dislodging a *Town and Country* magazine. It fluttered to the carpet, and she bent and picked it up. "Adan's children are my heirs. When I married him, he insisted, and of course I agreed. I don't have any family of my own. My share of the estate is only mine as long as I live." Twin creases appeared between her eyebrows. "I forget the legal term for that."

"A lifetime estate," Fitch said.

She beamed at him, her eyes shining. "Exactly. So Charlie, you *have* to stay. I can't live here all alone with people who... Well, they may not want to kill me, but they wouldn't be unhappy if something happened."

"Can you stay somewhere else?" I asked, impatient. Holli wasn't exactly poor. She wasn't trapped here. "You must be able to move out, get a hotel or somewhere else more permanent."

"But I have a lifetime estate in the house too. I can't move out."

"I don't think that's how it works," I said.

Holli shot Fitch a helpless look. On the delicate chair, he seem even rougher and larger.

"I get it." He nodded thoughtfully. "It's not fair to ask you to leave. But if you really believe you're in danger, it doesn't make sense to stay."

"Where else would I go?" she asked.

I shook my head. "A hotel," I repeated. "A B&B. A rental house." Honestly, she had good reason to be concerned. Holli should go somewhere safe. That was my old career talking though. My focus then had been more situational. It had been safer to keep clients out of bad situations than assume I could successfully fend off a bad guy.

Charlie rubbed the back of his neck. "I don't know. I don't think—"

"What the hell are you still doing here?" Arystarch stalked into the room and stopped in front of Charlie. He'd ditched his smock. Without it, he looked like a mime in his black turtleneck and slacks.

"Ary," Holli said, "that's unkind."

"Unkind, hell." He braced his fists on his narrow hips. "He doesn't belong here. He said he was leaving. I watched him go."

She straightened on the settee. "It's my house, and Charlie's my guest."

"Tea is served." Shelley minced into the room and set a tray laden with tea and tiny sandwiches on the coffee table between us. Holli removed her feet from the table.

Arystarch's eyes bulged. "Are you kidding me?"

"I know it's early," Holli said. "But in Germany—"

"Forget the Germans," he exploded and motioned toward my brother. "This fraud leeched off my father and now he's doing the same to you. Are you stupid?"

"No," she said icily. "I'm not." She leaned forward and plucked a scone from the tray.

Her step-son's lips whitened. Arystarch pivoted on his polished shoes and strode from the drawing room.

My eyes narrowed. I didn't think Holli was stupid either. This left two options. One: she didn't really believe she was in danger here. Two: she did believe it, and there was something going on she wasn't telling us. I suspected the latter.

"You see what I'm dealing with." Holli motioned toward the open door. "Charlie, you belong here. Please stay. Besides, this house is partly yours too."

"Actually," my brother said, "it isn't."

"What are you talking about?" Her coffee-colored eyes widened. "You're Adan's son."

"Yeah." Charlie scratched his neat beard. "But I'm not in the will."

"What?" She sat back on the settee and nibbled a corner of the scone. It looked like blueberry. And how was it possible I was hungry again?

"But that's not right," she continued. "He told me he was putting you in his will. There must be some mistake. Stay here with me, and I'll help you figure it out."

My brother grinned. "Really? You're sure? Yeah, I'll stay. It's a great idea."

Fitch shot me a warning glance and gave a slight shake of his head.

My mouth compressed, and I swallowed. The PI was thinking what I was thinking. What if one of the other heirs decided Charlie was a threat to their share of the loot?

"Oh," my brother continued, "but what about Alice?"

"Your sister can stay too." She turned to me. "You're a bodyguard, aren't you?"

"Surveillance specialist," I muttered.

"Then it's perfect," she exclaimed. "We've got plenty of room."

"I'm not sure that's such a great idea," Fitch said. "You've got work back in Nowhere."

"No, no," Charlie said. "We can do it."

"What about that project we're working on?" The PI asked meaningfully. "For the theater."

"It'll be fine," my brother said. "Staying's *exactly* what I want."

Fitch sank back on the sofa and scrubbed his hands over his face. He also may have growled, but I'm not a hundred percent sure on that.

"I've got a dog," I said desperately. "We can't."

"I *love* dogs." Holli finished the scone and wiped her hands on her jeans. "Bring him. I couldn't have a dog when Adan was alive—he was allergic. That's why he was so excited about the pet Rovers."

"He really designed them to be pets?" I asked.

"Oh, yes." She grabbed a mini sandwich off the tray. "I mean, they have other applications, obviously. But Adan designed them for fun. Bring your doggy."

"Yeah." Charlie popped a tiny scone into his mouth and swallowed. "It'll be great. Look at all the space Fredo will have to run around in."

She laughed. "Fredo? What a name! Oh, please come and bring him."

"Please?" Charlie said.

I grabbed a gold-rimmed plate and a blueberry scone from the tray. "Fine."

Back at my tiny apartment, I jammed a pair of socks into a duffel bag on my bed. Sammie watched me from the shoulder of my boxing dummy. Fredo tried to eat the socks.

"Cut it out." I pried the socks from his jaws, dropped them back in the bag, and zipped it up. Fredo growled, his bulging eyes rolling.

"Don't try that with me." The dog wasn't even knee high. Admittedly, the growling was more startling because his teeth stuck out in different directions. But I wasn't intimidated by an ankle biter. He gave a doggy shrug and dropped onto his belly.

"That's what I thought." I rummaged in the closet and pulled out a dog carrier. I'd gotten it used to take Fredo to the vet. I'd never managed to get the dog inside it though, and it had been easier to let him ride in my oversized purse than throw down with Fredo.

But I was taking him to a stranger's house and wasn't sure how he'd react. Today, he was going in the carrier, like it or not. Fredo made a more serious growl.

"We're not going to the vet, okay? It's just a ride."

The gray dog leapt to his feet. Sammie raised his head, interested. I stepped to my kitchen/dining area and opened a can of stinky dogfood. Scraping it into his bowl, I set it inside the carrier. Fredo sniffed and turned his head in disdain.

"Let's go." I picked him up.

Fredo twisted, springing from my hands. He darted toward my big leather purse on the floor and jumped inside.

"I'm not carrying you in my purse. It's undignified."

He barked once and panted.

I picked up the purse, and he shot me a doggy *I-win* grin. "You think you're so smart?" I set the purse and Fredo inside the carrier and reached for its wire door. He howled and scrambled from the purse.

Stabs of pain raced up my spine. "Ow!" I reared backward, flailing and spinning around like a drunk panda.

Sammie sprang from my back and to the window. The ebony cat sat and licked his paw.

I rubbed my back where the cat had landed. They were working together against me. This was not good. Not at all.

I turned toward the carrier. It was empty. I looked around the tiny studio apartment, then lifted the quilt and checked beneath the bed. Two amber eyes glared out at me.

At this point, fighting Fredo was just a matter of ego. "Fine," I said. "You can ride in my purse." I threw out the dog food, put away the carrier, and took Fredo for a walk down Main Street to calm him down.

Nowhere over the holidays wasn't as glamorous as Hot Springs. But the paper decorations in the shop windows were cheerful. White twinkle lights had been strung in the barren trees along the sidewalks. The lights were dim in the afternoon light, but they were there.

Fredo stopped to sniff the giant lawn flamingo's metal legs. Someone had tied a big red bow around its neck. The bow clashed with the pink, but it's the thought that counts.

"Sommerland," Gert barked, striding toward me. The older man looked lost in his oversized coat and scarf, but I wasn't fooled. Gert was trouble.

I paused, wary. "What?"

His glasses flashed in the sunlight. "I want intel on that miniature museum," our temporary mayor said.

"Just check the Hot Springs website."

"I have." He spat. "*Miniatures*. What the hell's wrong with people?"

I cast a glance at the four-story flamingo. "We have Big Things."

"Those are art. The Big Things combine incongruous imagery into new narratives that reflect on a tangible positivity, underpinned by a playful exploration of harmony and tension. I'm going to need more if we're going to stop this."

"That's just... That..." *What?* I shook my head. "Why stop it? People come to Nowhere, then go to Hot Springs. Maybe the miniature museum will be a complement to the Big Things."

"Yeah. A complement people will be paying for in Hot Springs. They need to spend their money here. Hot Springs is chiseling in on our territory, and I'm not gonna take it lying down. I'm calling in your marker. I want names. Background checks. The works."

"I don't have a marker," I said irritably. "Stop talking about a marker. It's not a marker. And I'm not a private investigator. I'm a surveillance specialist."

"Then what are you waiting for?" he asked. "Start surveilling." Fredo sniffed the mayor's scuffed brown shoe.

"Even if I wanted to, which I don't, I can't just work for free. I've got bills to pay."

"Good, you're here. What do you have to report?" Mrs. Malone, in a green track suit, thumped unsteadily toward us on her cane.

"Report?" I asked. She arched a menacing brow. "Oh," I said quickly. "Right." It was easier just to tell her, and it might divert Gert. "Charlie's moved back into the mansion, and I'm going to be staying with him for a while."

"Detecting and protecting," she said. "Smart. Though you'll need to keep a close eye on your brother. Is he sure he wants to do this?"

I sighed. "He seems to be."

"Alice and I were just talking about the new miniature museum in Hot Springs." Behind their glasses, Gert's blue eyes glittered with cunning.

"Of course you'll be providing intelligence," Mrs. Malone said. "You're perfectly positioned now that your brother's living in Hot Springs. No one will suspect you."

"Everyone will suspect me. They already suspect me. What do you expect to do with this so-called intel anyway?"

The two shared a look. "Better you don't ask," Gert said.

Fine. What was the worst that could happen? "No surveillance unless I get paid."

"Where's your holiday spirit?" Mrs. Malone asked. "This is for the town."

"Not unless I get paid," I repeated stubbornly. "Unless you want to knock a couple weeks off the rent..." I let the idea dangle.

"One week," Mrs. Malone said, and Gert threw me a triumphant look. I refrained from sticking out my tongue at him.

"Now what have you learned about the murder so far?" she asked.

Not a lot. I shuffled my feet. "I took a photo of Adan's calendar. But I was interrupted before I could get more than the two pages."

She snapped her fingers. "Let me see."

I excavated my phone from my jacket pocket and pulled up the picture.

She squinted at it. "How do you expect me to read that? Email it to me."

Obediently, I did, while she dug through her black purse. From it, she excavated reading glasses and a tablet computer. Her gnarled hands whizzed across the touch screen. She adjusted the glasses. "Ah. Much better. Hm."

"Hm?" I hadn't had a chance to look at it yet, and I came to stand beside her, studying the screen.

"Who's J. O'Reiley?" she asked. "Adan had an appointment with him scheduled for today."

"That's Adan's lawyer. He came to see Charlie. Apparently, Adan intended to include Charlie in his will. The lawyer had drawn it up, and Adan needed to sign it."

She sucked in her wrinkled cheeks. "But he was killed before he could? Suggestive, very suggestive. I see there's a line through an appointment for last Tuesday—DoD. Department of Defense?"

I jerked down the hem of my jacket. This was going too far. As much as I wanted to entertain Mrs. Malone, she was not a part of this investigation. "Adan built toy robot dogs. It's probably not that DoD," I said repressively.

She arched a brow. "Robot dogs could be put to all sorts of purposes. I hear the Hot Springs police department uses them."

"Bunch of jerks," Gert muttered. He wasn't a big fan of the heavy hand of government, even if he was temporarily our mayor.

"But only to record encounters," I said. The dogs were just another example of useless, overpriced technology.

"And you really think the HSPD spent all that money just for ambulatory video equipment?" She tsked. "Really, Alice. That's the Department of Defense, mark my words. But why did Adan cancel? And what does it mean, if anything?"

"Nothing," I said stubbornly. But the back of my neck prickled. What *did* it mean?

"Hi, Alice. Hi, Mrs. Malone. Hi, Gert." A white rabbit strolled up to us.

"Hi, Lilyanna," I said. "No snow making today?"

The rabbit shook her oversized head. "It's only a part-time job. I heard Charlie was coming back to Nowhere today?"

"Oh. Ah." I shifted my weight. Why did I feel like I was making excuses for my brother? And why did I feel so guilty about it? "There's been a change of plan. He's going to stay in Adan's house a bit longer."

"Oh," Lilyanna said in a small voice. "Is he okay?"

"He's trying to solve his birth father's murder," Mrs. Malone said.

"I guess I should have expected that," the rabbit said. "He's got a chivalric code."

Gert rolled his eyes.

"It's just a temporary thing," I said quickly. "His step-mother wanted him to stick around until things settled down."

The rabbit's head bobbed. "That makes sense."

But it didn't. Not at all. And that worried me.

Chapter Twelve

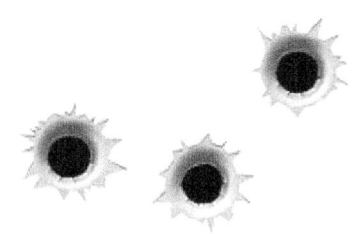

Fredo was an acquired taste. If he was ever entered in an ugliest dog contest, he'd win. His teeth stuck out at odd angles. We've seen a canine dentist, and she threw her hands up in despair.

His eyes bulged and rolled. His gray fur, despite my attempts at brushing, did what it wanted. Once you got over the shock and his tendency to eat clothing—while you were wearing it—he was okay.

Some people never got over the shock.

"Oh my God, what is that?" Holli recoiled, her heel striking the base of the foyer's curving, red-carpeted staircase. She pressed one hand to the chest of her I ♥ Rover tee.

"It's a dog." I shifted the oversized purse with Fredo in it on my shoulder. "It's Fredo." I set my duffle bag on the marble floor.

"That's no dog." She backed away toward the double stairs.

"No, really." I reached to pat his head, and Fredo growled. Thinking better of it, I jammed my hand into the pocket of my jeans instead. "It's Fredo."

"Are you sure?"

Fredo drooled happily, examining the high ceiling.

"Pretty sure," I said. "Where do you want me?"

"This way." She edged past, keeping her arms close to her body—a sign of intelligence on her part.

I picked up my duffle bag and followed her up the stairs. The room she led me to was about half the size of Charlie's. It looked like something out of a haunted castle. Portraits of lords and ladies in lace ruffs scowled down from the forest-green walls. A fireplace with herringbone brickwork stood opposite the four-poster bed.

My view overlooked the long driveway, which wasn't bad for surveillance purposes. I'd be able to monitor who was coming and going.

I eyed the Gone-With-The-Wind curtains and brushed a wisp of blond hair from my eyes. This wasn't the sort of place where I could leave Fredo alone. Not if I didn't want a massive repair bill at the end of my stay. "Who else is home right now?"

"Just me and Charlie," Holli said. "He's outside looking for Barney."

I glanced out the window. A gray Jaguar glided away from the house.

"Who's that?" I nodded to the window.

Keeping her distance from Fredo, she came to stand beside me. "That's Shelley. Today's his shopping day." She checked the clock on her cellphone. "He doesn't usually leave this late in the day though."

"I just remembered – I need to pick some things up. I'll see you later." I hurried to my Jeep. Settling Fredo inside, I followed Shelley.

Bringing Fredo along was a desperation move. Dogs can cause problems on surveillance. They can attract attention when you need to blend in. They may bark at inconvenient moments. But as long as we were in my car, I could deal with it.

The butler had gotten a head start, but I could handle that too. There was really only one way into town from here, so I didn't need to follow too close.

I trailed the butler to an open-air shopping center, designed like a Swiss village. From my car, I watched Shelley trek in and out of gourmet food stores and do absolutely nothing suspicious.

Shelley made his way back through the parking lot. I put Fredo in my purse, stepped from the Jeep, and approached.

"Shelley? Is that you?" I adjusted the oversized bag on my shoulder.

His shoulders hunched beneath his elegant gray coat. He turned. "Ms. Sommerland. What a surprise. Can I assist you with something?" His gloved hands clenched on the shopping bags.

"I don't suppose you've seen Barney this morning?"

"The last I saw him, he was out by the hot spring. But that was days ago, the day of Mr. Levann's death, to be specific. May I ask why you're so concerned about the dog?"

"He records everything, doesn't he?" I asked.

"I believe that's true."

"He may have recorded something the day of the murder." This was the more sinister explanation for why Barney had gone missing. A better PI might not have pointed it out to Shelley. But if Shelley had done away with the Rover, he already knew it.

He arched a brow. "You do realize that the video and audio recordings are stored in the cloud, rather than in the dog?"

That pulled me up short. I was an idiot. A fool. Of course they would be. I rubbed the back of my neck. "Naturally," I said. "Who would have access to the recordings from Adan's Rover?"

A movement outside the upscale butcher shop caught my attention, and my stomach tightened. Three Rovers marched past. Antlers had been tied to their heads with big red bows.

I squinted. A fourth Rover, sans antlers, wore a gray pad on its back, like Selina March's dog. I didn't see how it was possible Selina's dog had gotten to the shopping mall. It was miles from her house. But from a distance, it sure looked like hers.

Shelley's nostrils twitched. "I'd imagine— What the hell is that?" Shelley leapt backward, colliding with a parked Ferrari. Its alarm blared.

Fredo growled, his head sticking from my bag.

"That's my dog," I shouted over the noise. "Fredo."

He smoothed his scarf and straightened off the shrieking Ferrari. "Are you certain it's a dog?"

"Oh, come on. It's a dog." And that joke was getting tired. I plucked Fredo from my purse and snapped on his leash. The car alarm fell silent.

"If you say so," he said doubtfully and tugged his ear. "As to whom would have access to the recording, I suggest you ask Mr. Rich or Ms. Levann."

The Rovers turned in unison. They walked past a Christmas tree and deeper into the shopping area.

"Okay, thanks." I set Fredo down, and we hurried after the Rovers.

I wove through the luxury cars and strode into the shopping area. Fake snow lay piled in drifts against the faux-stone buildings, strung with holly garlands. I hurried beneath a giant mistletoe ball, hung above a walkway.

The pseudo reindeer trotted toward an open area with a massive Christmas tree. Children pointed and laughed. The robo-dog with the padding on its back trailed after them. The dogs moved toward a Santa's Village.

Children lined up inside the village for a photo with the big guy. Elves with cheerful, plastered-on expressions shuffled tikes through a candy-cane maze.

Fredo and I caught up to the Rover with the padded back. It was definitely Selina's. I snapped a photo of it with my phone, then took a step back for a wider angle. I'm not sure why I had the idea I should prove where I'd found it. It just seemed more thorough.

Using my foot, I tipped Selina's Rover over onto its back. Its legs kept marching in air, going nowhere. *Heh.* A real dog would have been able to roll over, antlers and all. "See?" I said to Fredo. "These dogs aren't that great."

The little dog barked, tail wagging.

"Let that be a lesson," I told him. "Flesh and blood beats hardware any day." I jammed the phone into the rear pocket of my jeans and reached for two of its paws.

Fredo coughed. A metallic growl sounded behind us, and my scalp prickled. Slowly, I looked over one shoulder. Three antlered Rovers stood behind us in a V-formation, their blue eyes glowing.

"Ah, I'm returning this Rover to its owner," I said, straightening. "Selina March."

I grimaced. Who did I think I was talking to? The robo-dogs couldn't understand me. But if someone was controlling them, maybe a mall security guard, talking to the Rovers wasn't completely inane.

The legs on Selina's rover rotated one hundred and eighty degrees. The dog rose, its head now upside down.

"Oh," I said, uneasy. "You can do that." It flipped over. "And that," I said, edging backward.

Fredo backed away. The four dogs stepped closer.

I retreated outside their closing circle. "Okay," I said. "This is all just a misunderstanding."

The dogs lowered their front ends toward the ground, as if preparing to spring. A greasy chill slithered down my spine. Drifts of fake snow lay piled against the planter boxes. *Santa Baby* played over the outdoor mall's speakers. A single ribbon of glittery tinsel coiled like a snake on the tile floor.

Fredo barked. The Rovers' blue eyes flared. Suddenly I was back in the woods, being chased by half a dozen robot dogs. My hands turned clammy.

"Okay-bye." Releasing Fredo's leash, I leapt sideways and pivoted, racing past the candy-cane maze. Under other circumstances, I'd feel bad about abandoning Fredo. But the dogs had been fixated on me. Fredo was better off on his own.

A woman shrieked. I turned so fast my feet skidded out from under me on the slick tiles. My fingertips touched the cold paving stones before I regained my footing and straightened.

The dogs tore through Santa's Village. Candy canes, snowmen and gingerbread people went flying. Children screamed, stampeding toward me, elves and parents thundering after them in hot pursuit.

And then the panicked crowd was on me. I raised my hands to protect my head—admittedly not my most valuable asset. The crowd charged past, buffeting me. I caught an elbow in the ribs, someone stomped my foot, and then they were past, and I was free.

I limped toward the village. An elf scrambled on top of a faux-gingerbread house. A robo-Rudolph snapped at him, pulling free a green felt boot. It shook the boot in its metal jaws. I knocked the robo-dog onto its back.

Its legs swiveled backward and over its head, then hooked in its antlers. The dog flopped around making mechanical, wheezing sounds.

"Save Santa," the elf shouted, pointing.

Santa stood on top of his throne. He swung at two robo-dogs with an oversized plastic candy cane.

"Stay there," I told the man in the red suit.

"Where do you think I can go?" he shouted, spots of color pinking his cheeks.

I waded through drifts of fake snow toward the mall Santa.

Santa brandished the candy cane. "Back! Get back!" He smacked one dog on its nose, denting the plastic and leaving a red streak on the robot's face.

I kicked a Rover over. Its companion dog pivoted toward me. It sprang, multicolored holiday lights reflecting off its steel casing.

I dove clear, leveling an artificial Christmas tree forest. Leaping to my feet, I promptly tangled one ankle in a fallen string of lights. The dog bounded toward me. I wrenched the lights from around my leg.

Nowhere had a rodeo every year. It was kind of a big thing, and also the source of my second-greatest humiliation. That embarrassment was neither here nor there, though it had to do with a mutton-busting event gone wrong.

The point is, I actually knew how to tie and throw a lasso. I hadn't done it in a while, and I'd never done it under pressure. Worse, my other lassos hadn't been lined with twinkle lights. But my fingers automatically tied the knot in the cord. The dog leapt, and I threw.

The lasso sailed over the Rover's head. I squeaked and ducked. The robo-dog landed in the pile of downed Christmas trees.

My neck corded. "Oh, come *on*!" Hastily, I reeled in my makeshift lasso and prepped for another throw.

The Rover swiveled and jumped. I threw the lasso.

The dog jerked in mid-air and crashed to the trees, sparking. My lasso fell uselessly on top of it. The Rover's legs kicked spasmodically a few times then wheezed to a halt.

Cautiously, I approached the dog. A string of twinkle lights had tangled around one of the dog's legs. It crackled, sparking. I froze. The fake trees had metal bases. If a part of the wire was touching them... I could be in a giant electrical trap.

A uniformed policeman zipped up on a Segway. "Halt!" He hopped from the machine.

I raised my hand. "Stay away from the—"

Zzzzt.

My hand fell to my side. "—trees."

Chapter Thirteen

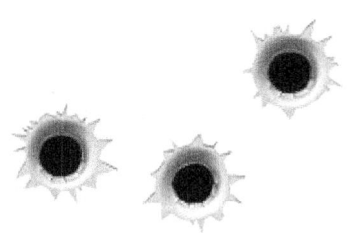

THE GOOD NEWS WAS the Hot Springs cop was only a little singed. Bad news? Getting a teensy bit electrocuted didn't improve his temper.

The Rovers had vanished. Santa was too busy tending to a hysterical elf amidst the candy cane wreckage to make much sense. I'd been left standing in a smashed Santa's village like Godzilla after a ramble through Tokyo.

"The Rovers don't attack people," a second police officer repeated. He was fit, and his uniform looked tailored. I was willing to bet the Hot Springs PD paid for his gym membership. A paramedic led the cop's semi-fried partner to a waiting ambulance.

A gust of wind whipped through the open-air mall. Fake snow scattered across the downed Christmas trees.

"Arrest that woman," the mall manager squawked. He was a portly man and would have made a good mall Santa. Though I suspected his face wasn't normally as crimson as it was now.

What was it with people and technology? Despite all the times we've *seen* it go wrong—lost computer files, wayward GPS's—no one wanted to believe it *could* go wrong.

My teeth clenched. "There must be some security footage." I adjusted the oversized purse on my shoulder. Fredo poked his head from the bag. He'd hightailed it into my purse once the Rovers had vanished.

"There isn't," the cop said. His nametag read HERNANDEZ. "Convenient for you, huh?"

"Trust me," I said. "Nothing today has been even remotely convenient."

He glanced at my purse and jerked away. "What the hell?" He pointed at Fredo.

"It's a dog," I snapped. "And why isn't there any security footage?" I nodded toward a camera beneath the eaves of a knife store.

"She did it." Edging away, the manager eyed Fredo. "She destroyed the video somehow."

"I did not," I said hotly. "How could I?"

"The cameras stopped working a few seconds after you came into the frame," the cop said.

"Well, I didn't do that," I said. "I don't have EMP powers. I can't neutralize security cameras with a look."

The mall manager folded his arms. "And yet, they're not working," he said, as if that settled everything.

My nails bit into my palms. "I'm telling you, I didn't mess with the cameras, and those Rovers went rogue."

The cop lowered his chin and looked up at me. "If someone attacked me, I'd react too."

"Well, yeah," I said, mollified. At last, someone who understood self defense.

"I meant why did you attack the dogs?"

"What? I didn't attack them." I pressed a hand to my chest. "They attacked me." It came out a little whiny, and my face grew hotter.

"Santa said he saw you knock one of the Rovers over before the incident began," the cop said.

I narrowed my eyes at Santa. He shrugged and patted the elf's shoulder. I guess I couldn't blame him for his honesty. He was Santa.

"That Rover belonged to Selina March," I said. "She hired my—the investigative firm I contract for—to... Whatever, to find it. The Rover company replaced her dog before we could find it, and she let us go. But I saw her Rover here and decided to investigate."

The cop arched a brow. "And you could tell it was her Rover."

"It had a sort of padding on its back. Gray."

"Then why'd you attack the mall Rovers?" the manager howled.

I gripped my head in my hands. "For the nth time, I didn't." This was getting us absolutely nowhere.

"Look at this mess." The mall manager motioned toward the felled trees and candy canes. "It's going to take us all day to get this back in order, and that means a closed Santa's Village. Who's going to compensate us?"

"Ask Rover," I snarled.

Things pretty much deteriorated from there. I got a ride to the police station. Selina was called. She phoned Fitch, and he turned up at the PD. The private detective had never looked so good. And it wasn't just because he was wearing a green Henley that brought out his eyes and emphasized his muscles. Finally, I had someone to vouch for me. But I didn't mind the shirt either.

At least they hadn't put me in handcuffs. They just bored me to tears sitting in an open office beside an empty desk. A gnome-like man with sleek, thick white hair and an expensive brown suit sat in one of the guest chairs. He stared at me through thick glasses. It was getting unnerving. Gert had given me the identical look on multiple occasions. It had never gone well.

Finally, Fitch and Detective Guthrie strolled from the latter's office, clapping each other on the back and looking pleased. My eyes narrowed.

"You're free," Fitch said.

"And I want my mug back," Guthrie said.

"I didn't do anything wrong," I said hotly. No one had offered me chai this time. I was feeling more than a little maltreated, maligned, and misunderstood. "And no take backs on the mug."

"It's not a take-back," Guthrie said. "I never gave it to you."

"The mug's mine. I like that mug. The handle doesn't get hot when you microwave it."

Guthrie shook his head at Fitch. "Better you than me, man."

Fitch chuckled. "You have no idea."

"Hey." I rose from my chair. "I provided a service. I saved Santa."

Guthrie folded his arms and managed not to crease his suit. "That's not what the mall manager says."

"Santa was fighting for his life. Did you see what happened to that candy cane?" I picked up my purse. Fredo wriggled inside it.

Guthrie shook his head, turned, and strode into his office. The door slammed shut behind him.

"But..." I sputtered. "The Rovers!"

The old man in the brown suit stood and went to Guthrie's door. He walked inside without knocking and shut it behind him.

"Come on," Fitch took my elbow and steered me from the room. "Let's get out of here before they change their mind."

Fuming, I let him. Maybe I was being overly sensitive. But when you've been falsely accused of something terrible, it's hard not to react when you're accused of a far more ridiculous crime.

"This better not be in the local papers," I muttered. I couldn't deal with any more bad press.

Fitch opened the police station door for me. "Oh, it will be." We walked outside and into a blast of cold, night air.

"Now I see why you stuck with surveillance," Fitch continued. We trotted through the police station's marble colonnade. "You suck at detecting."

I followed him down the marble steps. "I'm telling you—"

"There's something wrong with those dogs," he said grumpily. "I know."

"You know I told you, or you know there's something wrong with the dogs?" In my purse, Fredo sneezed. I was surprised the Hot Springs PD had let me bring him in, but they were dog friendly.

"Both. Selina's original Rover is still AWOL, and Adan's is still missing too. Something's obviously wrong, and hello? Haven't you noticed yet this is a company town?" He jerked his head toward a trio of robo dogs in police uniforms marching past.

"So? And it's not a company town. Rover's not the top employer."

"But it is a top donor."

I stopped beside his blue Explorer. "Not to the police department?"

"Yeah it donates to the police department, to the parks department... Who do you think pays for all this fake snow?"

I scrubbed a hand over my face. This was why public-private partnerships were trouble. "Okay. So kicking over a robo dog might not have been the most politically correct move. What was I supposed to do?"

He opened the passenger door for me. "Not attack one of the town's prize pets?"

"They're not even real!" I hate technology. The internet had pretty much ruined my life. Now artificial intelligence was gunning for me too? It was getting hard to keep up.

He drove me back to my Jeep, leaning across me to open my door. "Get your brother out of that house. It's not safe."

"You think I don't know that?" I got out, and I drove, grumbling, to the mansion. Maybe the dogs' weird behavior had nothing to do with Adan's murder. But what were the odds?

Holli, Charlie, and I had an awkward but delicious dinner together. Holli was doing keto tonight, which meant wagyu steak and asparagus. Adalina and Arystarch did not deign to join us.

Shelley hovered, ensuring our wine goblets were topped up and listening to every word we said. Not that our conversation was particularly illuminating.

The butler didn't bring up the disaster at the mall. Neither did I. Maybe he hadn't witnessed the destruction. Or maybe he was just keeping that knowledge close to his vest. The latter would not have surprised me.

After dinner, I followed Charlie up to his bedroom. Fredo took a look around the gloomily luxe room, trotted to the sleigh bed and jumped on top.

"Get off that," I said. The dog ignored me.

"Forget Fredo," Charlie hissed. "What happened?"

I told him about Shelley and the mall. "Fitch thinks it's going to make the local papers."

"The papers don't matter. You think Shelley had something to do with the dogs going crazy?"

"I don't know. He was there, and someone has to be controlling the dogs remotely. I don't know what the range is on those things—"

"Fifteen miles."

"Seriously?"

My brother nodded. "Adan told me. He was really proud of it. That and the battery life. So what's our next move?"

"I want to look for Adan's dog. Two people said they spotted him out by the hot spring."

"I can show you where that is. Come on, I'll get a flashlight."

I glanced uneasily at Fredo, curled on Charlie's bed. I didn't want to take him—odds were he'd howl or bark at exactly the wrong moment. But he did make a good excuse for wandering around outside. And I didn't trust him alone with expensive fabrics.

We both got flashlights—part of our usual travel kits. I dislodged an irate Fredo from the bed, put him on his leash, and the three of us snuck out one of the mansion's back doors.

Our flashlights were unnecessary. Spotlights illuminated the sloping lawn. I followed Charlie. Our long shadows rippled eerily before us, and I glanced over my shoulder toward the mansion. Icicle-style twinkle lights lit its gabled roofline. A silhouette moved in an upstairs window.

"We're not exactly being stealthy out here," I said. Fredo sniffed a bush.

"We have every right to go for a walk on the property," Charlie said. We continued on without speaking, our footsteps soft on the grass. "You didn't ask," he continued.

"Ask what?"

"About Mom."

Frowning, I kept walking. I wasn't sure I wanted to know about Mom and Adan. "No," I said. "I guess there's not much to say about it."

I half hoped, half dreaded Charlie would tell me I was wrong, that there were things to talk about. But he didn't. We continued down the low hill, our jackets rustling.

"The spring house is there." He pointed with his flashlight toward a wood and stone house about a hundred yards away. Frost glistened on its peaked roof. A thicket of pines speared from the earth behind it. I scented sulfur.

"The spring house is usually locked," he continued. "Think Adan's Rover went—?" He stopped abruptly, and I walked into him. "What's that?" he said. A low pine branch rustled. Fredo growled.

"Probably a squirrel," I said, glancing at the tree line.

"Here," he said, "give me the leash." I handed it to him. Fredo's rolling gaze ping-ponged erratically between us.

"What if it's Barney?" Charlie whispered.

"I don't see any glowing—"

"I'll be right back." He loped into the trees. Barking, Fredo raced beside him.

"Eyes." I swayed in place and stared at the pines he and Fredo had vanished into. Fredo's barks echoed through the woods.

I blew out my breath. The killer wasn't hanging out in the woods waiting for one of us to take a night-time stroll. Charlie would be fine.

I approached the spring house. The sulfur smell grew. A padlock hung from the latch on the door, so I was out of luck there. Someday, I'd really like to get Fitch to teach me how to pick locks.

Automatically, I tugged on the padlock. It snapped open.

My mouth puckered in a silent whistle. I pulled off the lock and opened the door. A cloud of sulfur-scented steam billowed out, and I stepped backward, making a face.

I switched on my flashlight and stepped inside, holding my breath. The flagstones were slick and shiny. I raised my light. It illuminated benches, rattan chairs sans cushions, and an irregularly shaped spring. Steam rose in curls from its inky surface.

The smell made my eyes water, and I pulled my shirt up to cover my nose. The scent had gone beyond rotten egg to something more acidic. No wonder no one used this spring anymore.

Pulse skipping, I glanced back at the open door, then edged to one side so my back faced a wall. There was no way I was closing the door in all this stink. But I didn't want anyone sneaking up on me either. No one was hanging out in the woods. But one of the Levanns or Shelley could have seen us leave the house and followed.

I shined the beam of my flashlight into the dark corners and opened low cupboards. But I didn't see any sign of Barney or anything vaguely resembling a clue.

Finally, I approached the spring. In several of the countries I'd traveled in for work, there'd been "gates to hell"—cave mouths or sulfuric springs with dark legends attached. Those other springs hadn't bothered me. They'd just been naturally occurring phenomena, like this spring.

But there was something about this place that was different, that raised the damp hairs on the back of my neck. Swallowing, I shined my light into the water. Despite the acidic smell, it was shockingly clear, the bottom smooth, black rock.

The beam of my light caught something metallic. I edged closer.

A Rover lay on its side at the bottom of the spring.

"So that's where you went," I muttered. "Charlie!" I shouted. "I found it!"

I turned toward the door. It slammed shut. A lock snapped closed.

Chapter Fourteen

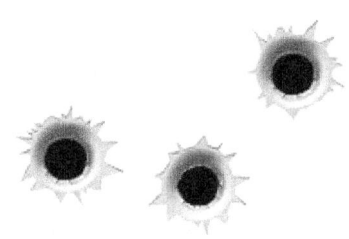

I rattled the spring house door. It was a dumb, futile gesture, so I kicked the door for good measure. Then I hopped around on one foot cursing and nearly fell on my assets.

I steadied myself against the stone wall. "Charlie!" I shouted. "Someone locked me in!" And that meant that someone was out there. With my little brother. My heart rabbited.

I scanned my light across the stone walls, and my flashlight wobbled only a little. Spotting two steamed and shuttered windows, I strode to them. The windows opened without much effort. I tugged on the exterior shutters. They seemed to have been latched from the outside and were made of solid, fitted wood.

"Alice?" Charlie's muffled voice came from the other side of the thick, wood door.

Unsteadily, I hurried to it, and one foot skidded from under me on the slick stones. I grabbed the back of a rattan chair and managed to stop from doing the splits. "Open the door," I said.

"I can't. It's locked. How'd you get inside?"

My jaw clenched. "Someone locked me in."

He rattled the lock. "Yeah, it's stuck."

"There's someone out there, Charlie. You—"

"I'm going to get some tools or a key or something."

"Someone—"

"I'll be right back."

My blood pounded in my skull. "Charlie? Charlie!" I beat my fist on the door.

Okay. I blew out a breath. This was fine. It was only a stupid prank, and there probably was not a murderer lying in wait in the darkness for my brother.

I kicked the door again and hurt the same toe. My eyes and throat burned. I adjusted my shirt over my nose. A headache blossomed behind my eyeballs. I swayed, reached for a chair, missed, and fell.

So. That wasn't normal.

I sat on the damp flagstones and thought about my sudden bout of clumsiness. I'd assumed the spring had been closed because it was too acidic for safe bathing. But maybe the air was bad too.

I choked out a laugh beneath my shirt. *Maybe?* The spring house literally reeked. The heat wasn't doing me any favors either.

I crawled toward the window I'd opened, clambered to standing, and pressed my nose to a crack in the shutter. I inhaled a pathetic rivulet of fresh air, and my headache eased slightly.

My heartbeat was elevated—maybe from the heat, maybe from something else. I didn't want to dwell on the something else. Dwelling would just freak me out. Freaking out would make it harder to get out of here.

I wobbled to a chair and picked it up. Angling it, I slammed one leg against the shutter. It didn't budge. I hit the leg against the shutter again. Had it moved a little? I didn't think I was going to break free this way. But maybe I could pry the window open enough to get more air.

I jammed the leg into the seam and used it like a lever. The rattan snapped.

"Dammit!" My head spun.

I made to use my flashlight as a lever, thought better of it, and returned to the door. Dropping to the paving stones, I laid my hand at its base. A faint current of cold air flowed across it. I lay flat, nose to the door.

There was a snort, and an exhalation of weapons-grade doggy breath.

"Ugh." I gagged. "Get away from the door, Fredo." The dog whimpered and scrabbled at the door.

"Alice?" Charlie asked. "You still there?"

Where else would I be? I shook my head. "I'm here. Charlie, hurry."

CRACK! The door shuddered. CRACK! There was a metallic screech, and Charlie yanked the door open. He dropped the sledgehammer he'd been holding. "What are you doing on the floor?"

I lurched from the spring house and rolled onto my back on the grass. The stars were really pretty. They usually are in the Sierras, even if they were a little spinny tonight.

"Hey." My brother bent over me, his hands on his thighs. "Are you okay?"

"That spring house is a menace," I said. Fredo dropped beside me on the lawn and panted.

"Did you see who locked you inside?"

"Of course not. Because that would have been useful." But if I moved now, I might be able to figure out who'd done it.

I really didn't want to move. My head hurt. My hair was damp and sticking to my skin. I was still a little nauseated. But I was definitely feeling better. I extended my hand, and Charlie helped me up.

"Who's home?" I asked. Using the corner of my shirt, I picked up the broken padlock and latch. I shook the latch free and dropped the lock into the pocket of my jacket.

My brother squinted. "Uh, everyone I think. Holli, Arystarch, Adalina and Shelley." He retrieved Fredo's leash.

"Let's see where they've been." My lips flattened. My heartrate was up again, but not because of the heat. Someone in that house had locked me in. It had to be one of them. And they all knew there was something seriously wrong with that spring. It might not have been attempted murder, but it had been attempted something.

Shelley met us at the mansion's back door holding a shiny toolbox. "I see you succeeded in your endeavor Mr. Sommerland?"

"Yeah. Thanks." Charlie handed him the sledgehammer. "I broke the lock."

"I shall repair it tomorrow."

"Did you see anyone outside?" I asked. "Aside from us."

"I do not generally monitor the rear doors."

Of course not. "This place needs more security cameras," I snapped.

"Mr. Levann felt they were too intrusive."

Yeah, yeah, yeah. Cameras *are* intrusive. But they could also be helpful. "Where are the others?"

"Mrs. Levann is in her room. Arystarch and Adalina are in the drawing room."

"Thanks." I brushed past the butler. Charlie at my heels, I strode down the carpeted hall and through the tall, open doors.

Adalina looked up from the striped divan, a teacup to her lips. "What happened to you?" She wore a black cashmere lounge suit. It looked crazy expensive.

"Someone locked me in the spring house."

Her dark eyebrows slashed down. "What were you doing in there?"

"Looking for Barney," I said shortly. "Where have you two been?"

"Here," Arystarch said beside the lit fireplace. Still in his black turtleneck and slacks, he and Adalina looked very matchy-matchy. Adalina's green hair was the only jarring note. "I was in my studio and then here," he continued.

The studio with a view of the back lawn. He could have easily seen us walking there. Though in fairness, the drawing room had the same view, and I couldn't see a damn thing. The windows were mirrors, reflecting us, the portraits, the elegant furniture. "Did you see anyone out back?"

Adalina sucked in a breath. "Is that a... dog?"

"Wha—?" Arystarch cringed away.

"That's Fredo," I said, my voice strained. "And did you see anyone in the back yard?"

Arystarch shifted his weight. "No."

But he could have seen me and followed. And then there had been that figure in the upstairs window. *Holli? Adalina?*

"And I don't appreciate your tone," he continued. "If you're accusing one of us—"

My neck corded, and I tried to force myself to relax. "Someone locked me in that spring house."

"I'm not surprised," he said.

"I was," I said.

"With your reputation, why should you be?" His nostrils flared. "Maybe one of your other associates followed you here. I don't know why Holli thought inviting you to stay was a good idea—"

"She thinks she'll get a free bodyguard." Adalina laughed unpleasantly. "She doesn't like to spend her money on things she needs, only things she wants."

"Does she need a bodyguard?" Charlie asked from behind me, and I started. He plucked a sandwich off the tea trolley.

"Of course not," Arystarch said sharply. "She's paranoid."

"Your father was murdered," I said. "Someone dropped his Rover into the hot spring."

Adalina jerked forward, spilling tea on her lounge pants. "What? You're sure?"

"I'm sure there's a Rover at the bottom of the spring," I said. "I suppose it could belong to someone else, but what are the odds?"

"Immersion in water like that would kill it," she muttered.

"Kill it?" I asked.

She set the teacup on a nearby low table and clawed both hands through her green hair. "Odds are, now nothing is retrievable from its hard drive."

"I thought the data was all in the cloud?" I asked.

"It isn't a constant upload," she said. "It only uploads as often as the owner programs it to."

"Who cares about that damned dog?" Arystarch complained, and I cut him a glance. By now he had to realize the dog might have been a witness. He couldn't really be this dense.

"How did it get into the spring house?" Adalina asked. "It's always locked."

"It wasn't tonight," I said. "The lock was in the clasp, but it wasn't shut. Who has the key?"

"It hangs on a board by the front door," she said.

"So anyone could have taken it." Charlie dropped into a chair that looked too old and too fragile for that kind of abuse. But the chair didn't wobble.

"This is ridiculous." Arystarch braced one elbow on the mantel. "Someone probably left the spring house door open, and the dog wandered inside." He tore a bite from his mini sandwich.

"And then put the lock in the door behind it?" I asked.

"Someone else must have done that after the dog fell in," Arystarch said. "No one goes in there. The smell is mind altering. They probably didn't even know the dog was in there."

"That's a lot of probably's." I studied him. He was hiding something. And locking me inside the spring house seemed like just the sort of trick he might pull.

His saturnine face contorted. "What exactly are you accusing us of?"

"I'm not accusing anyone of anything," I said. "I'm just trying to figure out what's going on."

"Nothing's going on," Arystarch said.

Adalina stood. "You can't believe that." She crossed the room and poured herself another cup of tea.

"And where the hell is Holli?" her brother said hotly. "She never misses a chance at an evening bite."

"She never misses a chance, period." Adalina's mouth twisted.

"What do you mean?" I asked, though I had a pretty good idea. A log in the fireplace popped.

"I mean she's a gold digger," she said, "but I'm sure you already figured that out."

"I dunno," Charlie said. "She's always been nice to me."

"Well, she would be," Adalina said, "wouldn't she? You're both the outsiders against—" She clamped her mouth shut.

"Against you two?" I asked.

Adalina set down her tea. "I'm going to see about that Rover." She strode to the open doors.

Holli rushed inside, bumping her step-daughter's shoulder. She stopped inside the doorway, her chest heaving. "My jewelry! Someone's stolen my jewelry!"

Chapter Fifteen

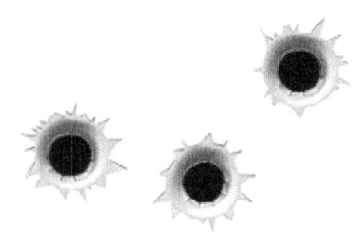

"Your jewelry?" Arystarch jammed his hands on his narrow hips and glowered. A shower of sparks shot upward inside the drawing room fireplace.

"My diamond necklace and ring set." Holli strode to the fire and knotted her fingers.

"Those belonged to Adan's mother," he said.

Holli folded her arms over her Rover tee. Her jaw jutted out. "And he gave them to me, and they're gone."

The tips of his nostrils whitened. "Those aren't—"

"Ary," Adalina said. "Come help me with the Rover."

A muscle pulsed in his jaw. His fists clenched. "Fine." He turned on his heel and followed his sister out the door.

"It's not my fault the jewelry was stolen," Holli said weakly.

"Have you called the police?" I asked.

"Not yet," she said. "But I thought maybe you could take a look at it."

"Oh." Charlie snapped his fingers. "Right. Because Alice is a PI now."

"I'm not a—" What was I saying? Sure, I wasn't officially a PI, but heck yeah I wanted to see the scene of the crime. Not that I had much confidence I could do anything about it. But I could at least get some pictures for Fitch. "Lead on."

Holli led us upstairs to the spacious bedroom she'd shared with Adan. I tried to look like the environment was new and surprising and I hadn't been inside the black and gold room already. A fur coat sprawled across the king-sized, four-poster bed. Fredo shot the coat an interested look.

"It wasn't just the necklace and ring set," Holli continued. "It was all Adan's mother's jewelry. At least, all the best pieces. She had some sixties costume stuff." She pressed a panel on the wall. "I think it's fun." The panel swung open, and she walked inside.

"Cool." Charlie followed her inside.

Chagrined, I stared at the opening. A hidden doorway? A secret room? And I'd missed it? I glanced at the picture windows. If memory served, they had a view of the spring house too. Could the person I'd seen been standing here?

Fredo and I walked inside the walk-in closet, and I gaped. The closet was the size of my apartment. Granted, my apartment was tiny, but this was ridiculous.

The closet doors were glass, so you didn't have to wonder where you put that sequined top. An ivory chaise lounge stood beside a shoe island in the middle of the closet. The wood floor was in a herringbone pattern.

Charlie dropped into a comfy-looking ivory chair against the wall. "Wow. This is amazing. I could live in here."

Her brow wrinkled. "You know, this house is your house. That's how Adan wanted it."

Fredo hopped onto a matching ottoman. He turned in a circle three times then dropped to his belly and panted.

"Yeah." My brother sat forward, his grip tightening on the arms of the chair. "I know. But it doesn't feel right."

Holli nodded. "I get it. It didn't feel right to me either when I first moved in." She motioned toward a squarish, lit shelf lined with jewel boxes. "Here."

I pulled my phone from my pocket and took photos of the shelf, the open jewel boxes. Empty velvet squares and rectangles marked where jewelry had gone missing. "Who knew about this room?"

"Everyone did," she said. "It wasn't a secret."

Then any of the family members could be the thief. "When's the last time you saw the jewelry?"

"This morning, when I got dressed," she said. "What do you think?"

I thought the odds were good the jewelry was still somewhere on the estate. "I think you should call the police now."

"Right." Holli nodded. "I'll need a report for the insurance."

"The pieces were insured?" I asked.

"Of course," she said. "Adan didn't get where he was by being a stupid man."

I angled my head. Holli wouldn't be out anything. In fact, the theft had been a neat way of turning the jewelry into cash. *If the jewelry really belonged to her and not to the other heirs.* "How much were the pieces worth?"

"A few hundred thousand," she said. "Like I said, they were quite nice."

"Don't worry," Charlie said. "We'll get them back."

"We can't promise that," I said quickly.

"We'll get them back," Charlie repeated, nodding.

I grimaced. Charlie's confidence was going to get us both into trouble.

"If you don't," Holli said, a grim set to her jaw. "I will."

"How?" I asked, wary. Did she suspect whodunit? Or did she have a plan destined to blow up in her face?

"I've got some ideas," she said.

"Like what?" I asked.

"It's better you don't know." She smiled tightly.

I crossed my arms. "No, I really think it's better if we do know."

But Holli wouldn't talk. Slide that one into the had-I-but-known category. I should have pushed her harder. But I was tired and damp and smelled of sulfur, and I didn't.

I didn't sleep well that night. The guest room was too big, and every creak of the house made me tense. Fredo didn't have that problem though. The dog's snores rattled the portraits on the walls.

Yawning, I wandered down to breakfast the next morning. Food was laid out in silver warming trays on a sideboard. I toasted a bagel, smeared it with cream cheese, and sat. The bagel was sourdough and fresh and delicious.

No one joined me in the breakfast room, so I went on a recon to see where everyone was. Arystarch was in his studio and wasted no time chasing me out. Adalina was in the garage but calling it a garage didn't do it justice.

My father had had a garage attached to our house. He'd used it to tinker and build birdhouses. Adan's garage was the size of a dance hall. Its floor was tiled. Most of the place was taken up by cars, but one large corner had been turned into a workspace. It wasn't the sort of workspace my father had had, lined with hammers and screwdrivers for home repair. This was a gleaming, high-tech wonder.

Adalina, wearing magnifying goggles, baggy jeans, and a loose gray cashmere sweatshirt, sat on a high stool. She bent over the Rover we'd fished out of the spring. It lay on its side on the counter. She'd removed panels on its side and stomach, exposing an array of chips and wires.

"Any luck?" I asked.

She straightened, raising her head, and removed the goggles. "None." Her round face pinched. "What the water didn't destroy, the acid did."

"What about the video it stored in the cloud?"

"It's not a constant stream. It uploads video every two hours. In the last video it uploaded, the Rover was with Adan."

"What was your father doing in the video?" I braced one hip against an Audi.

"Working at his desk, here at home. After that, nothing."

After that, someone had taken the Rover for a walk to the spring and kicked it in. I gnawed my bottom lip. "And there's no chance of retrieving the video on the Rover?"

"There's always a chance. That's why I'm still working on it. But this proves the Rover wasn't defective."

"There is something going on with the dogs though," I said. "They were running amuck at the mall yesterday, tore up Santa's village."

Adalina's mouth quirked. "Did they?"

"It wasn't funny."

Her expression hardened. "No. Robots for offensive purposes aren't funny at all."

"Offensive?" I remembered that DoD notation in Adan's calendar, as well as some other comments Adalina had made. "I thought they were just for fun? Pets?"

"First of all, they're stupid pets. Your dog..." She stiffened and looked around the garage. "Where *is* your dog?"

"Charlie took him for a walk."

Her shoulders relaxed beneath her sweatshirt. She ruffled her green hair. "As weird as he is, your dog's a real dog, with a real personality. These are... a Trojan Horse. They look funny and cute, and that's all Adan wanted them to be. He thought they could be helpers to people with disabilities."

Selina had certainly appreciated hers—enough to call Fitch when it had gone missing. A stab of irrational jealousy flared in my gut. "And Jameel?"

"Like I said, Trojan Horse. People get used to them, so no one blinks when the company gets a military contract. After all, why put real dogs at risk as military helpers when you can use the Rovers?"

And the military had bottomless pockets. "But there's more to it than that?"

"Of course there's more to it," she sneered. "You can't be that naive."

I ignored that. "Does Rover have any military contracts lined up?"

She returned her attention to the pieces of robo-dog on the counter. "They're in the works."

"You're a part owner now," I said. "If you feel strongly about it, couldn't you stop it?"

"Not me. Adan might have, but without him, the Rover board is all in on Jameel's plan. It's all about profits. And there are lots of profits to be had when the US taxpayers are paying."

"Would Adan have been able to stand up to them?" I asked. "Put principle over profit?"

"He had the shares. He could have done it."

I toed a pebble on the tile floor. "And now those shares…?"

"Are divided between Arystarch, Holli, and myself."

Her words were even, but there was anger in them. I just wasn't sure if it was anger at the division of spoils, anger at her father's murder, or anger at what would happen to the company. Maybe all three.

"And the family can't really hold the line?" I asked.

She arched a brow. "Do you really think Holli won't do what she needs to… How does Jameel put it? Maximize shareholder value? Do you think she'll put the good of society first?"

Cold fingers trailed up my spine. No. I didn't.

Chapter Sixteen

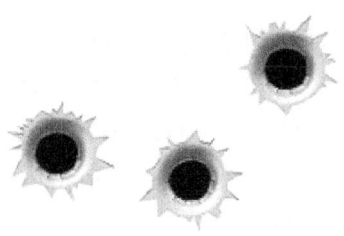

"You realize that the fingerprints on this lock are only helpful if you have your suspects' prints too?" Fitch lifted the padlock, wrapped in a plastic bag, off his office desk. He raised his brows. "And a lawyer would have a field day with this chain of evidence."

He wore a charcoal business suit, so I presumed he had an important meeting later today. It was not expensive, not designer. But in it, Fitch could hold his own against any of the men in Hot Springs. In the end, a suit could only go so far.

"Can you dust for prints or not?" I plunked down in the chair on the other side of his desk. The spider plant on the filing cabinet was in even worse shape than usual. The wall clock blinked three-fifty-four. It was only Saturday, but it seemed like Adan Levann had died years ago.

"Of course I can." He glanced at Fredo, drooling on the thin, gray carpet. "A lawyer from Rover called me."

"Why?"

Fitch rubbed his jaw. "They implied you were somehow responsible for the malfunctions. It seems the problems only occur when you're around."

"Because I'm such a tech genius," I said, sarcastic. "Someone's got to be controlling them." And I had some ideas as to whom.

"Yeah, and they seem to have an Alice Sommerland fixation. I'm going on the theory your reputation's once again preceded you, and whoever it is sees you as a threat. The question is, who?"

I shook my head. "Selina's Rover went haywire before Adan was killed. This can't be about me."

"Maybe not at first, but it seems to be now. You were the one locked in the spring house."

"In fairness," I said, "I was the only one *in* the spring house. They may have assumed my brother was in there with me. And there's more." I told him about the figure in the window last night, the missing jewelry.

He shook his dark head. "The jewelry could have been a crime of opportunity. And we can't ignore the Rover connection with Adan, who's now dead. Where's Charlie?"

"In Nowhere." I crossed my legs at the ankles. "He's playing the one-eyed man at the dinner theater tonight." I wouldn't have left the mansion if he'd still been in it.

"I don't like him in that house. You need to keep him away from Hot Springs."

I nodded unhappily. But Charlie wouldn't want to go, and I wasn't sure I could convince him otherwise.

"You said this was on a door?" He opened the plastic bag.

"The one to the hot spring house."

Fitch shook his head and dumped the lock onto his desk. "Private hot springs. What a life. Where's the latch?"

"The latch?" I was supposed to bring the latch?

"It could have prints too, and it should be a smoother surface than this lock." He squinted at the lock's metal ridges.

Briefly, I closed my eyes. *Of course.* "I'll get the latch."

He grinned. "Don't beat yourself up, Nancy Drew. You'll learn. Here's your next lesson."

I rolled my eyes.

"Normally," he went on, ignoring me, "you'd use white fingerprint powder to pick up prints on a dark surface. Black powder works on a light surface. Since this lock has uneven ridges, I'm going to use neither." He looked at me expectantly.

"If you're waiting for me to come up with the answer, we'll be here all night."

"Fluorescent powder," he said.

"Glow in the dark?"

"Under black light. It should work best. Come here."

I rose and walked to his side of the desk. The PI snapped on a pair of latex gloves. He laid a sheet of paper on the desk and the lock on top of it. Opening a desk drawer, he pulled out a flashlight and what looked like a petri dish filled with dark powder. Using a makeup brush, he dusted the lock. Flecks of powder drifted to the paper.

I leaned closer, interested. Fredo sat up, his collar jingling faintly. I could feel the heat from Fitch's body, and I swallowed. His cologne smelled like cedar and nutmeg, and it was really good.

Fitch turned the lock over and dusted the other sides. "Get the light, will you?"

I moved to the door, flipped off the light, and returned to my spot behind the desk. It was only four o'clock, but the winter light was already gloomy. The PI rose and closed the blinds, then he flipped on the flashlight. It shone purple. He turned the padlock this way and that beneath its beam.

"No prints," he said.

"Nothing?" My body grew heavy with failure. I'd hoped I'd found something useful. I should have known better.

He turned his head, and I realized too late how close we were. Our lips were inches apart. His chiseled face had the beginnings of a five o'clock shadow. The wall clock ticked. Something seemed to flicker in the depths of his green eyes.

Heart hammering, I stepped back and glanced away.

He cleared his throat. "On the positive side, your prints aren't on here either. You did a good job removing the lock without contaminating it."

"Unless I destroyed other prints in the process," I said, trying to slow my racing heart.

"If that was the case, they'd be smeared, not gone completely. Someone wiped this down before you touched it. Maybe after they locked you inside."

I turned on the desk lamp, shattering the spell. "Then it's useless."

"No. It validates your story."

I folded my arms. He hadn't believed me? That was just insulting.

"Hey," he said, "just because one of my contractors comes in with a wild story about being locked in a shed filled with poisoned gasses, doesn't mean I automatically buy into it."

I blew out my breath. "It was the part about nearly being overcome by the sulfuric fumes, wasn't it? Was that detail a bridge too far?"

"The melodrama factor was off the charts."

I walked to the door and braced one shoulder against its frame. "Fair enough. And yet, that spring *has* gone bad. Adalina told me its high acid content helped destroy that Rover's video files."

He rested his elbow on the desk, his chin in his hand. "Almost like whoever shoved the Rover in the spring knew what they were doing. Adalina?"

"Or Holli. She worked at Rover before she married Adan."

"And she invited you into the mansion to keep an eye on you?"

I shrugged. "I don't know. I'll go get that latch."

By the time I got back to the mansion it was full dark under a new moon. Instead of going inside, I walked around the house and across the lawn to the spring house. A shiny new lock and latch secured the door.

I swore. Shelley hadn't wasted any time repairing the lock. I tugged on it, making sure it really was closed. (It was). And then I returned to the house.

I found Shelley in the kitchen. The butler wore a pristine white dishtowel around his trim waist. He stirred a pot of something that smelled divine.

"The remains of the latch?" He cocked his head and kept stirring evenly. "It's in the dustbin behind the garage. Would you like me to retrieve it for you later?"

It would have Shelley's prints all over it. At this point, collecting it was probably a waste of time, but I shook my head. "I'll do the dumpster diving. But thanks anyway."

"It's rather dark back there," he warned. "You should take a flashlight if you're going to go now."

"I've got one. Thanks."

I strode along the covered walkway to the garage. Pausing, I turned on my red-light flashlight. I didn't really need it. Lights shone from inside the barnlike building, faintly illuminating the paving stone walk. Was Adalina still at work on the Rover?

More slowly, I walked behind the garage. A bear-proof wooden cabinet jutted out from the garage. A pyramid of neatly stacked bricks sat piled beneath it. I unhooked the open padlock from the cabinet, opened its wooden doors, and hefted out the garbage can.

The broken latch from the springhouse was near the top of a pile of dried pine needles. No composting for this house. I pulled on a pair of latex gloves I'd filched from Fitch's office. Plucking the latch free, I dropped it in a plastic bag I'd brought for the occasion.

I set the remains of the springhouse latch on the ground and wrestled the garbage across the bricks and into its box. Returning the lock to its latch, I left it the way I'd found it.

I stooped to retrieve the latch. The red light from my flashlight caught an uneven shape on the other side of the wooden cabinet. Frowning, I stepped backward and aimed the beam.

I sucked in a breath, my pulse thudding slow and heavy. A tennis shoe. A slim ankle. A pair of fitted jeans. A baby doll tee. Holli lay crumpled on the paving stones, a dark stain spreading beneath her head.

Chapter Seventeen

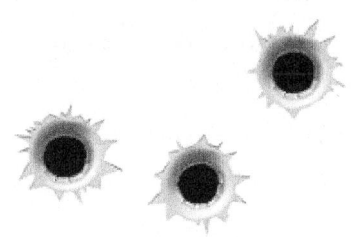

Holli was dead.

I was in jail.

It was, I had to say, a very nice jail. I smoothed the bed's down comforter and dropped into a modern, blue-cushioned chair. With its sand-colored walls and faux-wood floors, my cell looked like a tiny yoga studio. Aside from the heavy, metal door with a porthole in the top.

Maybe I'd try meditating later, or at least do some tai chi. I pressed a bell in the wall.

After a few moments, a uniformed female officer peered through the window. Locks clanked, and she opened the door. "Can I get you anything?" Her nametag read Sergeant Juarez.

I picked up the paper menu. "Do you really have cappuccino?"

"Yes. We've got a Keurig."

"I'll try a cappuccino."

"What about breakfast? We have scrambled eggs, oatmeal, or pancakes today."

"Oatmeal, please."

"Sure." She smiled and retreated, locking the door behind her.

I stretched back in my comfy chair. Hot Springs might be onto something. It was hard to feel violent amidst such luxury. But it was still a small, locked room, and I didn't want to stay here. My insides jittered unpleasantly.

The police seemed to be trying to work out how many crimes they could charge me with. And I couldn't entirely blame them. I'd now found two Levann bodies at the mansion. I looked suspicious as hell.

The oatmeal came with walnuts and berries on top. The cappuccino was pretty good too. I was mid-way through my tai chi practice when the same jailer unlocked and opened my door.

"You're free to go," she said cheerfully.

I let my arms drop to my sides. "I am?"

"All the charges were dropped. You'll want your things back, I'll expect." She turned and walked away.

Hastily, I pulled on my boots. I followed her to a wide window that looked more like a hotel reception desk.

The smiling sergeant handed me a plastic bag full of my things. "Be sure to double check that you got everything back," he said. "We try to be careful, but mistakes do happen."

I rifled through my things. "It all seems okay."

"Are you sure? You might want to doublecheck."

"It's fine," I ground out.

"Then sign here." He pushed a computer tablet across the high desk and handed me a stylus.

"Oh, good." Detective Guthrie strode toward me in another Armani suit. "You're leaving."

"I'm the wind, baby." I signed the form.

"You're a pain in my—"

"Ah, ah. You might offend my delicate sensibilities." I handed the sergeant the tablet.

"What sensibilities?" Guthrie asked.

"Was there something you wanted to ask me," I said, "or are you just here to gloat?"

"I'm here to make sure you go."

"If you think I'd hang around, you're grossly overestimating your station's charms. The coffee's good, but it's not that good."

He sighed and pivoted, striding down the hall. "This way."

"Sure. Why not." I followed Guthrie to the reception area.

Charlie leapt from a leather chair. "Alice! You're free!" He pulled me into a rough hug and stepped away, tugging down the hem of his yachting blazer. Today he wore plain, pale blue board shorts beneath it. I guessed he was going for a more dignified look than parrots.

"I know what it's like," my brother continued. "The walls closing in on you. The smells. Good luck getting any sleep in a place like that. And the food. Blech."

"Nothing I couldn't deal with," I said valiantly. "Finding Holli was no picnic, but…" But this wasn't about me, and heat prickled my face. "I'm sorry, Charlie. How are you holding up?"

I glanced at the elegant clock on the wall. It was a testament to Charlie's concern that he'd gotten out of bed before ten AM

"I didn't spend the night in jail," he said. His face fell. "But... Holli. I can't believe it." He swallowed.

I could. The sounds and smells hadn't kept me up last night. The holding cell had smelled like vanilla. What had kept me up was thoughts about what I could have done—and had failed to do—to prevent Holli's death. "How's Fredo?"

"He's fine. Fitch has him outside. They wouldn't let Fredo in the station. I mean, they did at first, but then Fredo attacked a Rover, and he had to leave."

I nodded thoughtfully. For the ugliest dog ever, Fredo had good instincts.

Outside the station, Fitch leaned against the side of his Explorer. His blue t-shirt and jeans emphasized his muscles. Like my brother, Fitch must have been impervious to cold weather. The sky was clear, but it couldn't have been more than forty-five degrees. I zipped up my jacket.

Fredo gnawed on a rear tire. His head jerked 'round to face me. He hesitated, then hurtled toward me. Eyes rolling, he attacked my bootlaces.

Gently I edged him aside, stepping into a little fluff of fake snow. My foot skidded sideways, and I steadied myself.

"We got some frost last night," Charlie said. "Careful."

Fitch straightened off the SUV. "You okay?"

"Yeah. If I ever get arrested again, I want it to be in Hot Springs. Why'd they let me go?"

"Holli was dead for about two hours when you found her. You were either on the road during that time or at my office in Reno. You're in the clear for her murder."

"They've already figured out time of death?" I asked.

"Hot Springs has its own coroner," Charlie said. "I don't think he's very busy."

What? It took *weeks* to get a coroner's report in Nowhere. "What happened to her?"

"Bludgeoned over the head with a brick," Fitch said.

I winced. The bricks beside the garbage bin. One of them must have been the murder weapon. I'd taken a few photos of the body, while I'd waited for the cops. But I hadn't gotten too close, unwilling to get my DNA on the crime scene.

My belly knotted, and I looked at the sidewalk. I should have taken Holli more seriously. She'd said she was going to do something about that jewelry. Had she? Had that precipitated her murder? Why hadn't I pushed her harder?

None of these were new thoughts. They'd hamster-wheeled through my head all last night.

"It was quick," the PI said quietly. "She didn't know what hit her."

"I hope that's true," Charlie said, his voice thick. Anger blistered through my chest. I'd never know if Holli had been sincere about Charlie, but he'd cared about her.

"It's time for you to leave that house," Fitch told him.

"No," Charlie said. "No way. This makes things even worse. We've got to find out who killed Adan and Holli." A Tesla drove past, followed by a Ferrari and a Rolls.

Fitch shook his head. "You may be the next target."

"Yeah," Charlie said, "well, we'll be ready. Right, Alice?"

"Fitch may have a point," I said. "As his wife, Holli would have gotten half of the estate. Now she's gone, and the money's split between three people—you, Adalina, and Ary." But only if my brother contested the will. Until then, they might be able to kick him out for trespassing.

"I told you," my brother said, "I don't want the money."

Fredo started on the hem of my jeans, and I scooped up the gray dog. "Adalina and Ary can't be sure of that."

"And we don't even know for sure if this is about the estate," Charlie said. "What about Adan's business, Rover Inc.? For all we know, someone from there like Jameel could have done it."

"And killed Holli?" I raised a brow.

"Maybe she knew too much," Charlie said.

"He's right," Fitch said. "We don't know enough yet to speculate. And the police are going to be watching you, Alice."

Charlie folded his arms over his navy blazer, his jaw jutting forward mulishly. "Well, I'm not going. And isn't the client always right?"

Fitch's gaze flicked toward the bleak blue sky. "No."

"But I'm still the client, right?" he asked.

The PI hesitated. He glanced at me, and I nodded. "Yes," he said.

"Then I'm staying, and we're still investigating." My brother sidled up to me. "We're still investigating," he said in a lower voice. "Right?"

I sighed. "For now," I hedged, worried. I had to get Charlie out of that house, and I couldn't force him to leave. But Arystarch and Adalina could. "Unless your step-siblings ask you to leave. We have no right to be there, not legally."

Fitch shook his head. "Alice..."

"We have to go back to the mansion in any case," I said. "Even if they're going to kick us out, I have a suitcase full of clothes there and so does Charlie. We may as well find out what everyone was doing when Holli was killed."

Fitch briefly closed his eyes. "Fine. But then you get out of there."

"Um..." Charlie angled his head and squinted.

"We'll figure out our next steps," I said. "Off site."

"I can't wait," Fitch muttered.

The PI drove us back to the mansion. My brows lifted when Shelley let us through the gates. With our hostess dead, there was no one who wanted Charlie and me in the mansion. But maybe Shelley hadn't gotten the word. Fitch dropped us at the front door and drove off.

We found Adalina and Ary in the sunny breakfast room. Ary's plate was piled high with food.

Adalina prodded an uneaten bowl of oatmeal with her spoon. The light streaming through the windows turned her hair fluorescent. The green clashed with her magenta lounge suit.

Ary, in black t-shirt and slacks, paused, fork halfway to his mouth. Carefully, he set it down. "What are you two doing here? Weren't you arrested? And what's with the dog?"

"No." I shifted Fredo on my hip. "I was held for questioning and released."

"Why?" Ary asked.

"Because she couldn't have done it," Charlie said. "Holli was killed two hours before Al discovered her."

Adalina swore. Her spoon clattered to the table. "Which means you're still a suspect." She stared hard at her brother.

"How do you figure that?" Ary squawked.

"Because you were here," she said. "Alice found Holli around six. You were here at four."

"Where were you exactly?" I asked her.

"At the Rover office," she said, "working. I had a meeting with Jameel at two, and then I was there the rest of the day."

"I saw lights on inside the garage when I found Holli," I said.

"And you think that proves I was there?" Adalina folded her arms and slumped back in her chair. "It's not my garage. Other people go inside."

"I went in there," Ary said.

Adalina's jaw dropped. "You were in there? What were you doing in there?"

"I thought I could find some materials for my work. My current piece is mixed media."

"Did anyone else see you at Rover?" I asked her.

Adalina shot me a bored look. "My secretary, all the video cameras in the parking lot... Need I go on?"

"No," I said. "And you were in your studio?" I asked Ary.

"Where else?" He brandished his fork. Bits of egg yolk splattered to the parquet floor.

"Was anyone else here, aside from Shelley?" Charlie asked.

"No," Ary said quickly.

"Are you sure?" I asked.

"You should ask Shelley," Adalina said. "In fact, let's ask him now." She reached across the table and rang a small, silver bell.

A few moments later, Shelley appeared in the doorway. "You rang?" he asked in a sepulchral tone.

"Did anyone come to the house yesterday afternoon?" she asked.

"No. No cars came to the gate," he said. "No one rang the bell."

"You're sure?" I asked.

The butler pulled aside his gray suit jacket and extracted a cell phone from the pocket of his matching vest. "I can access the gate and the front door remotely with an app from anywhere on the grounds."

But Holli had been killed outside the mansion. No one had needed to ring the bell to get to her. Adalina chewed her bottom lip and watched her brother through narrowed eyes.

"And you didn't see or hear anyone at the house?" I asked Ary.

His nostrils flared. "How would I know? Of course I heard someone at the house. Holli was here. But don't ask me if I remember hearing anyone after two o'clock. I wasn't paying attention and don't remember. Why should I have been paying attention?"

So Adalina was out of the running—if she was telling the truth. I'd need to confirm her alibi at Rover. I knew they wouldn't want to talk to me again, but I was confident I could convince them.

Chapter Eighteen

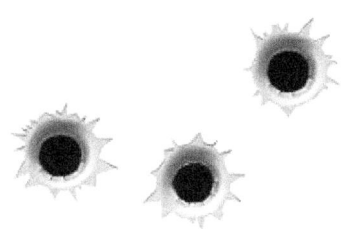

I HAD NO INTENTION of causing Rover trouble. But they didn't have to know that. Right now I was a wild card. And if they'd been worried enough to complain to the cops, they might be worried enough to grant me another interview.

"Just one moment, please." Jameel's executive assistant put me on hold. I'd been a little surprised she'd answered at all since it was a Sunday. But the Rover folks must have been burning the candle at both ends.

I paced beside the sitting room window, which faced the driveway. In the old days, this was where a butler would park unexpected visitors while he informed the lady of the house of their arrival. The room had a grand piano, maybe in case any of the guests got restless.

"Anything?" Charlie asked at my elbow. I shook my head and frowned.

Footsteps echoed in the foyer. Shelley passed the sitting room's open, white-painted door. Another door snicked open, and he walked outside.

He paced along the flowerbed, his head down as if searching for something. The butler shook his head and returned inside.

The phone clicked. "I'm sorry," the woman said. "Mr. Rich is not available."

"I have information about the Rovers he'll want to hear before the police do." So maybe I'd picked up a lesson or two from the blackmailer Toomas Koppel. It wasn't a pleasant thought.

"Just one moment, please." She put me on hold again.

I tucked my free arm beneath my elbow and stared out the window. There was a dusting of snow on the tops of the Sierras, but the lawn was green and untouched by frost. I was a little worried about the nonexistent information I'd claimed to have. But if they gave me an appointment, I'd work out that problem later.

Click. "Mr. Rich can see you today at three forty-five," she said.

"I'll be there."

But she'd already hung up, which seemed a little unprofessional. Or else she was letting me know they didn't really care if I showed up or not. But I had my appointment. So there.

Rover had managed to keep a lid on the problems with their dogs, but that couldn't last long. Too many people had seen dogs go haywire. The owners had to be complaining.

"Well?" Charlie asked, bracing his hand on a small round table. The bouquet of fresh flowers trembled atop it.

"I've got an appointment for this afternoon." I drew back the curtains and peered outside. A hawk sped low across the lawn. It swooped upward to alight in a stand of pines.

"What time? I'm coming too."

I dropped the curtain and turned. "Three forty-five, and you can't come."

"It's my investigation."

"You've got a show at the dinner theater. You have to get back to Nowhere. Sunday's a big night."

His face fell. "Oh. Right."

Heh. Now all I had to do was get Charlie to *stay* in Nowhere.

"I've got to work security tonight at the cannery afterward," he said. "I'll be back late."

Better and better. "Why don't you just sleep it off at my apartment over the theater?" Sammie would be there, but the cat had to be an improvement over the squirrels at Charlie's old treehouse.

His blue eyes widened. "Really? You wouldn't mind?"

"No," I said, pleased by my ruse. "I won't be using it." I should have known it was too easy. Once again, my optimistic nature was about to do me dirty.

Gina, elegant in a Vivienne Westwood mid-length black dress, strode into the room. I may not wear designer clothes, but I'd worked for women who had, and I knew high fashion.

The older woman stopped short. Her face tightened. "What are you two still doing here?"

The phone rang in my hand. It was a number I didn't recognize, and I declined the call.

"Ah…" Charlie shuffled his feet. "Holli thought—"

"Holli's dead," Gina said. "What she thought is immaterial. And your presence here is awkward, to say the least. I can't believe you don't have even a modicum of tact—"

My phone rang again, and again I glanced at the screen. *Another unknown number.* I muted my phone.

"What's going on?" Adalina slouched into the room. "Oh. Hi, Mom."

"Darling." Gina ruffled Adalina's green hair, and Adalina scowled. "I was just telling our guests it's time for them to move on."

"I think they should stay," Adalina said.

"Really?" Gina and I asked in tandem.

"It's a big house," Adalina said. "It's a little weird with just Ary and me in it."

Oh, *that* was believable. I crossed my arms. What was Adalina up to? Because if she was angling for easier access to murder my brother, she had another think coming.

Gina smiled, her shoulders relaxing. "That's understandable. But wouldn't you rather have someone staying here who was family?"

"Charlie is family," she said. "Sort of. He was Adan's family, at least. Now that Adan's gone, maybe... Maybe we should get to know each other better."

"Yeah," Charlie said eagerly. "That's all I want."

Her mother's mouth puckered. "Ye-es, but that's rather... Wouldn't it be better if someone who *knew* you stayed with you?"

Adalina dropped into a Louis XIV-style chair near the baby-grand piano. "Ary knows me, and he hasn't been a whole lot of help, to be honest. He's not very good with the emotional stuff."

"No," Gina said slowly. "Men usually aren't."

"Charlie is," I said. Sure, he spent all his money on medieval weaponry and donuts. But he connected with people at some weird, deep level that I didn't understand and wished I could.

"Aw." He punched my shoulder. "Thanks, Sis."

I shrugged. "Meh."

"He actually has been kind of nice to have around," Adalina admitted.

Gina blew out her breath. "But don't you think a *woman* in the house would be more comforting?"

I widened my eyes. "I can stay," I said with a straight face. "That was Holli's idea earlier anyway."

Gina's mouth crimped. It was obvious what she was trying to do—get back into the mansion herself. With Holli gone, she could play lady of the manor... And reinstate herself as queen bee, to mix my metaphors.

"I don't think that's such a good idea," Gina told me. "You're not even family."

Adalina responded with a string of paeans to my humble self. My years of experience in personal protection. That I'd been the one to find Barney the robodog and had nearly gotten killed in the process. They owed me after all the trouble I'd gone to. *And* I'd found poor Holli.

But one corner of Adalina's mouth quirked upward throughout her unconvincing monologue. She knew exactly what her mother wanted. For whatever reason, Adalina seemed to think it was good fun to thwart her.

Gina stomped her foot. "With all that's happening, you need someone you can trust. I should stay."

Adalina rose from the chair and rubbed her knuckles beneath her chin. "I dunno. Don't you think it will look weird?"

"I'm your mother. Of course it won't look weird."

"It might look a little weird," Charlie said. "What with Holli being killed and all."

Gina shot him a look that could have leveled Santa's village. "We need to talk privately." She grasped Adalina's elbow and guided her from the room.

Charlie rubbed his hands together. "What next?" The doorbell gonged.

"Let's see what's behind door number two." I walked into the foyer, where the two women were ascending the stairs. But Shelley beat me to the door.

"I'm here to see the Sommerlands," a familiar voice said.

"Let me see if they're at home," Shelley said.

"We're home," I said, and the butler pulled the door wider.

"It seems they're home." Shelley glided down the hallway and vanished behind the double stairs.

Fitch walked into the foyer and looked around. "Where's your stuff?"

"What stuff?" I asked.

"Your bags." He folded his arms. His muscles bulged. "We're getting out of here."

"Why? It's not any more dangerous than it was this morning," Charlie said.

"Yes." His dark brows slashed downward. "It is."

"Has something new happened?" I asked. My phone vibrated in my rear pocket. I ignored it.

"Yeah," Fitch said. "Time is passing, and either the killer has gotten what he wanted, or he hasn't. Your presence here is bound to rile things up."

Charlie shook his blond head. "No way. Adalina just asked us to stay. They want us here."

"That makes me even more suspicious," the PI said.

It made me suspicious too. "Can we talk?" I angled my head toward the open sitting room door. "Alone?"

"Oh," Charlie said. "Yeah. Got it." He winked at me and ascended a curving staircase.

Fitch followed me into the sitting room. "Well?"

I shut the high door. "I can't leave."

"Why not?" He glanced around, his gaze lingering on the piano.

"Because Charlie's not going to leave. Not after Adalina invited him to stay."

"You're going to have to convince him." He wandered to the piano and played a chord, his head cocked. *Huh.* The family had kept the piano in tune, so it was more than decorative. I wondered who played.

"It won't work," I said. "I know my brother. Once he gets an idea in his head, there's no dislodging it."

Fitch turned from the piano and cursed. "Pig-headedness must run in your family."

"Yeah..." I nodded to the instrument. "You play?"

"A little. My mom made me learn."

I could just see a young Fitch hunched over a piano. "You any good?"

He grinned. "Piano is my forte."

I laughed in spite of myself. "So since we're staying here, how do you suggest I play this?"

"It's not a game," he said, sobering.

"On the positive side, it doesn't look like Adalina could have killed Holli." I told him about her alibi and my plan to verify it this afternoon at Rover. "Meanwhile, Gina's angling to stay at the mansion. It's a good bet she'll succeed. So I'll be able to keep an eye on her."

"And she'll be able to keep an eye on you."

"Charlie's going home for the night, and I'm going to interview Jameel. Got any tips?"

He raked a hand through his thick, dark hair. "Find out where he was at the time of Holli's murder and verify it if you can. Probe him for reasons someone may have wanted Adan dead. He was the head of a billion-dollar corporation. He must have enemies. And find out more about those Rovers. Their behavior might not be connected to Adan's murder, but it might be."

"I wonder if Adan knew something was wrong with the dogs?"

"Stop wondering and start investigating." He scowled. "And write your interviews up in the report form I gave you. Keeping them in your head doesn't do me or a court any good. I expect to see a report on what you learned on my desk tomorrow morning."

I made a sloppy salute. "Yes, Sir."

He rolled his eyes and strode from the room. The front door slammed. *Huh.* I was starting to think he cared.

Charlie sidled into the sitting room. "That went well."

"You were eavesdropping?"

"Well, duh. You sure you don't mind about me staying at your place?"

"The cat will enjoy the company."

The front door opened and closed. Fitch strode into the sitting room. "We've got a problem."

My stomach tensed. "What's wrong?"

He jerked his thumb toward the front windows. "The press. They're here."

Chapter Nineteen

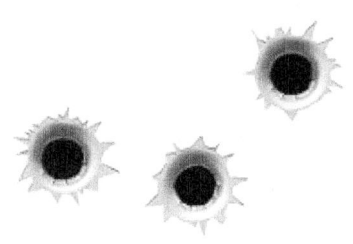

"No biggie." Charlie moved toward the sitting room's tall, double doors. "I'll go talk to them."

"No," Fitch and I said in unison and a little too loudly, because my brother winced. Charlie dropped onto the piano bench.

"How bad is it?" My recent run-ins with the press had gone colossally badly, and my stomach churned, which was just embarrassing. I squinted out the windows, but all I saw was driveway and lawn. The gates were around a bend and hidden by pines.

"National outlets and some local ones," Fitch said. "You can't see it from the house, but they're at the front gate. They must have arrived right after I did."

"Well, that's just swell," I said.

Gina strode into the room. "What's going on? Why haven't you two left yet?" She sucked in her breath at the sight of Fitch, and he smiled slowly.

Adalina trailed after her mother. "Ignore her. You two can stay."

"There are press vans outside," I said.

Gina smoothed a hand over her platinum blond hair and swore. "I'm surprised it took them so long."

"You didn't call them, did you?" Adalina asked sharply.

"Of course not. I'm only saying, your father was an important man."

"And two murders in a mansion is a bigger story than one," Fitch said.

"Who *are* you?" Gina asked him.

"Fitch. I'm a friend of Charlie's."

Gina pursed her lips and looked intrigued. It was a common reaction.

Adalina scanned the screen of her phone. "It's about more than two murders." She turned the screen so I could read the headline.

Killer Stalks Tech Family
Disgraced Koppel Bodyguard "Finds" the Bodies

I sucked in a breath. "Finds?" *In quote marks?* It was true, I *had* found the bodies, but the punctuation implied a world of suspicion.

"It's two murders plus a crooked bodyguard," Adalina continued. "That's why they're here. No offense."

"None taken." I pulled my own phone out of my pocket. A string of missed call bubbles popped onto the screen.

I unmuted it, and the phone rang in my hand. A prickly weight pressed down on my chest. This number I recognized. I'd considered blocking it, but a bad impulse had stopped me.

I answered the phone. "Hello, Kitty." Kitty Bannon was a reporter from Reno. We'd gone to college together and had never been friends.

"Alice! I heard you found Adan and Holli Levann. What can you tell me?"

"Nothing." I hung up.

"Why'd you bother to answer?" Fitch asked.

Because a part of me had needed to confirm for myself that the press really was on my trail. "They can't stop us from leaving," I said.

Gina's brown eyes widened. "Your name is now linked to ours. If they see you leaving, it will just solidify that connection." In other words, I was an embarrassment.

"More importantly," Adalina drawled, "you'd be giving them what they want. Video of you."

I nodded. There was that.

"We could take the trail out back," Charlie said. "You know, the one that connects to the road past the recycling center?"

"Hot Springs has a recycling center?" I asked, incredulous. I'd thought they'd have kept anything so pedestrian far, far away. And there was a trail behind the house?

"The *Town* of Hot Springs," Gina corrected. "And our recycling center has won awards."

"The only thing is," Charlie said, "you can't get cars down the trail through the woods. And once you hit the road, it's five miles back to town. The road's pretty twisty." My brother rested his forearm on the piano, and a clash of notes sounded. He jerked his arm away. "Sorry."

"You can take the e-bikes," Adalina said. "We've got enough for the three of you."

"Sounds like a plan," Fitch said.

I stared, disbelieving. I hadn't expected he'd be so quick to leave his car behind.

To me he said in a lower voice, "This works. And I want to see how well you ride." Somehow, he managed to make that sound dirty.

"We can't ebike all the way to Nowhere," I said.

"Once you get into the Town of Hot Springs," Adalina said, "you can call for a ride-share."

"Why can't we call for a ride-share once we reach the road to the recycling center?" I asked.

"No reception in that canyon," Charlie said. "Believe me, I've tried."

"This is ridiculous," Gina said. "I'm leaving and not on a bicycle. Shelley," she bellowed. The butler appeared in the doorway so fast he had to have been listening at the door.

"I'm leaving," she said. "Do what you need to do to keep the media jackals away from my car."

"Yes, ma'am."

She stalked from the room. Crouching like an obsequious minion, Shelley followed. I didn't think she noticed.

Getting the three ebikes ready was a bigger process than you'd think. There were a dozen in the spacious garage, but none were fully charged. We let them juice up while Fitch and Charlie had a late breakfast.

Ary wandered into the breakfast room, and the situation with the press had to be explained. He blamed me for the inconvenience.

Since he wasn't completely wrong, no one argued with him much. My sordid past likely had been the X factor inspiring the national press to take note.

Finally, around noon, the three of us got on the ebikes and drove across the back lawn. Charlie led us past the spring house and to a trail behind a folly.

Fitch stopped his bike and twisted on his seat, gazing back at the house. "If someone stuck to the tree line, they could circle around and get in through the back of the mansion. Odds are good they wouldn't be noticed."

So that was why he'd been interested in the trail. I should have thought of it myself.

We drove through the pines. Fitch stopped again when we reached the road. It had been less than a quarter mile from the trailhead to the narrow road. A person in good shape could walk it easily. And all my suspects were in good shape.

I scanned the ground. Beside a patch of melting snow, deep tire tracks from a car marked the soft earth at the side of the road. Fitch snapped a photo of the tracks.

"Does this trail continue on?" I asked my brother.

"No," he said. "It's not a real trail. It's just a deer trail. Town's this way." He glided down the road.

Certain mountain roads seem to suffer under a dark enchantment. Their twists and turns make no sense, and a few miles seems endless. This was one of those roads. Adan's house was only a couple miles from town. But every loop and bend seemed to take us farther away.

Uneasy, I scanned the curves ahead. At least there didn't seem to be any ice on the road.

"Are you sure we're going in the right direction?" Fitch shouted.

"Yeah. Look." Charlie pointed at an elegant blue sign.

Levann Recycling Plant

"Levann?" I asked, whizzing past thick pines.

"It's not Adan's," Charlie said. "But they donated the lot. They were basically behind building the plant."

"They? Holli and Adan?" Fitch asked.

"No," Charlie yelled over his shoulder. "The plant's older than that. Gina and Adan were involved. He's—" He swallowed, his posture on the bike loosening. "He was really proud of it."

We rounded a tight bend. A glittering white hill appeared before us, and I wrinkled my forehead. Had it snowed here last night? As we rode closer I saw my mistake. It wasn't a mountain covered in snow. It was a Matterhorn of plastic bottles.

"Is the plant actually working?" I asked.

"Yeah," Charlie said. "They sort the types of plastic. They've got it all mechanized, really high-tech. Adan explained it to me. Trust me, it's more detail than you want to know."

I swerved too close to the edge of the road. It dropped off into a steep, black rock canyon. Sucking in a breath, I re-glued my eyes to the road and got back in formation.

A green robotic arm whirred high above us. Its basket dumped a load of bottles on top of the pile. They skidded down the slope, stopping before reaching the bottom of the pile.

"They recycle the plastic bottles once a week," Charlie said. "The center's not open every day. I mean, it's open for deliveries, but it only runs on weekdays."

It looked like it was running today, and today was Sunday. "How many towns do they do the recycling for?" I asked.

"Just Hot Springs."

I gaped. "That's a week worth of bottles? From Hot Springs?" We were moving pretty fast at that point, and we still hadn't gotten past the bottles.

The robotic arm hummed. There was a plastic-y crash, and I glanced up. The green arm swept through the peak of the bottle mountain. Bottles cascaded downward making a sound like an ocean wave.

"Hit the gas," Fitch shouted.

A wave of bottles avalanched, rattling and rustling toward the road. My heart took a sickening plunge. The bottles weren't stopping.

I lowered my body closer to the handlebars and pedaled, but the pedals were loose beneath the pressure of my feet. I was going as fast as I could go.

A bottle plinked off my head, and I was skidding, engulfed in plastic.

Chapter Twenty

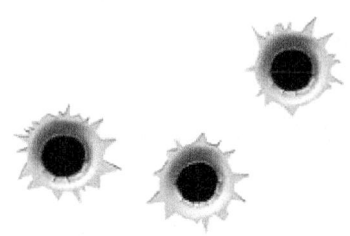

My ebike jerked to a stop. I flew over the handlebars and bit back a shriek. Ducking my head, I threw my arms forward to tuck and roll. Plastic bottles crackled beneath me, cushioning my fall and sucking me under.

Before I could make sense of much, I was drowning beneath a sea of bottles. Once, our parents had taken us on a trip to San Diego. I'd been in the chilly Pacific for all of two minutes before an ocean wave had driven me under and held me there. The blur of blue and sand. A sharp spike of fear. My body tossing helplessly, unable to breathe.

I flailed, unsure what was up and what was down. An iron hand gripped my wrist and jerked me to standing. I gasped, landing hip-deep in plastic bottles, and I sucked in a noisy breath.

A swathe of bottles cut the road in two. The mountain of bottles at the side of the road had eroded, but the avalanche was still moving. Plastic scraped and rattled and bounced across the street and waterfalled into the canyon.

"Bottles," I said shakily. "We were nearly taken out by plastic bottles. I *really* hate this town. This sort of thing doesn't happen in Nowhere."

A quick succession of emotions flashed across Fitch's chiseled face. Fear. Relief. Annoyance. His emerald gaze turned sharp and assessing. "You okay?"

Now I was just embarrassed and hoping he hadn't seen the panic in my eyes. "Yeah." I looked away, mainly to avoid looking at him.

Fitch skidded on a bottle and staggered. "Damn. You don't see that every day."

I frowned. "Where's Charlie?" I looked around. "Charlie?" I shouted, shrill.

"He was between us." Fitch moved toward me and thrust bottles away.

"Charlie?" I moved toward Fitch and roughly knocked plastic bottles aside.

We reached each other. Fitch frowned. "Where'd he...?" He looked toward the canyon.

My heart stopped. "No." I crashed clumsily through the bottles to the side of the road. The pile was lower here, ankle deep. My foot brushed a bottle. It rattled across the dirt and tumbled into the deep, black-rock canyon. My breath turned quick and harsh. "Charlie!" I peered over the edge. "Charlie!" My voice echoed.

Bottles crunched behind us. "Whoo-hoo!" Charlie burst from a hillock of bottles on the opposite side of the road. "What a ride!"

I sagged, my knees weakening. Bending double, I breathed deeply, my elbows on my knees. For a few awful moments, I'd thought— I shook myself and straightened.

"That was no accident," Fitch said, grim. "Come on." We waded through the bottles and onto the recycling center's grounds.

"Why isn't there a fence?" I walked along the side of a corrugated metal building.

"Oh," Charlie said. "You have to get a special permit for a fence in Hot Springs. They're really expensive."

"So only the rich get fences?" I asked, incredulous.

"Eh, pretty much," Charlie said. "But in fairness, only rich people live in Hot Springs, so..." He scratched his head.

"And the recycling center couldn't afford one?" Fitch stopped beside the machine that had started the avalanche. The PI craned his neck up at the arm's scooper attachment.

"I think they figured there were better places to spend their money," my brother said. "Besides, hardly anyone comes back here."

Fitch climbed into the machine. "Key's in the ignition." He hopped lithely to the ground.

"Hey!" A fifty-something man with a wild, reddish tonsure and handlebar mustache strode toward us. His face reddened. "This is private property. You can't..." He took in the bottle avalanche, and his eyes bulged. "What have you done?" He fumbled with the radio on his belt.

"We didn't do anything," I said. "We were on our bikes, and someone used that arm to knock the bottles into the road."

"Nice try." He flipped a switch on the radio. "No one uses that road."

"Our bikes are under those bottles." I pointed.

The guard paused, radio at his jaw. "You got bikes?"

"Under that mess." Charlie pointed.

"Whatever," the guard said. "I'll let the police sort it out."

My stomach hit my trail runners. I couldn't afford another visit with the cops.

"Hold on," Charlie said. "We can figure this out, right? We're all law enforcement here."

The guard lowered his radio. "You're a cop?"

Charlie pulled a tattered wallet from the rear pocket of his board shorts. It had been our father's wallet. Charlie had kept it. My throat closed. I looked away, blinking. Now was not the ideal time for a sentimental reaction, and I wasn't sure why that wallet had triggered one.

Charlie hurried forward and showed the guard an ID. "I work security at the cannery in Nowhere."

"Heh." The guard shook his head. "I remember that cannery. I worked there as a teen. That was before it shut down." He paused. "I hate canned peas."

"And Fitch is a PI." Charlie motioned toward the detective. "Show him your ID."

"Yeah. Right." Fitch handed the guard his license.

The guard eyed me suspiciously. "And what about you?"

"I got nothing," I said. And if I was lucky, he didn't watch TV, didn't understand the internet, and had no idea about my past association with the recently and horribly deceased Toomas Koppel.

"That's not true," Charlie said. "Alice used to be a bodyguard. She worked countersurveillance for Toomas Koppel."

Charlie. I hung my head. The wonderful thing about my brother is he believes in me. The terrible thing is he doesn't understand why other people think I'm rotten. He believed the world was basically good. That taking a payoff and letting a crooked client get killed was something rare and unusual.

The guard snapped his fingers. "I knew I saw you somewhere. You got railroaded for that hit job. The stinking FBI let it all happen. Probably covering for the politicians themselves." He shook his head. "Man. That must have ruined your life."

I blinked. He hadn't believed what he'd heard? Only tinfoil-hat types didn't believe what they saw on TV. This guard was... A slow smile spread across my face. *Awesome.* "Um, yeah."

"Can't trust the government, man." The guard tapped his balding dome. "They condition us to think they're our friends. But all the time, they're robbing us blind, keeping us down. The little guy can't get ahead. Doesn't matter who's in power. They're all in on it."

"Exactly," Charlie said. "So, uh, speaking of in on it, was anyone else hanging around here earlier? Someone who could have used the bottle moving machine? Or whatever it's called."

"No one," the guard said. "I keep the key in the security shed."

"It's in the ignition now," Fitch said.

"That's not possible." The guard climbed into the machine and pulled out the keys. He stared at them. "I stand corrected."

I exhaled slowly. And he'd just smeared any fingerprints that might have been on the keys. "Who has access to the security shed?" I asked.

"After hours, only the guards. We keep it locked when we're alone here."

"Are there any other guards working today?" I asked.

"Just me. Hold on—you don't think I did this?"

"No," Charlie said quickly. "We just thought maybe we could ask the other guard if he'd seen anyone. But there isn't another guard. So... Did you see anyone else?"

"Nah. I was on the back porch when I heard the crash."

"Back porch?" I asked.

"For the employee café," the guard explained. "It's got a great view of the mountains." He motioned toward the snowy peaks to the west.

"Mind if we look around?" Fitch asked.

"Not at all. I'll give you a tour."

The guard led us to the front entrance—ungated— and to the café. It really did have a spectacular view. From there we ambled past patches of dirty snow to the corrugated metal security shack. It was unlocked. Outside its closed door, he scratched his head. "I don't get it. I'm sure I locked it. I always do."

"And only the guards have the keys to get inside?" I asked.

"Yeah, like I said." He smoothed his bushy mustache. "Which means... One of the other guards is a dirty traitor."

Or the guard had forgotten to lock it. Fitch bent and studied the lock.

"Could someone have picked it?" I asked.

"Sure," Fitch said. "It's a simple lock."

"Really?" the guard asked.

"Trust me," Charlie said. "He knows."

"All right," the guard said. "You three get out of here. I'm going to conduct a little sub rosa investigation, try to figure out whodunit. I'll let you know what I find out."

My stomach tightened. I did not need another helpful detective on the case. It was hard enough wrangling my brother.

"You don't have to do that," Fitch said quickly. "It could be dangerous."

"That's true." The guard rubbed his chin. "Never mind then. What are you going to do?"

"We think this may be linked to the murders of Adan and Holli Levann," Charlie said.

I winced. "Ah, that's a jump. We're not sure."

"What else could it be?" Charlie asked. "Adan started this recycling center. He was killed. We were investigating the murders and just left his house. And then someone sneaks in here and tries to bury us in recycling? Of course it's connected."

"It sounds connected to me," the guard agreed. A crow landed on the guard shack's corrugated roof.

"And we'd rather keep it quiet," Fitch said.

"Oh, yeah," the guard said. "I get that. I won't say anything. I'll take it to my grave."

"You don't have to go that far," Fitch said.

"No, really," the guard said. "It's no problem."

"Thin blue line, man." Charlie held out his hand, and the guard clasped it.

"Yeah," the guard said. "We're like outsiders, but we're insiders too. We're like, liminal people. In between."

"Yeah." Charlie nodded.

"Yeah," the guard said.

Yeah.

Chapter Twenty-One

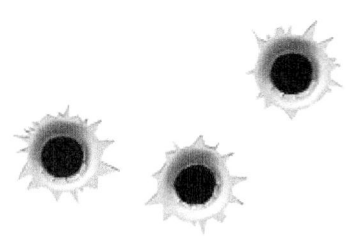

"You can't come." I glanced at the wall clock above my boxing dummy. I had to get moving if I was going to make my three-forty-five appointment with Jameel.

Charlie glared at me through one blue eye. The other was covered with an eyepatch. Along with the white suit and Panama hat, it was a key accessory for his role as the one-eyed man tonight. The scrapes from today's adventure at the recycling plant added to his rakish appearance.

"We totally have time to get to Rover, Inc. and get back before the show starts," he said.

I walked to my apartment's closed door. Studying myself in the long mirror there, I tugged down the cuffs of my navy blazer. "That's assuming everything goes according to plan. And when has that ever happened?"

"Oh." He scratched his head. "You may have a point."

I grabbed my bag off my bed. On the pillow, Sammie lazily flicked his black tail. Gnawing noises emerged from beneath the bed. Fredo had recovered his favorite bone. "I'll let you know what I find out."

"You promise?" he asked.

"Promise."

"Why can't Fitch go with you?"

I checked the mirror again and adjusted the collar of my white blouse. "Because he's busy with another case, and I'm a mature adult. It's a corporation. The worst that can happen is they throw me out. But they won't because I have an appointment."

"I guess," he said uneasily.

"I'll be fine." I clapped his shoulder. "Break a leg tonight."

He sighed. "Yeah, yeah, yeah."

I strode from my tiny apartment. "The show must go on," I called over my shoulder. Before he could follow, I hurried down the stairs and through the back of the theater. My Jeep was still at the mansion, but fortunately, I had a wheelman I trusted.

A blue Honda Accord glided to a halt behind the theater. The car window rolled down. A seventy-something woman with her gray hair in a braid down her back leaned out. "We following anyone today?"

"Don't think so." I walked around the car and got into the passenger seat. "But you never can tell."

Perella grinned. "Good. I haven't had an interesting ride in months. How's the detecting coming?"

We drove down the mountain and south along the highway to the Rover campus. Along the way, we discussed junior detecting and life as a rideshare driver. FYI, Perella was doing a lot better in the earnings department than I was.

The guard let us in the gate, and the car glided to a halt in front of Rover's glass front doors. "I'll wait in the guest parking lot," she said. "Anything I should be on the lookout for?"

"Robot dogs."

She snorted. "Right." She blinked. "Wait, that was a joke, right?"

"Nope." I stepped from the car. "This company makes them, and some have been going haywire. My guess is they're being hacked. So if any approach your car, use your instincts. I expect to be done in thirty minutes."

She nodded. I closed the door, and the Accord threaded its way through the parked cars.

I walked inside Rover, Inc. This time, there was a receptionist at the desk. She gave me a security lanyard, and a uniformed guard escorted me to Jameel's office. The guard raised his hand to knock, and the door opened beneath his fist.

The wizened man who'd been staring at me in the police station barreled from the room. His white hair was smooth and gleaming over his skull. "Watch it," he snapped. He flicked an imaginary speck of Alice Sommerland cooties off his brown Versace suit.

The man turned to the office's open door. A trio of cowed-looking women with clipboards hovered just inside it. "Free wi-fi for the museum," he said. "That's the deal." He pivoted, glasses glinting, and strode past us.

The three women glanced at each other. They hustled after him, their heels clicking on the floor tiles.

I frowned after them. It wasn't just the mystery man's attitude that reminded me of Gert. Aside from his fashion sense, he kind of looked like him too. "Who—?"

"Come in," Jameel called. The guard nodded to me. Bemused, I walked inside. The big windows framed steel-blue clouds massing over the mountains to the west.

Jameel rose from behind his polished, modern desk and smoothed his red tie. His suit jacket hung over the back of his executive chair. His shirt sleeves were rolled to the elbows. "Ms. Sommerland. Thanks for coming."

Since I'd been the one to set the appointment, I arched a brow. "Who was that?"

"The mayor of the Town of Hot Springs, Aanselmi Vertanen."

That explained why he could walk into Detective Guthrie's office without knocking. "He's not, ah, Estonian, is he?" Maybe he and Gert were long-lost cousins.

"Finnish, I believe. Why?"

"No reason." I wasn't sure if I should be relieved or terrified that Gert had a Finnish clone. But for the first time, I was feeling some sympathy for Jameel.

He motioned toward a leather chair on the opposite side of his desk. "Please have a seat," he said.

"And he's negotiating for free wi-fi? For the new miniature museum?" I sat and crossed my legs. A robodog by Jameel's wide desk raised its head, and I nearly jumped out of my seat. The dog cocked it playfully.

Jameel grimaced. "He drives a hard bargain. It looks like we're going to be a sponsor." The door closed behind me, the guard leaving us. The COO sat and nodded to me. "I'd like to apologize. We didn't take your complaints about the Rovers seriously. We should have."

I leaned back in the leather chair. His apology had come too easily. I didn't trust it. "Do you know what's causing their malfunction?"

"It appears to be a hack."

I'd guessed as much. The behavior of the robo-dogs had been too focused on me for it to be random. "Who could have done something like that?" I asked.

"It's a good question, one which I've posed to your colleague, Mr. Rhodes."

"Fitch?"

"He's agreed to take the case."

I wrinkled my brow. Since when had Fitch become an expert in cybercrime? Or maybe he had been all along, and I just hadn't noticed. He could play the piano. The PI might have all sorts of hidden talents. "I'd have thought you'd have people on your team qualified to fix the hack."

"We do, and they're working on it with Adalina's assistance. But there's a difference between fixing the hack and finding the hacker."

That sort of... No, that didn't make sense at all. What *did* make sense was that if we were working for Rover, we'd have to keep our mouths shut. No blabbing to the press about what we learned. My mouth pressed together. Why the hell had Fitch agreed to it?

"We've sent the paperwork to Mr. Rhodes, but since you're here, you can sign it now." He pressed a button on his phone.

"Paperwork?"

He leaned back in his executive chair. "Confidentiality agreements, that sort of thing."

Bingo. This was a pay-off to keep our mouths shut. "If news of the hack leaks," I said, "how much damage will it do to Rover's share price?"

"Our customers need to know they can trust their Rovers."

"And your military contract?"

He stiffened. "We don't have a military contract."

"Yet?" I guessed.

He didn't respond.

"But you are in talks," I guessed.

The door behind me opened. A middle-aged woman in black slacks and a sensible blue blouse walked inside carrying a folder.

"Ah," he said. "Helen. You have the agreements?"

"Right here, Mr. Rich." She set the folder on the desk.

"Thank you," he said.

She left the room. He slid the folder to me. I flipped it open.

I skimmed the page, then texted Fitch. Jameel says we work for them now. Wants me to sign confidentiality agreement?

"What are you doing?" Jameel asked.

"I work for Fitch Rhodes. I can't sign anything without his approval."

My phone pinged. If you want in, you'll need to sign.

I sighed. I didn't *want* to sign. But I did want in. And the confidentiality agreement didn't cover any criminal activity. If I learned anything that implicated Rover in Adan's murder, it was going to the police. "Have you got a pen?"

Jameel's shoulders dropped beneath his elegant suit. He handed me a Mont Blanc pen.

I signed where all the yellow sticky tabs told me to and returned the folder and pen to his polished desk. "And the military contract?" I asked.

"We don't have—"

"Not yet. If I'm to catch whoever hacked your dogs, I need to know about possible motives. Scotching a military contract could be one."

His long fingers twitched. "Why? Who would want to?"

"You tell me." I uncrossed my legs.

"This contract would double our capital," he said. "It would transform the company."

So Adalina had been right. The military *was* sniffing around. "Not everyone can be happy about that."

"Our shareholders certainly will be."

"I heard Adan wasn't keen on it."

He angled his chair away from me. "That's ridiculous."

"Do you normally work on Sundays?" Outside the windows, cars streamed past along the highway at the base of the hills.

"When there's a big project on, I work every day. This business with the Rovers is an all-hands-on-deck situation."

"Who else might want to sabotage them?" I asked.

"I expect we'll get a ransom message soon enough," he said coolly.

"Give us money and we'll let you know how we hacked your dogs?" I asked, skeptical. It wasn't that it was impossible. But it didn't track with the murders of Adan and Holli. Those had been personal.

"It's happened to other corporations," he said. "Why not Rover?"

I shook my head. "No. You may get a ransom, but that doesn't explain why the Rovers have been coming after me." I motioned toward the Rover beside the desk. It didn't react. "Why not take control of *your* Rover? If I was a happy hacker, looking to cause trouble, I'd go after that one to make a point."

He laughed lightly and steepled his long fingers. "We don't know the Rovers have been coming after you, as you put it."

The thread of doubt in his voice raised my hackles. "Have other customers been complaining?" I asked.

"Other customers' dogs have gone missing, so yes."

"But no one's been attacked by their Rovers."

"No," he said, drawing the word out.

"Have there been any other instances of violence or destruction on the part of the Rovers?"

"No."

Then it was personal. "What about Adan's Rover, the one that went missing. Have you been able to retrieve any of its data?"

"We haven't found it yet."

I canted my head. But we *had* found it. Adalina was working on Adan's dog. And some of the data had to be in the cloud—even if it wasn't the latest. Why hadn't she informed her company?

I asked Perella to drive me to the trailhead that led to the rear of the mansion. As we passed the recycling plant, a mini bulldozer moved bottles into the recycling center yard. The red-haired guard driving it waved. "Trust no one," he shouted.

"You know that guy?" Perella asked.

"Yeah…" I braced my elbow on the window frame and my cheek on my fist. "It's a small town."

It was almost dark when she dropped me at the trailhead. I paid her, waved goodbye, and hiked through the pines to the mansion. A final beam of sunlight gleamed through the high branches. It vanished behind the Sierras.

Shelley greeted me at the mansion's back door. "I saw you hiking across the lawn."

"Too bad there are no cameras on this side of the house," I said casually. "It would make it easier for you." And for me. Hell, a camera might have solved the case already.

"As I said, Ad—Mr. Levann liked his privacy."

I eyed him. In his gray suit, he looked like he'd stepped out of a costume drama. "How long have you worked here?"

"Six months."

"Have you been a butler long?"

"I spent eight years with Lord and Lady Feltingham at their London home."

And hopefully Fitch would have a way to verify that. At my ex's company, he had an entire department devoted to background checks. I rubbed a hand over my face. I should have paid more attention to that department, but the work had seemed boring.

"Are the press still at the gates?" I asked, stepping inside.

"Sadly, yes. Ms. Levann is in her garage workshop. Mr. Levann is in his studio." We walked down the hallway, our footsteps absorbed by the thick, crimson carpet.

"And their mother?"

"Has not returned yet."

"Do you expect her to?" I asked.

"That was her stated intention."

"And mine is just to collect my car."

He stopped inside the high-ceilinged foyer. "Will you be returning tonight?"

Not if I can help it. Because if I came back, Charlie would insist on returning too. "I don't think so."

An expression of relief flitted across his face and as quickly vanished. He nodded.

Shelley opened the front door for me and watched from beneath the portico as I got into my Jeep. Grabbing a hoodie from the passenger seat, I pulled it on over my blazer. I flipped up the navy hood and set a pair of big, dark glasses on my nose. It was way too dark to see anything through them, so I took them off again.

Starting the Jeep, I cruised down the long driveway to the iron gates. The solar lamps had come on, guiding my path.

A press van sat parked outside. A familiar black van was parked behind it, and I smiled. Not all the press got their jollies insinuating I was a killer. There was one guy who'd given me a fair shake. And that was his van.

The gates swung slowly open. I inched through, wincing despite my glasses at the flashes and shouted questions. No one was dumb enough to throw themselves in front of my wheels. When I glanced in my rearview mirror, no one followed me.

I turned the corner and checked my side mirror. The bushes along the roadside shivered, and I frowned, slowing. A Rover raced along the other side of the bushes, pacing me.

Chapter Twenty-Two

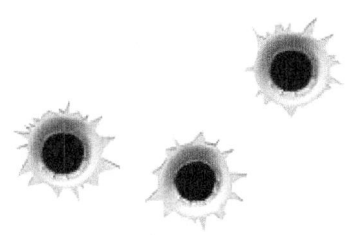

Even the tough guys in personal protection can freak out when things get weird. They weren't immune. But they learned to control their anxieties, using them to stay sharp rather than being overwhelmed by fear.

I *was* freaked out by the Rover, and I wasn't ashamed to admit it. But in the end, this was just a tail. And I knew how to handle a tail.

I edged up to thirty miles per hour on the residential street. The Rover leapt a manzanita bush and landed beside my car. Blue eyes glowing in the darkness, it kept up with my Jeep. That was all kinds of weird and disturbing.

If a Rover could do thirty, the ones that had attacked me when I was on foot could have taken me down. Why hadn't they?

I dropped back to twenty-five. This wasn't the sort of street where kids might dart out chasing a ball. But there were a lot of deer.

I rolled my shoulders and adjusted the seatbelt across my chest. And why was this one following me? Had the police sent it to surveil me? Somehow, I didn't think so. But if the person who'd hacked the Rovers was controlling this one, what was the point? To shake me?

They'd succeeded at the latter, at least at first. Now I was just curious about how fast the thing could go.

I checked my rearview. The black van that had been waiting outside the mansion was behind me. It flashed its high beams.

The Rover and the van followed me through town and onto the highway. I gunned the gas. At forty-five, the Rover began dropping back. By the time I hit fifty-five, it was a speck in the rearview mirror. At least the Rovers had some limits.

I rolled down the window and waved to the van, then pulled over at a rest stop. The black van followed.

A young man in a dark blue knit cap and thick parka hopped from the vehicle. I stepped from my Jeep and stretched, waiting beneath a parking lot lamp.

Zed Kelley glanced over his shoulder, his dark brow furrowed. "You had a shadow." He was a YouTuber and part of the new journalism movement. The reporter was making a name for himself breaking stories corporate media wouldn't touch. He'd been fair to me after the Toomas Koppel incident. But he was still a reporter and not a friend.

"Not a very good tail," I said. "Robot dogs stand out."

He scratched his knit cap. "What was that about?"

"I'm not sure yet. What are you doing here?"

"I was in Vegas," he said. "When I heard about your connection to the Levann murders, I thought I'd stop by. What can you tell me?"

"Not much. I just signed a confidentiality agreement with Rover, Inc." I didn't bother denying the connection. Zed was too good to bother lying to.

"And the Rover following you was making sure you stuck to it?" He raised a dark brow.

"That is a mystery I've been trying to solve since Adan Levann's death," I said. The parking lot lamp above us flickered.

"There's been a Rover following you since his death?" he asked.

"I don't think I said that."

The reporter grinned. "So you had nothing to do with the destruction at the Hot Springs mall?"

Oh. He'd heard about that.

The confidentiality agreement I'd signed covered the Rovers, but not Adan's or Holli's murder. And Jameel's attempt to coerce me into keeping my mouth shut made me want to do the opposite.

Wary, I eyed the reporter. Zed could come in handy someday. He'd already helped me out once. But I needed to choose my words carefully. "The murders may have nothing to do with Rover," I said.

"Is it true your brother was Adan's son?"

I nodded. So he'd found that out too. Though Charlie hadn't exactly been keeping it secret. "It's been..."

"A real brain bang?" he asked.

"Yeah," I said, surprised. "I mean, Charlie's my brother. That hasn't changed." Just everything I'd thought I'd known about our parents. And since they were both gone, there was no one I could ask.

My brows drew downward. Actually, there *was* one person...

Zed shook his head. "Those DNA tests are the worst."

I leaned against my Jeep Commander. "Tell me about it."

"How's your brother doing with all this?"

"I'm not sure." The cold from the black Jeep seeped through my blazer and hoodie, but I didn't move. "He was thrown, just like I was, when he learned about Adan. And then Adan seemed to accept him. Charlie was excited about meeting new family."

"And then someone killed Adan."

"Yeah." I studied the pavement between my boots. "Charlie didn't know Adan long enough to grow really attached I think, but it had to hurt. He's determined to—"

I dipped my head and clamped my mouth shut. Charlie was a client too, and he *was* covered by our confidentiality agreement. I'd only forgotten because Zed was very, very good. Cars hummed past on the highway. The first stars, cold and bright, appeared above.

"Find out whodunit?" Zed guessed.

"Wouldn't you want to know?"

"I do want to know. I've been looking into Rover, Inc. Their P/E ratio is out of whack."

"Price to earnings you mean?"

"Yeah. The stock price is a lot higher than the earnings warrant."

"Which means?"

"Which means the price is running on the expectation of future earnings. Word is Rover's about to sign some government contracts."

I straightened off the Jeep. "Adan was vocal about not wanting those contracts. When did the stock price go up?"

"Two days after his death. There was a drop the day after he was killed, which was to be expected. And then there was a major rebound. The stock price tripled, and it's still going up."

A gust of wind flapped our jackets, and I shivered. "Who are the majority shareholders?" I asked.

Zed adjusted his navy knit cap. "Who do you think? Adan and Jameel Rich."

"You're saying Adan's estate tripled after his death?"

"Not quite," he said. "Adan had other assets aside from the stock—that enormous house, for example. But according to an article I dug up last year, most of his wealth is in Rover. Even split three ways, your brother is going to be a very wealthy man."

"What about Holli's heirs?"

"She didn't have any relatives. Word is, she left everything to Adan's kids too."

I nodded. That confirmed what she'd told me.

He zipped up his hoodie. "Her will might affect Charlie's share. He may not get her chunk, depending on how the will was worded, but he'll still do okay. Is it true you're working for a PI now?"

"Contract work. Surveillance," I said, thinking hard. Money had always been a potential motive for the murders. I wasn't sure this new information changed anything. But it was interesting. "Why are you telling me this?"

"Why not? We're just two professionals chatting." He winked and ambled to his van.

I watched it cut across the highway and turn toward Hot Springs. Then I got in my Jeep and drove to Nowhere.

The theater parking lot was full. Lights gleamed through the old-west building's windows. I let myself in through the back and climbed the wooden stairs to my apartment. Charlie would want to hear what I'd found out, but not in the middle of a performance.

Fredo greeted me with frantic barks, his stumpy tail wagging. Then he remembered himself and attacked my boot laces. Sammie raised his sleek black head from my bed and yawned.

I ate a toasted bagel and cream cheese and sat at my computer. I searched for articles on Rover. Zed was right. The consensus was the company's finances were in better shape without Adan in charge.

I mulled that over and searched for more online intel. But I came up with a frustrating bupkiss. Downstairs, doors slammed. Car engines started. The show was over, people leaving the theater. I made my way downstairs.

Lilyanna, dressed in a safari dress and pith helmet, waved to me through the departing crowd.

"Hey," I said. "How'd it go tonight?"

"Fine," she said. "I love the Adventurer's Club mystery. Part of me wants to be in a Victorian adventurer's club. But of course they wouldn't allow women in back then."

"Which would make being in one even more delicious for a woman of that era." I scanned the dinner theater. Waitstaff pulled crimson tablecloths from the round tables. A few guests remained clustered at the open doors. "Have you seen Charlie?" I asked.

"He was the second victim tonight," she said. "I haven't seen him since he was carried off stage."

A sickening shiver trembled through me. But he wouldn't have gone back to the mansion. He didn't have a car, and he had his second job at the cannery tonight. "Thanks."

I hurried into the kitchen. The industrial dishwasher was chugging away, steam escaping through its closed door. Jane, the stage manager and restaurant owner, frowned at a computer tablet.

"Hi, Jane. Have you seen Charlie?"

She looked up from her tablet, and her plain face brightened with a smile. "Hi, Al. Um... He left."

I stopped short beside the gleaming dishwasher. "To the cannery?"

"No, he got a lift from one of the waiters who works in Hot Springs."

My heart jumped. "He went to Hot Springs?"

"That's what he said. I guess there was some mix-up with his schedule at the cannery."

"But he... When was this?" Steam heated my arm, and I jerked away from the dishwasher.

She checked her watch. "About an hour ago."

"Thanks." I jogged to my Jeep.

"Alice!" Gert strode toward me, a thick scarf around his neck and chin. "What have you got for me."

"I'm in a hurry, Gert."

"You must have learned something by now."

I opened the Jeep's door and got in. "The mayor's pushing Rover, Inc. to donate free wi-fi to the miniature museum."

His glasses glinted in the moonlight, and he hissed a breath. "Excellent."

"Is it?" I shut the door and pulled from the parking lot, then I called Charlie on my car's phone. My call went to voicemail.

"Charlie, I'm in Nowhere, headed back to Hot Springs. Where are you? Call me ASAP."

I peeled from the parking lot. My brother was fine. I was worrying about nothing. His phone battery had probably died. It happened all the time. That was why he wasn't picking up.

And just because Charlie might be a lot richer than I'd thought, he was fine. That was no reason to kill him. He wasn't going to challenge the will. He'd already told the lawyer.

And the lawyer had told him to think on it before deciding. I gripped the wheel so hard I thought it might break off.

Elbows pressed close, I swore and sped down the mountain highway. I took the turns too fast, passing slow-moving cars where I shouldn't have. I reached the north-south highway and turned toward Hot Springs.

I stepped on the gas, hitting ninety on the straightaways. Again, I called Charlie. Again, my call went to voicemail.

I turned on the road into the Sierras toward Hot Springs. A low shadow darted from behind the *Welcome to The Town of Hot Springs* sign.

A *deer*. I braked and sucked in a breath. The animal swerved, cutting the edge of my headlights. My jaw tightened. Not an animal—a Rover. Had it been waiting for me this whole time? Because that really was creepy.

The robot dog followed me all the way to the mansion's iron gates. They stood open, and a fresh burst of fear seized my heart.

Without slowing, I cannoned down the driveway. Gravel pinged against the bottom of my Jeep. I slowed to a stop in front of the mansion's stone steps. Hopping from the Jeep,

I glanced toward the gates. The Rover hadn't followed me inside.

I opened the door and strode into the house. A small crowd of people at the base of the stairs turned to stare. Jameel. Gina. Ary. Adalina. Shelley.

The butler hurried toward me. "Ms. Sommerland. You're here."

"What's going on?" I grabbed the sleeve of his gray suit. "Where's Charlie?"

The others parted, revealing my brother, lying unmoving at the base of the stairs.

Chapter Twenty-Three

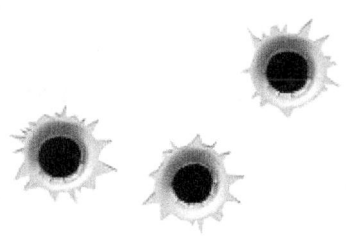

Buzzing filled my ears. I couldn't speak. Couldn't move. No. This wasn't happening.

"Charlie?" My voice sounded odd, distant. The scent of the red and white roses on the foyer's circular table was cloying. The bouquet looked waxy, unreal—as unreal as the people standing around my supine brother.

"We just found him there." Shelley motioned toward my brother at the base of the foyer's twin curving stairs.

Releasing his arm, I brushed past the butler. I couldn't be too late. The others moved away from my brother's still body.

"We haven't touched him," Jameel said.

"Have you called an ambulance?" I asked sharply.

"Not yet." Jameel smoothed his red tie and tucked it inside his buttoned-up blazer. "We just got here."

"Charlie. I told him... This was exactly the sort of..." My legs gave out, and I crumpled beside him. For some stupid reason, the sight of his yachting jacket sparked hot anger at the base of my skull.

And then my training kicked in. I swallowed and lightly ran my hands over his blond head. There was a massive lump on the top right. His neck—

He groaned and stirred.

"Charlie." Unsteadily, I sat back on my heels. He was alive. *Thank God.*

My brother lifted his head, a silly expression on his face. "Alice?" He smoothed his beard. "What's going on?"

"He appears to have fallen down the stairs," the butler said.

"I can see that," I snapped. "Did you see who pushed you?" I asked my brother.

"What?" he asked groggily.

"Pushed?" Gina, in black Dolce and Gabbana, arched an elegant brow. "Why ever would you suggest that?"

"Oh, I don't know, Mom." Adalina crossed her arms over her green cashmere top. "Because this is a houseful of killers?"

"Shut up," Ary snapped. He was dressed all in black again—no painter's smock tonight.

"What happened?" I grasped Charlie's shoulder.

He sat up and looked around. "Oh, hey."

"You've got a concussion." My face tightened.

"No, I'm fine," Charlie slowly folded sideways, landing face down on the stairs. "I'm fine," he mumbled into the red carpet.

I ran my hands over his arms, legs, and torso. Nothing was broken or bleeding. I took my brother's arm. "Shelley, help me get him into my car."

"With pleasure." He grabbed Charlie's other arm, and together we steered him outside and to my Jeep.

The others trailed behind and stood on the stone entry steps. We maneuvered Charlie into the passenger's seat.

I buckled Charlie in. He could have been killed. I wasn't there, and he could have been killed. Anger boiled inside me, but I forced myself to stay calm. "What really happened?" I asked Shelley in a low voice.

His blond brows drew together. "I was in the kitchen. I heard several loud thumps in the foyer. When I came to investigate, I found your brother at the bottom of the stairs." He rubbed a hand over his face.

"Was anyone else there?"

"Ms. Levann exited the drawing room at approximately the same time I arrived in the foyer."

"Which Ms. Levann?" I asked.

"Adalina."

"When did Gina get to the house tonight?"

"She arrived in time for dinner at six. I believe she intended a sort of council of war."

"About what?" I asked.

He tilted his head toward my brother, who was pulling the seatbelt from his chest and letting it snap back. "Cool," Charlie mumbled.

"And Jameel?" I asked.

"Arrived thirty minutes ago. He asked to speak with Adalina."

"But he didn't come out of the drawing room with her?"

"No," he said. "I don't know which room he came from when he arrived in the foyer. My attention was fixed on your brother."

I closed Charlie's door. "We'll talk more later."

"How ominous."

Ignoring the barb, I strode around the car and got in. I didn't want to take Charlie to the local hospital. At this point,

I didn't trust anything or anyone in Hot Springs. But all Nowhere had was an underfunded clinic. The next nearest hospital was in Reno, an hour away. We were stuck.

I drove down the driveway. Only once I'd passed through the open gates, did I call Fitch. When I explained what happened, the PI cursed. "And your brother doesn't remember anything?"

"It doesn't seem like it. He hit his head pretty hard."

"Your brother's lucky he didn't break his neck. Where are you taking him?"

"The hospital here in Hot Springs."

Fitch was silent a long moment. "Okay. You staying with him?"

"What do you think?"

"I'll see you in the morning."

Charlie was still loopy when we reached the emergency room. But he managed to pull a ratty wallet from the back pocket of his board shorts and extract an insurance card. "Adan put me on the family plan," he slurred.

It must have been some plan. The staff got a lot more respectful after that.

Charlie was eventually moved to a room in a tasteful blue gray. It was more luxury hotel than hospital—leather armchairs and floor tiles that looked like wood. It even had an extra bed for guests. Since I'd spotted a Rover downstairs, I took the bed.

I called the police from the hall so as not to wake Charlie. Twenty minutes later, Detective Guthrie in Gucci pushed open the door to my brother's room. "How is he?"

"Loopy," I said.

"I'm great," Charlie said groggily.

"What happened?"

"Someone pushed me," Charlie said.

"You see who?"

"It's all fizzy. Fuzzy. Wuzzy."

I cocked my head toward the hallway. Guthrie nodded and strode outside and to the waiting area. I followed him.

"What happened?" He stopped in front of the faux-stone fireplace. Poinsettias lined the mantel. A gas fire flickered, the flames casting rippling shadows on the thick carpet.

"He was found at the bottom of the foyer stairs at Adan's house. I got there just after it happened. Gina, Adalina, Ary, Jameel, and Shelley were there, and no one saw anything."

"Should they have?"

"Come on. What are the odds?"

"People do fall down stairs," he said blandly.

"And sometimes, they're pushed."

"Yeah." He lifted a single eyebrow. "Funny you should come across two victims of that in as many weeks."

"What's that supposed to mean?"

"What do you think it means?"

"Are you a psychiatrist now too?"

His face darkened. "I'll look into it." He pivoted and strode to the elevator.

Uncertainly, I returned to Charlie's room. Okay, I'd been a little short with Guthrie, but I hadn't been that bad.

After that, I didn't get much sleep. Charlie had a concussion. Machines beeped and blared at random moments. At around three AM, the door to his room opened three inches. I swung my feet from the bed and stared at it through scratchy eyes.

The door silently closed. I sprang to my feet and peered into the blue-gray hallway. A nurse in soft shoes padded past, but I didn't see anyone else. An overhead light flickered.

I closed the door behind me.

A nurse came in to check on him at five AM. I watched her with folded arms and burning eyes, and she left hastily.

The door opened again at seven, and Fitch walked into the deluxe room. He took in Charlie's sleeping form, jerked his head toward the hallway, and walked back out. I joined him there.

Another man, built like a bouncer, stood beside a supply closet door. I did a double take. The newcomer *was* a bouncer. He worked at the speakeasy in Nowhere.

"How is he?" Fitch asked me in a low voice.

"Concussion." I tore my gaze from the bouncer. "The hospital wants to keep him here for another day, at least."

He nodded. "I brought Phil to keep an eye on him."

"I see," I said slowly. "Mind if we have a word?" I smiled at Phil then walked down the hall to the plush waiting area. The fireplace had gone out. It was all I could do not to drop into one of the leather chairs and close my eyes.

"What's up?" Fitch asked. "Was he able to tell you who pushed him?"

"No. How well do you know Phil?"

"Pretty well. We met when I was on that job in Nowhere that went south. He's done a few protection gigs for me since."

My mouth compressed. There was a certain skill set when it came to personal protection. It was miles away from throwing drunk and unruly guests out of a speakeasy. Okay, I was kind of a protection snob, but I *had* worked in the industry for over ten years.

"Don't get your panties in a bunch," Fitch said. "You're lucky I was able to get anybody on such short notice and on Charlie's budget."

"Charlie has a budget?" I asked, surprised. When had my brother ever had a budget?

I glanced down the hall. Phil was gone.

"See?" I snarled.

I stormed to Charlie's room and flung open the door. Phil sat in a chair beside Charlie's bed. Charlie said something in a voice too low for me to hear, and Phil laughed.

"Hey, Al." Charlie grinned. "Phil's here."

I exhaled slowly. So. They were friends. I should have expected it. Nowhere's the sort of town where everyone knows everyone. Intimately. Fitch shot me a self-satisfied look.

"It looks like you're feeling better," I said to my brother.

"It was nothing a good night's sleep couldn't fix." Charlie squinted at me. "What's wrong with your eyes?"

I glanced in the gilt wall mirror opposite his bed. My eyes were red and puffy. The color clashed with the dark circles beneath them. "I didn't have the benefit of being knocked unconscious," I said. "This hospital is loud. What do you remember from last night?"

Charlie looked at the ceiling. "Ah... I hitched a ride with a friend to Adan's, and Shelley let me in. The others were finishing dinner in the dining room. You wouldn't believe how many rooms that place has," he said as an aside to Phil. "You should stop by some day."

I cleared my throat. Really? We were doing chit-chat?

"Right," Charlie said hurriedly and pulled the sheets higher. "So they were finishing dinner. Everyone got really quiet when I walked in. I think I'm not the best reminder for them about Adan. I mean, it's been weird for me finding out I have another family. But it's got to be even stranger for them."

That was putting it charitably. "And then?" I asked, impatient.

"They left. Shelley came in with a tray of dinner for me. Man, for a butler, that guy can cook."

My fingers twitched. "And then?"

"Then I broke into Adan's safe."

"Excuse me?" Fitch said.

A *safe*. I clawed a hand through my hair. And he hadn't thought to mention it to me, even though he knew I'd been snooping. *Charlie.*

"It wasn't hard," my brother said. "I'd kind of seen the combo one day when Adan opened it. It's hidden in the floor of his study, under a rug. Cool, huh?"

"What did you find?" Fitch asked.

"Nothing. It was empty." He shifted in the hospital bed.

Fitch's brows drew downward. "Completely empty?"

"Yeah," he said. "Though it wasn't when Adan opened it two weeks ago. It was full of all sorts of papers and stuff."

"One of the kids probably opened it," I said. "Anything inside is theirs now."

"But," Charlie said, "they didn't know about the safe, because of the gun."

"The what?" Phil asked.

Charlie nodded, then winced and rubbed the back of his head against the pillow. "Adan had this cool gun, with a thing you stick against your shoulder that flips out."

"A shoulder brace?" I asked.

"Yeah," Charlie said. "That. And a laser sight. He told me the kids didn't know about the safe—he didn't want them to know about the gun in the house."

"But he showed you," I said, disbelieving. And why not let his children know? They were a long way from being minors. Unlike a lot of my old colleagues, I was never that into guns. But when things went wrong, I'd rather be the woman holding one. They were useful tools if you knew how to handle them.

"It was sort of an accident," Charlie said. "I didn't know no one was supposed to go into his study when the door was closed. I walked in on him."

"Obviously someone else did know about it," I said, my fingers twitching. And now that someone had whatever had been in that safe... and a lethal weapon.

Chapter Twenty-Four

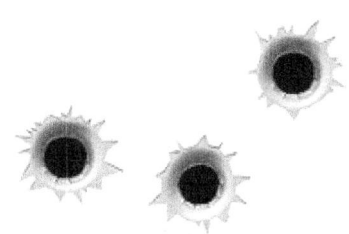

We hashed over the mystery of the empty safe. But it was clear Charlie wasn't in much shape for the talk. Reluctantly, Fitch and I left Charlie's hospital room and took the elevator to the first floor.

"Thanks for getting Phil," I said, stepping from the elevator. I met the PI's gaze. The amused look in his eyes changed to something else. I stilled and reminded myself we were only colleagues. This was business.

Fitch broke eye contact first. His brow creased. "Your brother's a target. Of course I took care of it."

My muscles loosened, warming. One of the best things about my old career had been the camaraderie. I'd been part of a team. We'd had each other's backs. I felt that now, but I wasn't sure I should. I worked for Fitch, and only as a contractor. That was all we were. Nothing more.

"Have you talked to the police yet?" he continued.

"I called them last night. They didn't believe it was anything more than an accident." My mouth compressed.

We crossed the high-ceilinged lobby. The glassed atrium was decorated for the holidays. Twinkle lights twined artfully through the greenery. Maybe it was the early hour. Maybe Hot Springs citizens were too healthy to visit the hospital much. But I'd never been in a hospital this quiet. I tugged down the hem of my jacket.

"Don't underestimate them." Fitch touched my arm, and a shiver rippled through me. "I'll call and follow up."

I nodded and stared ahead at the hospital's sliding glass exit doors. I should have been irritated he assumed they'd listen to him and not me. But with the state of my reputation, it was true. Fitch had a better chance. "I'm not sure I'd trust them if they did follow up. The Hot Springs PD seems a little too cozy with Rover, Inc."

Fitch grunted. "Maybe. I ran a background check on our principles. They all checked out."

"Even Shelley?"

"This is his first job as a butler. He was an actor before that."

I stopped a few steps from the glass doors. Shelley had lied. "No Lord and Lady Feltingham?"

"He didn't lie about that. Shelley worked at their theater company."

My neck tightened. "Son of a..." I missed it. I'd known something was off and I hadn't pursued it. Briefly, I shut my eyes. "This is why I should stick to surveillance. I need to get back to personal protection."

"Did you ever leave it?"

"Are you kidding me? They kicked me to the curb so hard I'm having trouble sitting down."

"What exactly do you think you're doing now?"

"I have no idea what I'm doing," I said. "That's the problem."

"You saved Mrs. Stanton's life, and she isn't the first person you've saved. As to Charlie, you know as well as anyone that if a client is determined not to be protected, you're not going to protect him."

"That's not..." Hell. I *was* doing personal protection and surveillance. How could I not have seen it?

He clasped my shoulder. "Sorry I can't give you the expense account you've been accustomed to. Now go home and get some sleep. You've had a long night. You okay to drive?"

"Yeah." I was at the point where I was so wired I was twitching, but I knew it wouldn't last.

I left Hot Springs and chewed over what Fitch had said. I'd spent a lot of time feeling sorry for myself about losing my old career. What a waste that had been. And now... what? Was I building something new? Did I *want* something new? I liked the people I encountered in Fitch's world more than the ones I'd dealt with in personal protection.

Back at my apartment, I took Fredo out to do his business. After feeding the animals, I shoved Sammie aside on my bed and fell asleep.

I woke up feeling worse than I might have if I'd just powered through. The clock on the wall behind my boxing dummy read twelve o'clock. Watery sun streamed through my window.

My stomach growled. I left the theater in quest of food. The day was gloomy. A thick fog blanketed the streets and reduced the giant lawn flamingo to two pairs of legs. I bypassed the pizza parlor in favor of a place marginally healthier—The Sagebrush.

The bell over the glass front door tinkled as I walked inside. Conversation stopped for a beat, then resumed. Molly, the owner, motioned me toward a corner booth, away from other diners. I sat, yawned. Christmas carols played tinnily from the café's speakers.

A cup of black coffee and a menu appeared on the table before me. I stared at them blearily.

The bell over the front door jingled. The diner again fell silent and quickly resumed. A cane thumped rhythmically on the linoleum, and I looked up.

Mrs. Malone, in a powder blue track suit and fleece jacket, slid across from me into the booth. "Good. I thought I'd find you here."

And I'd thought I'd find her at her cabin. If anyone knew the story about my parents, it would be Mrs. Malone. But before I could ask, a yawn swelled in the back of my throat. I covered my mouth with one hand.

"You've been derelict in your updates about the murders," she said. "What's happened?"

I studied the line of white roots that framed her wrinkled face. "Someone tried to kill Charlie last night."

She drew back. "Good God. Is he all right?"

"He will be. Charlie's in the hospital. Someone pushed him down the stairs at the Levann mansion. He didn't see or can't remember who. He's got a concussion, but the doctors say he'll be fine in a day or two."

"Concussions are serious." Her lipsticked mouth puckered. "As is attempted murder. I suppose it was only a matter of time before one of the heirs tried something. Charlie cuts into their share of the treasure."

"Treasure?"

"A figure of speech." She motioned to a passing waitress in blue. "I'll have the chicken salad sandwich and a glass of iced tea. Alice?"

"Ah..." I hadn't had time to really look at my menu. "I'll have the breakfast burrito."

"For lunch?" Mrs. Malone's gray brows sketched upward. But the waitress had already swished away.

"I haven't had breakfast yet," I said. "And I'm not so sure this is just about an inheritance. Well, it is, but maybe not only because of the money."

"Why do you say that?"

"The Rovers. There's something going on with them. Jameel hired Fitch and me just so we'd sign a confidentiality agreement. He wants us to keep our traps shut." It was heartening anyone had faith in my signature, given my rep as a dishonorable bodyguard.

She lowered her chin. "An agreement which I see you're not too particular about honoring."

I waved a hand negligently. "You're not going to the press."

She harumphed. "Does Charlie inherit a share of the company?"

"He doesn't inherit anything. Adan never got around to changing his will."

"And in Nevada, children must be legally recognized to inherit. But the court may recognize that the omission was unintentional. If that's the case, he would inherit."

"That's probably why his estate attorney suggested Charlie challenge the will. Apparently, the lawyer had drawn up a new will and was just waiting for Adan to sign..." I cocked my head. Mrs. Malone wasn't a lawyer, but she seemed awfully knowledgeable.

"If his attorney was in the process of revising the will, Charlie would have an excellent case. It would be obvious the omission was unintentional. What are you thinking?"

"How do you know so much about Nevada inheritance law?"

A second glass of iced tea appeared before Mrs. Malone. "I looked it up, of course, as soon as I heard Mr. Levann had been murdered. Didn't you?" She sipped from her white mug.

Of course she had. I massaged my temples.

"You learned something new regarding our case, haven't you? What is it?" she demanded.

Our case? I mentally shrugged. "Charlie broke into Adan's office safe last night," I said, "before the stair incident. He said it was empty."

She hissed an indrawn breath. "Someone stole the new will. Who had access to that safe?"

"That's a leap." I rubbed my burning eyes.

A plate crashed in the kitchen. Everyone looked in that direction, then away.

"Has anyone found the new will?" she asked.

"If they have, they haven't told me. Or the lawyer." But it didn't matter. Any competent lawyer would have a copy of it at his office. The question wasn't whether the will existed, it was whether the court would accept it if it hadn't been signed. And if the change in the will was a motive for murder.

"Adan told Charlie his kids didn't know about the safe, but he could have been wrong. I knew all sorts of things my parents didn't think..." I trailed off again, my tired brain failing to keep up with my mouth. I'd forgotten what I was trying to say.

She took another sip of her coffee. "You look like something the cat dragged in. *Try* to finish a sentence, will you? It's only polite. Now, what about Adan's business partner?"

A dozen sharp retorts caught in my throat, and I swallowed them down. I was too tired to argue. "Jameel Rich? What about him?"

"He may have known about that safe, and the combination."

"I don't think so," I said dully.

"Why not?" She sat back against the diner's sky-blue booth. "If Adan was keeping work-related documents in that safe, he may well have kept information about the safe in his office. In case of emergency, someone from the office might need to retrieve it."

"I suppose it's possible," I said. "And Jameel *was* at the house when Charlie had his fall."

"What was he doing there?"

"Shelley—that's the butler—said he'd come to see Adalina. She works at Rover."

"I'm well aware."

I smothered another yawn. "Sorry. I'm not thinking clearly. Their mother was there too—Gina."

"In other words, any one of them could have robbed the safe and pushed Charlie."

"If Adan didn't change the safe combo after the divorce..." I frowned. Ary had implied he and Gina had lived in that house together. But if they had, why hadn't she gotten the house in the divorce? It wasn't required, but it seemed sort of traditional. Though they'd divorced later in life. The courts wouldn't have been worried about providing Ary and Adalina a stable home life. Still, it was interesting.

Mrs. Malone tapped a crooked finger on the table. "You need to find out."

"What do you know about my mother and Adan Levann?"

"What does it matter? That was all over long ago."

My hand spasmed on the table. "What does it matter? My brother's not..."

"Not what?" Her eyes widened innocently.

The waitress slid our plates in front of us. The scent of cheese and beans made my nose twitch. "Can I get you anything else?" she asked.

"No, thank you," Mrs. Malone said to her, and the waitress left. Mrs. Malone met my gaze. "Now, what about Charlie?"

"He's struggling to figure out what went on between Adan and our mother too. I mean, we know what went on, obviously. Just not why."

"What did Adan have to say?"

"I don't know."

Her brows shot skyward. "You didn't ask?"

I pretended to study my coffee. "I guess I didn't want to know," I admitted. And why *had* asking Mrs. Malone seemed easier than asking my brother?

"And yet you're asking me about it. Your father loved Charlie, raised him, taught him to be a good man. He was Charlie's father in every way that counted."

"Did my father know the truth about Charlie?" I asked quietly.

She sighed. "I have no idea. I honestly knew nothing about any of this until you and Charlie told me. And if I may give you some advice..."

I sank against the blue seat. She was going to give it to me whether I wanted it or not.

"This issue of your brother's parentage is only as big as you make it," she concluded.

Heat flushed through me. "Of course I'm not going to make a big deal about it," I said. "Charlie's still my brother." Mrs. Malone turned her glass on the table and didn't respond.

My anger deepened to shame. Because a small part of me had feared something had changed between Charlie and me, that we were no longer the Sommerland kids. Charlie had a new family, another brother and sister and father, and I was outside.

I'd made Charlie's revelation about me, about my relationships, about who I was. And that was crummy. Charlie would always be my brother. But I'd been afraid I wouldn't always be his sister.

Had Charlie sensed it? He was surprisingly sensitive, so... He probably had. I hung my head and groaned.

She patted my hand. "You'll fix this. Now... let's talk about our suspects."

Chapter Twenty-Five

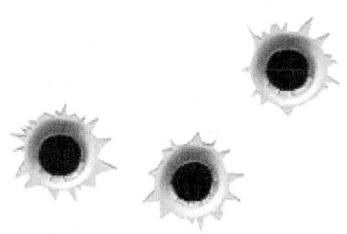

Mrs. Malone and I reviewed the suspects and agreed further investigation was needed. Investigation by me. Her little gray cells needed more data, and I was the one to provide it.

We finished our lunches, and I returned to my apartment. Curled on the bed, Fredo and Sammie ignored me. I sat at the card table in my kitchen/dining area/workspace and called Charlie. Phil answered my brother's cell phone.

"Hey, Alice."

"Hey." I glanced at the boxing dummy. "How is he?"

"Sleeping. I figured I should let him, but I guess you want to know what's been going on?"

"Yeah."

"Charlie wants to go to the holiday parade in Hot Springs tomorrow."

"Isn't going to happen."

Phil cleared his throat. "Also, a doctor was here earlier. He said Charlie was doing well."

"That's good. Thanks."

"Yeah, well, I owe him."

"You owe Fitch?"

"Charlie. Someone sent flowers."

I grimaced. I should have thought of sending flowers. "Who?"

"It's a weird name. Adalina?"

I bit back a curse. Then the whole family knew exactly where Charlie was. Not that it would have been a leap to figure out. And since one of them was probably a killer, I was glad Phil was there.

"How long are you going to be there?" I asked.

"Until someone relieves me."

"Okay. I'll be there in a few hours."

We rang off. I grabbed my bag, got in my Jeep, and headed toward Hot Springs. I didn't bother calling the mansion to warn them I was coming. There was a chance no one would be home. But if someone was, a surprise interrogation might get me more honest reactions.

There was also a good chance that the reaction would be to toss me out on my rear. But Adalina *had* sent those flowers. Stopping by with news about my brother's recovery wasn't so off the wall.

I didn't spot any Rovers as I drove through Hot Springs. After seeing so many of them, their absence seemed a little weird. I decided I was making something out of nothing and shrugged it off.

I pulled up to the mansion's iron gates. Three news vans were parked along the road. Reporters hustled to my window as I leaned out and pressed the intercom.

The gates swung open before I could speak. Ignoring the shouted questions, I drove through, my tires crunching on the gravel. I glanced in the rearview mirror. No reporters tried to slip through the closing gates after me.

Shelley greeted me at the door. "Mrs. Levann is here," he said before I could speak. "She is unaware of your arrival. I felt it would be prudent to allow you inside rather than subject you to the reporters."

I forced a smile. In other words, they didn't trust me to keep my mouth shut. Or was Shelley really trying to do me a solid?

"How is Mr. Sommerland?" he asked.

"Recovering. But the timing of his fall is suspect. Charlie had just discovered someone had emptied the floor safe in Mr. Levann's study." I stepped into the foyer. Its curving staircases seemed menacing now, arms reaching out to crush me.

Shelley blinked and drew backward. "Safe?"

"Did you know about it?"

"I assure you, I did not." He closed the arched front door.

"It's hidden under a rug." Which a good housekeeper would have moved at some point to clean. Shelley wasn't the housekeeper, but he did manage the cleaning crews.

"That would explain why Mr. Levann was adamant about being in the study when housekeeping was there," he said. "I was only aware of the safe in the master bedroom closet."

"Everyone's aware of it now," I grumbled. "You said Gina was here last night for a council of war—to speak to Adalina and Ary when Charlie fell?"

The butler nodded.

"But Adalina was in the drawing room with Jameel," I said. "Where were Gina and Ary?"

"I'm afraid I don't know. As I said, I was in the kitchen, cleaning up."

"Who's here now?"

"Aside from Mrs. Levann? Mr. Levann is in his studio, I believe."

"I'll see him there."

Shelley didn't try to stop me or to announce me, as a good fake butler should. I strode down the carpeted hallway. A burning desire to punch someone built inside me. Since that's a good way to break a hand and get arrested, I tabled that impulse.

The door to Ary's studio stood open. The scent of fresh paint wafted from the room and stung my eyes. I knocked on the door frame.

Ary didn't turn from his seat before the easel. "I told you, no more." He faced the floor-to-ceiling windows looking out over the rear lawn. He wore his artist's uniform of black clothes/white smock.

"It's me."

He swiveled on the wooden stool and scowled. "Can't you see I'm working?" He motioned toward his canvas.

I walked deeper into the room and glanced at the clash of colors. The painting was a crude version of American primitive. But its colors were glaring, garish. "Interesting," I said. "What are you trying to do here?"

His frown deepened. "I'm ironically deconstructing Americana."

These days I wished the world had a bit less irony and more beauty. "Modern art is the means by which we terrorize ourselves," I quoted.

He gave me a startled look. "That quote's not quite right, but close enough. You know Tracy Emin?"

"One of my clients was a collector."

"Who—?" He shook his head. "Never mind."

"What appeals to you about this style?" *Make nice. Gain rapport. Don't bite his head off.*

"The need to tear down the old to make way for the new. That's what appeals."

My heart heavied. It was stupid to get upset about the state of the art world. I had bigger things on my plate. But why were so many people hell bent on destroying what was old and beautiful? "Why not just make something new and lovely?"

"Art isn't supposed to be lovely." He sneered. "Its goal is to create an emotional reaction in the viewer."

In this at least, Ary had succeeded. "Charlie's doing well."

"Oh." He lowered his paintbrush to his side. "Good to hear."

"Where were you when he fell?"

"Here." He motioned with the brush around the studio, finished canvases stacked against its walls.

I glanced at the wall of windows. "It was a little dark at the time for painting, wasn't it?" The lighting wasn't great now either, clouds blocking the sun.

"It's a good place to think. It's private."

"You were alone?"

"No," he said. "I was talking to my mother."

"So, not so private after all." I hesitated. "It must have been tough, growing up in this house." Actually, I couldn't imagine anything easier than being waited on hand and foot. But everything's relative, and we all have our childhood wounds.

"Yes," he said eagerly. "It was. You have no idea."

"Especially after the divorce?"

He laughed harshly. "They divorced three years ago. We weren't children."

"Is that why Adan kept the house?"

His mouth twisted. "No. He kept it because my mother violated the terms of the pre-nup. With his business partner."

I sucked in a breath, my head jerking backward. Gina and Jameel had had an affair?

Arystarch laughed at my reaction. "You're wondering how Jameel and Adan kept working together? Easy. Adan cared more about his precious company than he did about our family. He needed Jameel. He didn't need our mother."

I couldn't imagine Adan would have kept working with Jameel unless his marriage had been long done. But I didn't know Adan. Maybe he was that obsessed with Rover. Gina and Jameel were still single, so their affair hadn't gone much farther. Or was it still quietly going on?

"Before Charlie had his fall," I said, "he discovered Adan's safe was cleaned out."

He turned back to his painting. "That's happened already, remember? Poor Holli and her jewelry," he said without much sympathy. He dotted the canvas with orange.

"Adan's other safe, in his study."

"He had another safe?" Adan reached for a knife and smeared more orange on the canvas. "I had no idea. Where was it?"

"In the floor beneath a throw rug."

"He never liked us playing in there."

"You're not at all curious about what was taken?"

"Of course I am," he said. "But you said it was cleaned out before Charlie got there. I'm assuming you can't fulfill my curiosity. Unless you were the one who emptied it?" He swiveled on his wooden stool to face me.

"No," I said dryly. "It's an honest to goodness mystery. But it might have something to do with the new will."

He sucked in a loud breath. "What new will?"

"His lawyer had drawn one up including Charlie. All Adan had to do was sign it, but it seems he never returned the signed will to his lawyer."

"And so your brother's out of luck." He pulled a face. "What a shame."

Charlie wasn't out of luck if Mrs. Malone was right about Nevada law. The lawyer had drawn up a new will at Adan's request. That went to intent. "I really don't think Charlie cares about the money."

"He'd be a fool not to."

"A fool not to what?" Gina asked from behind me.

Chapter Twenty-Six

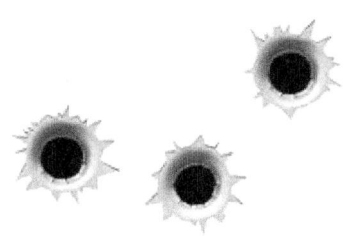

"How's your brother?" Gina asked, surprising me. I hadn't thought she'd cared.

Like her son at the easel, she wore black—a tasteful silk pantsuit with low heels. Her equally tasteful gold earrings glimmered faintly against her platinum blond hair.

"He's fine. And well protected," I added for good measure.

The older woman strolled into the studio, her charm bracelet tinkling. "I'm glad to hear it."

I didn't quite believe that, but I thanked her anyway. "I'm glad too."

Ary angled his head and scratched his cheek with the end of the brush. "Alice wants to know where we were when Charlie had his dramatic fall. Of course, I told her I was with you, here."

I studied him. His expression was even, but it had sounded like a warning. To keep his alibi?

"I see," she said. "You've graduated from bodyguard to detective."

"Not quite." No offense to detectives, but it didn't sound like much of a promotion.

"That friend of Charlie's is really a private detective," she said, and I started. "She and that detective have been using Charlie to snoop around this house."

How had she found out about Fitch? "And what was Jameel doing here last night?" I asked.

Her mouth twisted. "Trying to save his precious business, no doubt."

The venom in her voice was impossible to miss. I'd been speculating about Adan's ability to work with Jameel after the betrayal. But how must Gina have felt? She'd lost her marriage over another man. And then that man had remained partnered with her ex-husband and left her on the proverbial side of the road. Jameel had betrayed her as well as Adan.

"What was the working relationship like between Adan and Jameel?" I asked.

"I wouldn't know," she said coldly. "And I think you should leave."

"I'm looking for Adalina," I said.

"She's at Rover," Arystarch said. "I'll call her if you like." Before I could respond, he pulled a phone from his pocket and pressed it to his ear. "Addy? Yes... No... Alice wants to interrogate you about your and Jameel's whereabouts last night. Yes... I'll tell her." He set his phone on a nearby table. "She'll see you at Rover."

"Thanks," I said uncertainly.

"I can't speak for Jameel though." He arched a brow. "I presume you intend to quiz him as well?"

"If I can."

Ary turned back toward his painting. "Tell your brother to be more careful."

Unspeaking, Gina followed me to the front door. She watched my Jeep glide down the gloomy drive, the light from the foyer lengthening her crooked shadow across the stone steps.

The Rover at the company gate trotted beside my car until I parked. It sat and waited while I exited the Jeep, then walked beside me into the building. I pretended not to be unnerved by the escort.

A receptionist printed out a lanyard badge and waited while I hung it around my neck. She escorted me to Adalina's office and closed the door behind me.

Adalina's corner office was on the top floor too. Her view wasn't as spectacular as Jameel's. The windows aimed toward low, barren hills to the east instead of at the Sierras. The office was a mess of cheerful clutter, tables strewn with metal parts I couldn't identify.

"How's Charlie?" In a black cashmere sweatsuit, Adalina sat on a wooden stool beside one of the tables. Her goggles magnified her eyes, which bulged, insect-like.

"Bummed he's going to miss the holiday parade tomorrow."

She laughed. "Hot Springs puts on quite a show."

"Thanks for the flowers."

She shrugged. "Least I could do. Your brother's..." She shook her head. "I thought he was just another grifter, but he's the real deal. I'm sorry I didn't see it sooner."

"Yeah, he is." I removed what looked like the back half of a Rover from the stool opposite and sat. "Even though he didn't know your father well, he's upset about his death."

"I get that. Charlie never had a chance, did he?"

I stiffened. "He's done okay."

"I meant with my father, not..." She shook her head.

My face heated. My old defensiveness had returned, in spite of my determination not to let it. "No, I'm sorry. It's been harder for Charlie than it has been for me."

"But it's been hard for you too." Adalina pulled off the goggles. "I get it. Your brother's now a half-brother. Worse, you can't ask your parents about it, because they're gone."

It had been a near perfect echo of my own thoughts, and I wanted to hug her. I wanted to trust Adalina's sympathy. I wanted Charlie's new family to be good. But I couldn't quite bring myself to do any of it. "The important thing is Charlie's my brother. I want him to be happy. And to stay alive."

"Which is why you didn't just come here to give me news about his recovery. Ary said you wanted to know where Jameel and I were when he fell down the stairs." She massaged the reddened goggle rings around her eyes. They didn't look funny on Adalina. They made her look vulnerable, endearing—green hair and all.

"If you don't mind," I said.

"I was in the drawing room. Jameel had left to use the bathroom."

"How long was he gone before you heard Charlie fall?" I asked.

"About five minutes, I think. Though honesty, I wasn't paying that much attention." She pulled a metal gadget from her loose pocket. "I was playing with this."

I leaned forward and squinted at the object. It looked like a tiny metal cat. "What is it?"

"A miniature robot. Some people get on their phones when they're bored. I tinker with these." She dropped it in her pocket.

"I've been trying to figure out who would have the tech skills to hack the Rovers *and* keep the company's tech team from figuring it out." I folded my arms. "I only came up with one name."

She tilted her head and didn't respond. But what hung in that silence didn't feel like tension. It felt a little like hope.

"Yours," I finished.

She glanced at the closed door behind me.

"You're trying to scuttle the military contract," I said. "Aren't you?"

She stared at me, and I stared back, but there was no hostility in her gaze. Warm air from the office's nearby heat vent tossed strands of her green hair.

Her shoulders slumped. "Adan didn't want the Rovers to be used against people. I don't either."

"And you can't stop it."

"The Rovers were supposed to be fun. The police Rovers... We were both hesitant about that. But Jameel argued that it would be good for the community, a positive gesture. It would help people get used to seeing them around town. And they were only there to record events. But of course, none of that was true," she added bitterly.

"They were there to give the military an inkling of how they could be used," I said.

Adalina nodded. "The Rovers never would have hurt you," she said quickly.

"One nearly took my foot off." I should have been angry, but I just felt exasperated. I was starting to see the resemblance between Adalina and my brother. Both acted without thinking. Maybe nature over nurture really was a thing.

"But it only got your shoe," she said. "That's how precise they are."

"That was *all* it was meant to do?"

"I thought..." She bit her bottom lip. "I thought if they went haywire, if they seemed dangerous, people would wake up. And I thought you could take care of yourself."

"The attack on Santa's Village was, in a certain light, mildly hilarious," I admitted.

A smile flashed across her rounded face. "Thanks. Your brother actually gave me the idea." She returned the tiny robot cat to the pocket of her sweatpants.

"To attack Santa's Village?" I hooked my feet in the stool.

"No, to do *something*. To take action, even if it was over the top. In fact, the more over the top the better. Charlie's so... He just seems to believe everything will work out if you *do* something. He doesn't worry about the bad things that might happen. He just goes for it."

Which was how he'd wound up at the bottom of her stairs with a concussion. I forced a laugh. "Yeah, that's how he broke his arm when we were kids. He went for it and jumped off our parents' roof."

One corner of her mouth lifted in a smile. "Maybe I shouldn't have leaped before I looked either. But I had to go big. The board isn't interested in my professional opinion."

"Even now that you're a part-owner in the company?"

"Especially now."

"I need to see the video from Adan's Rover."

"I'd like to see it too. But I wasn't controlling Adan's Rover."

"Come on," I scoffed.

"I mean it. I wasn't." The soft sigh of the heater faded, and Adalina's blowing hair stilled.

"Then who was?" I pulled my ankles free of the stool and rested my shoes on its wooden crossbar.

"I don't know who was controlling it, but someone hacked it."

"So you're telling me that two genius hackers got the same idea at the same time, and there's no connection..." I trailed off. *Two tech geniuses...*

"That's exactly what I'm saying. What's wrong?"

The half-formed thought evaporated, like half-formed thoughts do. I'd caught onto something, figured it out, but couldn't figure out *what*. "Nothing."

"Even if I could figure out the hack under normal conditions," she said, "the sulfur spring destroyed that Rover. There's no way I'll be able to figure out what was done to it. And believe me, I've tried."

"What about the cloud?" I asked. "You said something might be there."

"The last video was dated the day before Adan died. I'll send it to you if you like, but I didn't see anything suspicious."

"You know Jameel hired me to try and figure out who the hacker is?"

She drew a quick breath. "No, I didn't know that." Her gaze flit about the office. "You're not going to tell him about me, are you?"

I wasn't sure what I was going to do. Adalina could be lying about everything. And Fitch had signed a contract. It was Fitch I reported to though, not Jameel. And now Adalina was family. Screwed up family. Possibly murderous family. But family.

She leaned forward, her torso pressing into the table. "You've seen what the Rovers can do. You know this is a very bad idea."

Someone once told me the definition of tragedy is when you're left with no good choices. This seemed a lot like that. "If you don't sell to the military, some other robotics maker will."

"I know," she said, "but why does it have to be us? Why do we have to be a part of it?" She drew her hand through her green hair, and it stuck up in tufts. "This wasn't what Adan wanted. It's not right."

The door opened behind me. Jameel strode into the office studying his phone. "The mayor isn't letting up. He—" He looked up and caught sight of me. "What are you doing here?" Jameel straightened his blue tie. He was out of his usual suit jacket, his white sleeves rolled nearly to his elbows.

"I'm investigating," I said. *So there.*

"Jameel, did you see anything when Charlie, er, fell?" Adalina asked.

His jaw set. "That's what you're investigating?"

"Before Charlie fell," I said, "he discovered an empty floor safe in Adan's study. Do you have any idea what sort of paperwork he would have kept there?"

"Business documents would be my guess," Jameel said.

"Why keep them at home?" I asked.

"To review there. Both of us took work home. You did say the safe was in his study. What does this have to do with the Rover hack?"

"I don't know yet," I said. "Adalina, you didn't empty that safe by any chance, did you? Take the documents away to review them for the estate?"

"I didn't even know there was a safe in his study," she said, eyes wide.

"Ms. Sommerland, may we have a word?" Jameel held the door open for me. Adalina's face creased. I nodded to her and followed Jameel into the hall. After the casual chaos of Adalina's office, it seemed stark.

He closed the door. "What are you really doing here?"

My neck stiffened. "I'm really investigating."

"Are you investigating your brother's fall? Or the Rover hack?"

"They may well be connected," I said. "Did you see anything or anyone unusual in that house before Charlie fell?" A Rover rounded a corner. It trotted past, its metallic paws clicking on the floor tiles.

"No."

"Because someone pushed Charlie down those stairs." The thought of it returned angry heat to my face.

He folded his arms. "I didn't see the fall, and this isn't what I'm paying you for."

"If these incidents are connected—"

"They're not. And it's clear you're not working for me. You're working in your own interests."

My stomach hardened. "That's not—"

"It doesn't matter. I'm going to have to let you go."

"You what?" I stared, the breath catching in my throat.

"You're fired."

Chapter Twenty-Seven

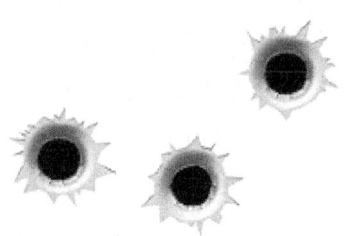

Being fired, even when you didn't trust your client or really want the job, is an ego blow. The only bright spot was I was the only one who'd gotten the chop. Jameel told me he'd call Fitch and let him know why.

Getting ratted out by Jameel didn't bother me much. But it did make me curious. If he wanted me out because I was getting too close, why keep Fitch in?

Life was so much easier in executive protection. You watched. You defended. Simple. Clear.

I drove to the hospital and took the elevator to Charlie's room. The sounds of masculine voices and laughter flowed through the open door. I pushed aside the curtain guarding it and walked inside the blue-gray room.

Charlie was sitting up in bed. A half-eaten tray of hospital food rested on the arm-table beside him. Phil lounged in the nearby leather chair.

I smiled. "You're looking better."

"Thanks," Phil said.

"Ha, ha." I frowned. He grinned, unrepentant.

"I feel better," Charlie said. "What'd you find out about who pushed me?"

"Everyone has an alibi except Jameel and Adalina."

Charlie's brow furrowed. "One of them pushed me?"

"Maybe," I said.

"*Someone* pushed me," he said stubbornly.

"You remember what happened now?" I moved toward the window. Charlie's collection from well-wishers had grown. The sill was lined with flowers.

"Sort of," he said. "I remember sensing someone behind me, and then... Things get confused."

Phil grunted. "That happens a lot around here."

"Tell me about it." Charlie rolled his eyes. "Hey, the doc's going to release me tomorrow."

"That's awesome." It was one more day I could guarantee my brother's safety. I glanced at the card on a modest bouquet of mixed flowers. It was from Adan's lawyer.

"I might be able to make the Hot Springs holiday parade after all," my brother said.

Not if I had anything to do with it. My phone rang and I checked the number. *Fitch.* "Sorry. I should probably take this." I edged into the hallway and answered. "I take it you heard from Jameel." I strode to the waiting area.

"You're just making friends and influencing people everywhere."

"It's a talent honed by years of experience."

"You got fired from the job on purpose?"

"Of course not, but Charlie's my first priority." I dropped into a blue leather chair and felt my muscles unwind. Even the waiting room chairs were top of the line.

"He's mine too," he said mildly. "Where are you?"

"The hospital."

"Is Phil still there?" Fitch asked. A nurse walked past pushing a cart filled with trays of food.

"Yeah. I'm here to relieve him."

"Good, he can use a break, and you can do what you're best at. What did you do to set Jameel off?"

I lowered my head, my chest tightening. "He didn't tell you?"

"He said you weren't attending to the job he'd assigned."

Alright. That was fair. "I asked where he was when Charlie had his fall. He wasn't with Adalina. He'd left to use the bathroom."

"So Adalina was on her own as well."

I crossed my legs in the chair. "I hadn't missed that point. Charlie was unconscious after the fall. She could have run past him to the drawing room then emerged with the others. He wouldn't have noticed."

"Does he remember anything?"

"He remembers someone behind him before he fell, but that's it."

"You focus on your brother. I'll keep poking the bear." The PI hung up.

He hadn't given me a chance to tell him about Adalina's confession. And, okay, I hadn't exactly been eager to tell Fitch about it. I stared at the floor. I'd have to tell him eventually—fair was fair. But... not today.

I returned to Charlie's room. Phil left mumbling about food, and I snagged his chair.

"You don't have to keep watch over me," Charlie said.

"Someone tried to take out my little brother. I'm not leaving you alone."

"I'm safe in the hospital."

"I'm still a protection specialist." I reached for the windowsill and fingered the petals of an orchid. *Classy.*

"I thought you were executive protection specializing in surveillance."

"I'm a lot of things."

"I'm just glad you're my sister."

Sister. Not his half-sister. His sister. "Yeah," I said. "Me too."

The hospital released Charlie the next day. I'll never understand why releasing someone from a hospital takes so long. It wasn't like his departure was a surprise, and the forms were all standard. But we didn't escape until late afternoon, when the sun was dimming on the horizon.

I brought Charlie to my apartment to recover. Returning to the mansion was out of the question. Fredo yapped excitedly and Sammie twined around my brother's ankles. Ignoring the chaos, I filled the table and windowsills with Charlie's flowers. He'd gotten a simple bouquet from Lilyanna, and I smiled.

I settled him on my bed, then opened my laptop on the table. The cat and dog snuggled against my brother.

"What are you going to do?" Charlie asked.

I booted up the computer. "Just some research on the Levann family." I'd spent last night going over the video Adalina had sent from Adan's Rover. I hadn't seen anything suspicious in it either, but I'd sent it to Fitch, just in case.

"Don't forget Jameel," Charlie said.

"Trust me, I haven't." I opened a popular career website and typed in a name.

"So... What do you think of Ary and Adalina?"

I thought they were pains in my butt. "I think they're dealing with a lot and not at their personal best," I said, typing.

"Yeah," he said. "Yeah. I think so too."

I pressed the ENTER key. The website considered my request. An online resumé appeared on the screen.

"Do you think...?" He trailed off.

I sighed and turned to face him. "Think what?"

"Do you think they'll want to spend Christmas with us?" He shifted his weight. "I mean, not all day," he said quickly. "Just maybe dinner. Or lunch."

An ache swelled in my chest. How did he do it? How did my brother stand the disappointment he constantly set himself up for? "I don't think they're there yet."

He deflated. "Oh. Remember Mom's Christmas breakfast?"

Boy, did I. I looked around the cramped room. There was no way I could pull off that sort of feast here. Not with my toaster and wonky hotplate. Suddenly my life seemed pathetic.

"I'm thinking of renting a vacation house for Christmas," I said, surprising myself. "Then we could do some real baking, have a good holiday dinner."

"That'd be cool. What are you thinking? Somewhere in Hot Springs?"

Any other time, that would be the logical choice. But I didn't want him anywhere near that town. "I'll check some websites, see what I can turn up," I hedged. "Maybe Doyle, in California."

"I don't think Lilyanna would feel comfortable in Doyle."

I arched a brow. "Are you two a thing now?"

He blushed. "We're, you know, taking it slow."

"Gotcha." I turned to the computer and grinned.

Jameel's page was impressive, with professional blog posts about the tech industry. I guessed someone else had written them. I couldn't imagine someone in Jameel's position having the time. Jameel had—

Phil knocked on my open door. I'd left it open because my apartment was too small for two people. The open door gave the illusion of having more space. At least, that's what I told myself.

"Hey." Phil pulled the other dining chair away from the card table. Making himself at home, he put it near the bed and sat. "I heard they cut you loose."

"I'm a free man, man." Charlie laced his hands behind his head.

I shut the laptop. "They told him to take it easy," I said sharply.

"So no ax throwing," Phil said.

"Why not?" Charlie leapt from the bed. "It's Tuesday. We can throw for free today."

I didn't bother arguing. How much trouble could they get into throwing axes?

Don't answer that.

They departed, leaving me with Fredo and Sammie. The black cat sneezed and strolled through the open door.

"It's just you and me now," I told the dog. He sniffed, hopped onto the bed, and turned three times. The gray dog tucked into a sleeping position, his back to me. "Fine then. I can finally get some work done."

I typed another name into the professional website's search engine. With the exception of Arystarch, my suspects all had accounts. And their pages told me what I'd expected.

I sat back in my chair and frowned. It was interesting background, suggestive even, but it wasn't proof.

I rose and punched the boxing dummy half-heartedly. *Proof... How to get proof...*

Charlie's appearance in Adan's life had set a lot of things in motion. Adalina hacking the Rovers. The change to Adan's will. The change to his family structure. And now the change to Rover, Inc. I wondered, murder-wise, which was more important in the scheme of things.

I stopped in front of the mirror behind the door. And I realized, with dawning horror, that the killer didn't need to get rid of Charlie to get what they wanted. There was someone else, someone closer.

In the mirror, my face turned ashen.

Someone unprotected.

Chapter Twenty-Eight

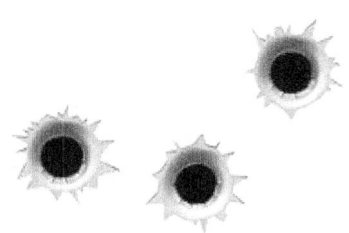

I CALLED, FINGERS DRUMMING on the small table, but there was no answer. Grabbing my jacket off my bed, I hurried from the theater. The sun was lost in clouds, and a gloomy twilight had settled on the town. Twinkle lights had come on in the stand of barren aspens nearby.

"Alice!" Mrs. Malone waved her cane in greeting. She strode across the parking lot in a lurid pink workout jacket and thick hiking leggings. "Good job on the museum investigation. We can work with that. What data do you have for me on the murders?"

Museum investigation? I shook my head. *Whatever.* "Can't talk. If someone was trying to kill Charlie so he wouldn't inherit, they may go after Adan's lawyer." Now that Holli was dead, the lawyer was the only proof left Adan had intended to include Charlie in the will. "I've got to go."

"Go where?"

"To warn the lawyer, Mr. O'Reilly." I said, walking backwards towards my Jeep.

"But where?"

"His office. It's Tuesday afternoon. If he's not in, his receptionist should know where he is." And I was a little worried that the receptionist hadn't answered the phone. But maybe he didn't have a receptionist.

"Wouldn't it be simpler to call?"

Roughly, I yanked open the door to my Jeep. "I've tried that. No one's answering."

"I'll call the Hot Springs police."

I climbed inside. "Good luck with that," I said sincerely. I really hoped she did have luck, because I knew they wouldn't listen to me. Not with anything so nebulous.

Forcing myself to keep to the speed limit, I pulled from the lot and drove down Main Street. A group of tourists in Santa hats spilled from the speakeasy.

I'm not sure what it says about me that I hadn't considered calling the police. But right now, all I had was a bad feeling and circumstantial evidence. I didn't think it would motivate them to act. Maybe Mrs. Malone would have better luck.

I cruised past the park. Giant plastic candy canes glowed beneath its oversized mushrooms. There was someone else who might be able to help. I called Fitch.

"What have you got?" he asked.

"Now that Charlie's protected, I think the killer may go after Adan's estate attorney, John O'Reilly. Can you track down his office address for me?"

"Has something happened?" he asked sharply.

"Yeah, my brain finally kicked into gear. Here's what I think." I explained my theory. The timing fit, and the personalities fit. The murders, the theft of the jewelry, Adan's Rover... It all pointed to one person.

"It makes sense," he finally said. "But we've got no proof."

"I know. But if I'm right, O'Reilly may be in danger. He can show intent to include Charlie in the estate. I'm headed to Hot Springs now."

"Where are you?"

I turned south onto the highway. "On the road, about twenty minutes from Hot Springs."

"Here's O'Reilly's office." He rattled off an address. "I'll find his home address and number and see if I can catch him there."

My muscles unknotted. I wasn't in this on my own. I wasn't sure why I'd been denying that for so long. Fitch wasn't just my occasional employer. He had my back. Though he was also getting paid by my brother, so... there was that.

"And we'll talk about your reports—and lack thereof—later," he said.

I winced. "I've been filling them out," I said.

"Then you need to *send* them to me. Let me know what you find at the office." He hung up.

I programmed the address into my phone. Speeding down the highway, I turned up the winding road toward Hot Springs. My hands squeezed the wheel.

The sun flashed, a thin line of gold above the Sierras, and vanished behind the mountains. The clouds shimmered briefly like a storm-tossed lake then darkened to molten lead.

I passed the *Welcome to The Town of Hot Springs* sign. No Rover greeted me. I'd half wished one would, even one of the police Rovers. "There's never a cop around when you need one," I grumbled.

"Obstruction reported ahead," my phone chirped.

Drums and horns sounded. A police car sat parked across the road beside two barriers. A uniformed policewoman motioned me onto another street.

I craned my neck. A Christmas float strung with lights lumbered behind the police barricade. Snowmen waved from its deck.

"Re-routing," my phone said.

"Well come on and re-route," I snarled, gliding along the detour route. The screen remained blank.

Hot Springs had good cell service—for the mountains. But it was still the mountains, and slow by comparison to big city streets. Finally, my phone figured out where I was and how to get me to the lawyer's office.

Shifting in my seat, I turned down a residential street of Greek-revival houses set well back on their lawns. After half a dozen twists and turns, I found myself back in the commercial section of town.

A few flecks of white dotted my windshield. The wipers automatically turned on and screeched across the near-dry glass.

By some miracle, I found a parking spot on the street. Not bothering with the meter, I ran to the door of the lawyer's low, brick office building. It was locked.

I cursed. It wasn't five yet. Where was O'Reilly? I called Fitch again.

"I'm on my way to his house," he said before I could speak.

"I'm at the office. The front's locked up. I'm going around to the back."

"Keep me posted." He hung up.

I rounded a box hedge and strode into a parking lot ringed by low pines. A figure beside a silver Jaguar was struggling to put a box inside the trunk.

"Mr. O'Reilly?" I trotted forward, relief flooding my system. I wasn't too late. Though it was still quite possible I was wrong and about to make a fool out of myself. But I was sort of used to that.

He slammed shut the trunk and turned. "Ms. Sommerland. What a surprise. I'm afraid I'm rather in a hurry."

"Someone tried to kill Charlie."

His eyes widened behind their glasses. "What? I knew he was in the hospital—I sent flowers. But I thought it was some sort of accident. How is he?"

"He's in Nowhere and being protected. I tried calling you this afternoon, but—"

"I've been ignoring calls, I'm afraid. I promised my wife I'd meet her at the holiday parade, and I had to get some work done... What happened?"

"My brother was at Adan's house," I said, impatient. "Someone shoved him down the stairs. He doesn't know who."

"Have you told the police?"

"Yes. But like I said, he didn't see who did it and doesn't remember much. I'm afraid he didn't make the most convincing witness."

He straightened. "I'll talk with the police. After two murders in that household, they damn well should take this seriously. Charlie's an heir. There's motive."

The tension in my neck and shoulders released. He believed me. I got why the family wanted to deny the truth—the truth hurt. But it was nice to be taken seriously. "Is it true that if Adan had demonstrable intent to include Charlie, that would be enough to include him in the estate?" A distant trumpet blatted.

"Yes," he said, "that's why I told Charlie he had a good case. I'd drawn up the amended will myself at Adan's request. If that doesn't demonstrate intent, nothing does."

"Even if the will is gone?"

"I've got a copy in my office. But even if I didn't, my testimony would be enough."

"Mr. O'Reilly, I think it's possible you may be a target."

He blinked. "Excuse me?"

"Gina can't get to Charlie now. But she can get to you." I pulled my cell phone from the rear pocket of my jeans. "If you don't mind, I'd like you to meet a private investigator I do some work for."

"I thought you were a bodyguard?"

"Executive protect—Never mind. I do surveillance work for this PI on occasion. It's only contract work. He's not my boss or—" And why was I babbling about that now?

He shook his head. "Wait," he said. "Gina?"

"I know it's hard to believe. But I think she's doing it for her kids."

"No." He pointed behind me. "I meant... *Gina.*"

I turned, and every muscle in my body tensed. Gina smiled at us in the darkening parking lot. She wore a mid-length mink coat and low-heeled shoes. They clashed with the Sig Sauer MCX she aimed at me, the folding brace tucked against her shoulder.

I looked down. A red dot wavered on my chest.

Chapter Twenty-Nine

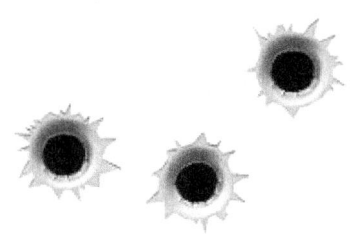

I'VE MANAGED GUN TAKEAWAYS. Mostly in a dojo, but on a few rare occasions in real life. Long guns like rifles and shotguns required a different technique than pistols. The gun Gina pointed was somewhere in between both, and my hands went clammy. I wasn't sure how to take away this gun.

The laser sight didn't make me happy either. The gun might be a nine millimeter, but the bullet would go right into my chest, where all sorts of important organs hung out. I was screwed.

The low trees blocked much of our view of the street. The odds of someone seeing us in the parking lot were low. I licked my lips. The twilight shadows had deepened. Everyone, including most of the police, was at the holiday parade. Despite the early hour, the streets were deserted.

Trumpets sounded—I guessed the Hot Springs High School band—and a cheer went up in the distance. I swallowed. If she pulled the trigger, would anyone even hear it?

"Mrs. Levann," the lawyer began. She swiveled the gun toward him. He gulped, his gaze lowering to the laser site on his chest. "How can we help you?"

I'll give the guy this, he was cool under pressure. No wonder Adan had hired him.

"You can't help her," I said, pulling her attention back toward me. "She's come too far. Haven't you, Gina?"

She shook her head. "You have no idea." Her eyes had the determined glitter of a person who'd gone over the edge. I'd seen it before. It never ended well.

"I know you killed your husband." I was pleasantly surprised to hear my voice was steady. "You found out—how *did* you find out he was changing the will? The Rover?"

She barked a laugh. "I've been controlling Adan's Rover for months. He had no idea. He met me the same way he met Holli—at work. I used to be a damn good engineer. I still am. Where do you think Adalina got the idea of hacking one?"

"She knew?" I asked.

"My daughter has no idea. But can you imagine how I felt? Adan should have told me. So typical. He thought it didn't affect me. In short, he didn't think at all."

"But it did affect you," I said.

A chill breeze ruffled her platinum-blond hair. "Of course it did. They're my children. They're Adan's children too, but he somehow thought they were all equal. He actually was going to push them aside for your brother."

The lawyer cleared his throat. "Not aside. They would have shared equally."

"I know that," she snapped. "It would have made their shares significantly smaller. They grew up with Adan and me. We *raised* Ary and Addy. To treat Charlie as an equal is a, a..."

"Insult?" My thumped in my ears. If I could get close enough, I could try for the gun. I'd no idea if I could succeed, but it would give O'Reilly time to run. She shifted her stance.

"So you snuck into the mansion crossing the property from the back," I said. "There are no security cameras there. You used his Rover to keep tabs on Adan, know where he was, what he was up to. While he was safely out of the way, you stole the will from his safe. Did you get the combo from the Rover's video too?"

"He hadn't changed that combination since we were married." Her crimson mouth twisted. "The combination was the date we adopted Ary and Addy."

"And then what?" I asked. "Hacked off after reading the new will, you tracked him down in Charlie's room and bashed him in the head?"

"That part was spontaneous," she said dryly. "Do you know that was one of the reasons he divorced me? He said I was too predictable."

"That and your relationship with his business partner," the lawyer muttered.

The murder may well have been spur-of-the-moment, but it didn't make much difference. She'd killed twice and was going for two more. "What was Adan doing in Charlie's room?" I asked, stalling.

"Leaving him a note," she said.

"You took it?" I scanned the parking lot without seeming to. The pine trees blocked the view of the street. What I did see was depressingly empty.

"I had to," she said. "I didn't know what it was. For all I knew, he could have been telling Charlie about the new will. So I grabbed it and left."

"Makes sense." I nodded and tried to slow my racing heart. "What was in the note?"

"It said he had a surprise for Charlie. Three guesses what it was."

The change in the will. "What I don't understand is why you came back to steal Holli's jewelry."

Her eyes bulged. "Because if I didn't, the little tramp would have sold it. That was *my* jewelry. She had no right to it."

So many reasons to kill. I imagined Gina cycling them through her mind, working her way up to the act. Maybe Adan's murder hadn't been so spontaneous after all. "Ary knew you took it," I said. "He was covering for you when he gave you your alibi that night."

"Ary always understood me. He's a good boy."

A shadow prowled at the edge of my vision, and hope jolted through my body. "But Holli wasn't as dumb as she acted," I said more loudly. "She was an ex-engineer too. She caught you sneaking out of Adalina's garage workshop, and you killed her."

The lawyer cleared his throat. "I suspect it was more than that," he said shakily. "While Adan was alive, he was paying you alimony. But with him dead, a share of his estate would go to Holli and the alimony would end."

"You'd be cut off," I finished. "But you sort of did that to yourself when you killed your ex."

Her lips whitened. "This was never about me. It was always about the children."

A Rover emerged from behind a silver Lexus, and my breath stopped in my chest. It didn't have a police jacket on. Was it one of Adalina's? If it was filming, we might have a chance.

CHAPTER TWENTY-NINE

"I assume you were in Adalina's workshop to check on the Rover we'd retrieved?" I asked.

"I had to make sure the sulfur spring had done its job," she said. "Fortunately, it had. Not even Adalina, for all her brilliance, could bring that dog back."

"Ary covered for you again when you shoved Charlie down the stairs," I said. "Did he know what you were planning?"

"Of course not. He's an artist. He doesn't concern himself with things like that."

"But he must suspect you're involved in the murders," I said.

"He doesn't know anything," she repeated. "Now. Get in the car." She motioned toward the Lexus.

The Rover was nowhere to be seen. But it was somewhere, and it had good ears. My leg muscles tightened.

"The car?" the lawyer repeated weakly. Even he must have known nothing good happens when you get in the car.

The Rover emerged from behind Gina. Head low, it crept toward her.

"What about Jameel?" I asked. I didn't think he was involved, but I'd been mistaken about people before.

"What about him?" Her forehead wrinkled. "He's irrelevant."

"I take it you're not seeing each other anymore," I said.

"Are you kidding? After he gave me up for his job? I wouldn't give him the time of day if I had three watches on and was standing under a clock."

"He gave you up?" I asked.

Her mouth twisted. "You don't think Adan would have allowed us to continue on if he could stop it, did you? My ex-husband was a vindictive narcissist. Never mind that he'd cheated on me with your mother. He didn't get caught, so it was all right for him. If I'd known when I divorced him…"

"Your indiscretion wouldn't have mattered," the lawyer finished for her. "He'd cheated first."

"But Charlie turned up," I said. "And you knew the truth too late."

"I lost *everything* in the divorce. What price did Adan pay? Nothing. He got his new son. Kept his big house." She clamped her mouth shut. "And you're stalling. Get in the car."

"I don't think you really want us to do that," I said.

"Why not?"

"First, because you left evidence at the crime scene. A single thread from your suit that night. It was navy, and I assumed it was from Charlie's jacket. But it was yours."

"And second?"

I pointed at the Rover behind her. "Because the dog's been recording everything."

One corner of her mouth tilted upward in a crooked smile. "Don't worry about that. Rovers, herd."

My stomach cratered. Two more Rovers emerged from behind cars. They prowled toward O'Reilly and me.

Chapter Thirty

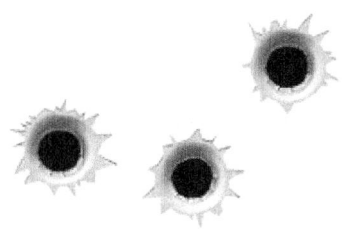

A PAINED SIGH ESCAPED my throat. She had *three* attack robot-dogs? Talk about bringing a cannon to a knife fight. Running was pointless. Unlike the dogs Adalina had been controlling, these three meant business. And I knew how fast they could run.

A fourth Rover emerged from behind a Tesla. My fists tightened. "Oh, come *on*."

"Get in the car." Gina angled her head toward the Lexus. "Rovers, herd." The Rovers encircled us, moving us toward the car.

Some say when you raise people's hopes then dash them, that's when people break. Finding out the Rovers were controlled my Gina had been a disappointment all right. But I wasn't broken. I was just mad.

"So what's the plan here, Gina?" My neck tightened.

"You're going to kill O'Reilly," she said, "and then kill yourself."

"No one's going to believe that," I said. A Rover snapped at me, and I hopped backward.

"Maybe not," she said, "but it doesn't matter. Whatever happens to me, no one will be able to prove Adan intended to include Charlie in his will. My children will get what they deserve."

"They'll know when they search my computer files." The lawyer backed toward the silver car.

"Files?" Gina cocked her head. More flakes of snow drifted downward and stuck in her pale-blond hair.

"You didn't think he'd make backups?" I asked, scornful.

"Good point," she said. "Rovers, heel." The dogs stopped.

She angled her head toward the low office building. "Rovers herd. Inside." She rattled off an address and office number. The metal dogs changed direction, pushing us toward the back door.

"What are you doing, Gina?" I asked, heart thumping. Keeping the gun trained on me, she backed toward the building.

"The building's locked," O'Reilly said.

"But you have a key," she said.

Indoors might work. She'd be closer to me as we passed through the door, and I might have a chance to take that gun from her. Assuming a shotgun takeaway would work on a weapon this short. And that was a big assumption.

But Gina edged sideways, and the dogs surrounded us. They forced the lawyer and me past her, out of reach. The opportunity evaporated.

I hated this technology. And I *really* hated the fact that the dogs understood her commands so well. Gina stood well back as the lawyer fumbled for his keys.

"Do you have any ideas?" he asked me in a low voice, his head bent.

"Yes," I lied without moving my lips.

"There are cameras in the building," he murmured. "Help will come."

It might if anyone was actually watching the cameras in real time. Hope raised its head and fluttered in my chest.

"Hurry up," Gina said.

O'Reilly unlocked and opened the door to a long hallway lined with closed doors.

"The downstairs offices are all locked," he said quietly.

So no escape through doors number one, two, or three. I'd have to make my move soon though. The deserted office was an ideal place for murder. Nice, thick walls to muffle the shots, and no witnesses... Aside from the cameras, which apparently Gina didn't know about.

Cold washed across my skin. If we could survive, there'd be evidence. If we didn't survive, there'd still be evidence, but I wouldn't be able to gloat about it. And right now, gloating about it was what I lived for.

"Inside." Gina closed the distance between us, and my heart sank. Two snapping dogs stood between me and Gina. We were closer, but not close enough.

The dogs were depressingly nimble on the wide stairs to the lawyer's second-floor office. O'Reilly let us inside his office with a key. His reception area was sleek and modern. With the three of us plus four Rovers, it was also cramped.

"Where's your computer?" Gina asked.

"In my office." He motioned down a beige hallway. "But stealing it won't be enough. We have cloud backups."

She smiled. "That won't be a problem."

I turned to her. Two Rovers stood side-by-side between us. "I'm surprised you didn't hack into his computer and delete the file remotely," I said.

She tossed her head. "This takes less time. Move."

The lawyer started down the hall.

"O'Reilly," I said, unmoving.

"What?"

"Get down." I leapt forward, stepping on the left Rover's back and using it as a springboard to land beside Gina. I grabbed the barrel of the Sig Sauer with my right hand and pushed it away from the lawyer. Reaching under the gun with my left hand, I grabbed the stock and yanked it down. The barrel circled up and over and raked Gina's face.

She shrieked and let go. I took a quick step back, flipping the gun over and shooting a Rover in its head.

I swiveled toward the Rover I'd stepped on. It leapt, filling my vision, and time did that weird slo-mo thing. I had enough time to realize I couldn't get off a shot without risk of hitting the lawyer, to see the changing angle of the overhead light glinting off the Rover's metal sides.

Then time returned to normal. The robot hurtled into me and knocked me to the carpet. It grasped the barrel of the Sig in its mouth, clamping down.

"Retrieve," Gina shouted.

But the command came too late. The Sig groaned as the Rover crushed the barrel between its jaws. The dog turned, wrenching it from my grasp. It dropped the wrecked gun at Gina's feet.

The lawyer raised himself off the floor and adjusted his glasses. "Well."

Gina pointed at me. "Attack."

The three Rovers raced toward me. I scrambled to my feet and made for the nearest door. It opened. I bolted into the office and slammed the door.

Inside the office, overhead lights flickered on. Two more doors banged shut outside. I hoped one of those was the lawyer barricading himself in an office.

A Rover slammed into the door. It shuddered, and I jumped a little. I told myself to get a grip.

The office had a desk and chairs and shelves lined with books. Its floor-to-ceiling windows overlooked the parking lot. There was no way to open the windows, and no helpful fire escape for me to climb down even if I could.

The door shuddered, splintering. A metallic nose jammed through the hole in the door. I hurried to the other side of the desk, picked up the phone, and called nine-one-one.

"Nine-one-one, what is your emergency?" a woman asked.

"I'm being attacked by a robot dog."

The dispatcher sighed. "Is this Alice Sommerland?"

"What does that have to—?" *Never mind.* I shouted an address.

A Rover thrust himself through the widening hole in the door. Involuntarily, I stepped back against the window. The metal dog leapt over the desk.

I ducked. The window shattered behind me—safety glass pebbling my back and the wooden floor.

I straightened and stared out the window. Outside, snow was falling more thickly. The Rover lay unmoving beside a Hummer. In the darkening parking lot below, Gina raced toward her car. Another Rover growled behind me.

Thinking is usually a good thing. But sometimes, it just slows you down. I would never admit this to my brother, but there are times you need to leap before you look.

I jumped through the open window and hit the Hummer's roof hard. Its car alarm blared. I'd like to say I tucked and rolled. But my knees buckled of their own accord, and I sort of fell off the SUV and onto the pavement. Miraculously, I landed upright. I swayed, stunned by this unusual spurt of good luck.

Something crunched into the pavement beside me. I flinched and glanced over my shoulder. A Rover lay crumpled onto its side, unmoving. *Ha.*

"So you can't jump." I panted. "Good to know." I sprinted toward Gina. A third metallic thud resounded behind me. The Hummer chirped, and its alarm fell silent.

Gina opened the car door at the same time I threw myself at her, which just goes to show how mad I was. Tackling someone was a rookie move with a high risk of minor but debilitating injuries. We bounced off her open door and fell to the pavement.

I'll spare you the details of our fight. Suffice it to say, it wasn't easy duking it out with someone flailing and clawing. But I finally got Gina in an ankle lock. I held her there until the police arrived.

They surrounded me, guns aimed at my head. "On the ground!" one shouted.

"I am on the ground," I snapped. An ankle lock isn't a particularly dignified position. We were both on the pavement, my arms wrapped around her leg and one foot somewhere I didn't want to think about much. In spite of the guns, I wasn't quite ready to give up my advantage. I was still pretty mad.

"That woman attacked me," Gina said. "She killed my husband. She's crazy."

"Oh no, she's not." Mr. O'Reilly strode toward us. "Gina Levann just tried to kidnap and kill me to get at the draft copy of Mr. Levann's will."

"What he said." I gave Gina's ankle an extra tug, and she winced.

A pair of polished Gucci loafers stopped in front of my nose. "Aw, screw it," Detective Guthrie said. "Arrest them all."

Chapter Thirty-One

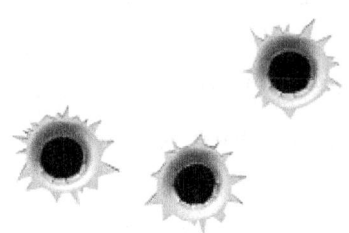

Charlie, Fitch, and I sat in a corner booth at the Sagebrush Café. Cheerful voices rose and fell in the diner. It smelled of burgers and fries and other homey scents. Christmas carols played on the overhead speakers.

I ached. Muscles I'd forgotten I had hurt. Muscles that had no business hurting hurt. This is what came of jumping out of a window without thinking.

"So," Charlie said dully. "That's that."

"You knew it was going to be ugly," Fitch said in a low voice, "no matter who was responsible."

Charlie toyed with his coffee mug. "Yeah. I guess. It's just... It's real now, you know? I never wanted Adan's stupid money," he burst out. "But... Okay, I mean, the Tesla's nice. But that wasn't what this was about."

I glanced out the front window. The blue Tesla sat on the street outside. And it *was* nice. He'd let me drive it earlier.

The skin bunched around my brother's blue eyes. "That wasn't why I wanted to meet Adan."

"I know," I said.

"So what are you going to do?" Fitch asked. "About the will, I mean."

"I don't know," Charlie said. "I'm no saint. I could use the money. But I don't want to have to fight my brother and sister for it. Half brother and sister..." His face squinched up. "Step?"

"Does it matter?" I asked. "Gina killed for her children. The fact that they were adopted didn't enter into it at all. Family's about more than birth."

Charlie met my gaze and smiled. "Yeah."

Warmth flooded my chest, followed by hot shame. I'd said the words. I'd *believed* the words. Mostly. A part of me had doubted them for too long.

The bell over the café's door jangled over the laughter. Shelley strode into the diner wearing a high-collared navy turtleneck and matching slacks. At the counter, Gert swiveled on his barstool. He stared, his eyes narrowing behind his thick spectacles.

"And speaking of which..." I waved to Shelley. I hoped this was a good thing. But good thing or not, it had to happen. "I invited Shelley to join us."

The butler nodded and strode to our table, sliding onto the bench beside me.

"Hi, Shelley," Charlie said. "What do you mean, speaking of which?" he asked me.

I swiveled in the sky-blue booth to face Shelley. "Do you want to tell him, or shall I?"

"I suppose I should," Shelley said. Even though I'd known it had been a fake, it was weird hearing him without his British accent. He rubbed the spot behind his ear. "So, uh..."

"You're not really a butler?" Charlie asked.

Shelley straightened on his seat. "How did you know that?"

"You were a little too perfect," my brother said. "I mean, you were good, don't get me wrong. But I know acting when I see it. And that was really good acting."

"Thanks," Shelley said. "Because I'm an actor by profession."

"No way." Charlie's blue eyes widened with delight. "So am I."

"Yes," Shelley said, "I know." He looked around. "It sounds like you've got a sweet gig at the mystery dinner theater."

"Five nights a week." Charlie frowned. "I missed a few nights what with everything going on though. You should see a show. I'll get you tickets."

"Thanks, but, uh... There's something I should tell you first." Shelley reddened. "So... The thing is..." He cut a sideways look at me. "Adan was my father too. An affair with my mother. Well, obviously with my mother or he wouldn't be my father. She was a waitress in San Benedetto when they met. Things ended badly. When she realized she was pregnant, she decided not to tell him. He'd been taking a break with Gina when he met my mother – or at least, that's what he told her. After he and my mother split up, he married Gina. I wasn't sure if I wanted to tell him who I was, so I took a job with him to check him out."

Charlie blinked. "But that's... That's, uh..."

"So, I guess what I'm saying," Shelley said, "is I'm—"

"I've got another brother?" Charlie slid from the booth. He jerked a stunned-looking Shelley to his feet and gave him a bear hug. "This is amazing!"

I sagged in the booth and exhaled slowly. How could I have been worried? This was Charlie. Of course another brother was a good thing.

He released Shelley and stepped backward. "I wonder if we've got any other family out there?"

Shelley grimaced. "It wouldn't surprise me."

"Do Ary and Adalina know?" Charlie asked.

"Uh... Not yet," he said. "It didn't seem like the right time."

"I want to see them," Charlie said. "But I'm not sure if I'd be welcome. But I think..." He squinched up his face. "I think we need to try, you know? They need family right now."

Lilyanna, in her beekeeper's outfit, walked up to us. "Hi, Charlie," she said, her voice muffled beneath the netted hat. "Is this a bad time?"

"Are you kidding?" Charlie beamed. "I've got another brother. Shelley, this is Lilyanna. She's an actress at the theater too."

Shelley scratched his cheek, his brows drawing downward. "Are you playing a beekeeper?"

"No," she said. "It's for the weight."

Shelley angled his head, the lines on his forehead deepening. "The weight?"

"This seems like a bad time," Lilyanna said. "I'll come back."

"No, no, no," Charlie said. "You're like family. You're... Um..." He turned to the table. "Do you mind if we step away for a couple minutes. Have a sidebar?"

"No problem," Shelley said. "It's a lot to take in."

"That's not it," my brother said. "It's just... We'll be back. Don't go anywhere." He led Lilyanna through the door to the patio. A cold gust of wind blew through the closing door, and I zipped my jacket higher.

"He seems to be taking it well," Shelley said.

"After getting to know Charlie," I said, "are you that surprised?"

He smiled. It made him seem a lot more human. "No, I guess I'm not."

"I take it you never got a chance to let Adan know who you really were," I said.

"No." He bent his head and stared at the tabletop. "No, I didn't. I regret that now." He met my gaze. "And not because of the money."

"Right." Fitch folded his arms and sat back against the sky-blue booth. "You'd need to show there was intent for Adan to include you in the will. If he didn't know about you, there's no intent." His green eyes narrowed. "But I suppose Charlie will share with you."

Shelley stiffened. "That's not why I'm here."

"No," I said lightly. "He's here because I invited him. I thought we should put our cards on the table. There've been enough secrets." And I was sure Charlie *would* share—if there was anything to share. But that was Charlie's business. "Of course, if you hurt my brother, you'd make me very angry."

"She's not the only one," Fitch growled.

Shelley swallowed. "Scout's honor. I'm only here because I lost my chance with Adan. I don't want to make that mistake again. I don't want anything from Charlie."

Gert slid from his barstool and strode to our table. "Who's this?"

"Charlie's brother," I said.

"The artist?"

"Charlie's other brother."

"Whatever," Gert said. "Good job in Hot Springs. The miniature museum is DOA."

"What?" I asked. "How?"

He rocked on his heels. "Let's just say some key investors had second thoughts."

"What did you do?" I asked.

Gert studied his chipped fingernails. "Nothing illegal."

"What did *you* do?" Fitch asked me.

"Nothing," I said, baffled.

"Then what's he talking about?" Fitch said.

"You don't wanna know." Gert strolled out the door, and a chill wind knifed through the diner.

"Do I want to know?" Fitch asked. "Because I'm really curious."

"I don't even think I want to know," I said.

"I have no curiosity whatsoever," Shelley said. "What happened to Charlie?" He twisted in the booth to frown at the closed patio door. "It's freezing out there, and neither of them are wearing jackets. Though I've no idea how warm those beekeeper outfits are."

I rose up in my seat to look out the window. Lilyanna's beekeeper hat tumbled across the patio's concrete floor. Wind blew flecks of snow around the two. It was a pretty good bet they didn't notice, their arms tight around each other in a passionate clinch.

I smiled and turned from the window. "They're fine."

A Hot Springs Murder RPG

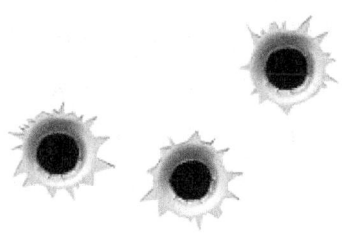

Introduction

A HOT SPRINGS MURDER RPG Game is a mystery role playing game (RPG) based on the book and characters created by Kirsten Weiss in *Big Bucks*. This short mystery is set at an imaginary town in the Sierra Nevadas and is suitable for two to six players but may be adapted for more.

You can download a printable, PDF version of the game HERE: https://bit.ly/BigBucksRPG. The downloadable version includes a printable brochure to help players navigate the town and a worksheet so they can keep track of their life points.

The player most familiar with the game acts as the Mystery Maven, leading the players through the game by reading the game story aloud and playing the roles of non-player characters. The Mystery Maven should review the game before playing and should also track the life points of the players.

Players choose roles to play (see the next page). Each player role has certain advantages and disadvantages when it comes to rolling the die. Players will interview suspects and confront danger. Everyone is encouraged to ham it up—the game's more fun if there's actual role-playing involved! (Players may read this rule sheet).

You will need one 6-sided die to play this game. Any roll *over* a three (i.e. 4-6) is a successful roll. Each character can throw the die once per round, unless there is only one player playing, in which case they get two dice rolls per round.

Interrogations:

When interviewing suspects and witnesses, any roll *over* a 3 (i.e. a 4-6) gleans an answer from the witness or suspect. If a player rolls a six, they get to ask two questions. Players with + charisma may add that number to their die roll during questioning. If there is no more information to be gleaned from an interview, the player(s) who did not have a chance to interview the suspect start play in the next round. Players may keep rolling, taking turns, until all the clues have been exhausted.

Searching for Clues:

When searching for clues in a room or space, a roll **over** a three (i.e. 4-6) gets players one clue. Players with + awareness may add that number to their die roll when searching for clues. If there are no more clues to be gleaned from the location, the player(s) who did not have a chance to search for more clues start play in the next round. Players can keep rolling, taking turns, until all the clues have been exhausted.

Fighting for survival:

Players with + strength may add that number to their die roll when fighting. Any roll over three (i.e. 4-6) is a successful defense. A roll of a three loses a player one life point. A roll of a two loses the player two life points. And a roll of a one loses a character three life points. When life points reach zero, the player is dead.

Rounds:

A "round" is one cycle of die rolls. For example, there are three players in the game plus the Mystery Maven. The players take turns questioning a suspect. After three die rolls (as there are 3 players), one round is completed.

Healing:

Once per round, the doctor can heal one player by rolling the die and adding the number that appears to the player's life points until the player reaches his original life points. I.e. the player's original LPs are six and the player is down to four points; the doctor rolls a five, and the player will be restored to the player's original six LPs. If the doctor rolled a one in the same circumstances, the player would get one LP, bring the player's total to five. During the same round, the doctor may also roll to search for clues or ask an interview question.

The game's afoot!

List of Non-playing Characters:

Armando Alejandro – The victim, a sixty-something jeweler

Adoracion Alejandro – The victim's ex-wife and owner of the Treeline

Bart Berkeley – Owner of Zodiac Boots

Clementine Colorado – Volunteer at the Hot Springs Info Center

Jewel Jones – A jeweler

Hank Hunter – FBI agent

Jan Walken – Manager of the Historic Hot Springs Hotel
Krystal Devons – Manager of Pur Mineral
Melania Mezzes – Art dealer
Snowbird – Fashion designer
Stockley Stanton – Waiter at the Sky High Café

Player Characters

[The Mystery Maven may wish to give a copy of this sheet to the players in advance, but if you do, ask the characters to introduce themselves, telling the other players their name and one or two things about themselves. Players will have more fun if they're able to interact with each other while acting out their roles]

Players will be searching for clues and interviewing suspects. Players will be more successful if they ask open question, which do **not** lead to yes/no answers. Possible open questions include:

- Where were you when…? [time of death]?

- What can you tell me about…?

- Who might have wanted to kill [the victim]?

- Who else should we talk to?

- What else can you tell me?

You may find clues in surprising places (including the brochure), so be sure to explore the areas listed on the brochure after you get it from the Mystery Maven.

To better roleplay your characters, pay attention to the notes in italics at the bottom of the character description. You'll find fun opportunities during the game to let your character quirks shine.

Lennon – Graphic Designer

+2 Awareness

+1 Charisma

Life Points: 6

Lennon has an eye for beauty—whether it's a painting, a well-plated meal, or interior design. Self-employed, Lennon is always on the lookout for a new gig. The merchants of Hot Springs look like excellent clients for Lennon's (web) graphic design services! Favorite phrase: *How is your website working for you?*

Arden – Holistic Healer

Arden can heal one life point for any player once per round **in addition to** Arden's die roll (i.e., the healing doesn't take the place of Arden's die roll).

+1 Charisma

Life Points: 9

As a holistic healer, Arden is excited about trying out the town's healing hot springs and is happy to pay for quality organic food. Favorite phrases: *Americans eat too many chemicals. What's in that?*

Dale - Engineer

+3 Awareness

Life Points: 7

Fiscally conservative Dale is skeptical of this uber-expensive town. Everything seems way overpriced. There's no steak worth two-hundred dollars, and putting gold on a hamburger is just silly. You can't even digest it! Dale is not a risk taker. In fact, Dale is just the opposite. Favorite phrase: *Not worth it.*

Robin - Chef
+1 Awareness

+2 Strength

Life Points: 7

Robin is looking forward to trying all the great food in Hot Springs and getting away from work. In fact, Robin really doesn't want to talk about work at all. This trip is supposed to be an escape. Favorite phrase: *Just relax.*

Blake - Professional Skier
+3 Charisma

Life Points: 6

Blake is an adrenaline junky, and investigating a murder sounds like a thrill ride. Blake is all in, ready to take risks and push the envelope. Favorite phrase: *Let's do it!*

Plot

The Town of Hot Springs, Nevada is a luxury ski resort on the eastern slope of the Sierra Nevada mountain range. The core of the small town is its shopping street, lined with expensive shops and restaurants, as well as the Historic Hot Springs Hotel.

You are a group of friends vacationing together, but you've gotten a little bored. Spas and hikes are wonderful, but you've done it all before. What you need is a little something to spice up your vacation.

Players begin the game relaxing on the outdoor patio of the Sky High Café, watching pedestrians in designer wear amble past and reading about the latest Hot Springs news. [Mystery maven should give the players a copy of the below newspaper article to read]

Sky High Café

On the paving stone patio, waitstaff wheel carts past serving coffee and oxygen from the Swiss Alps

A waiter stops beside your table. "Hi, I'm Stockley, and I'll be your waiter today. What can I get you?"

PLAYERS EACH ROLL TO ASK STOCKLEY QUESTIONS ABOUT THE THEFT. Players with + charisma may add that number to their die roll. Any roll over a 3 gets a clue.

Mood: Nervous. You're an ex-con. An FBI agent blackmailed you into stealing the jewels and leaving them in a secret niche by the Hot Springs. You should probably get out of town, but you want to know what's going on first and make sure you're not going to get railroaded for this.

Objective: Don't get caught.

If Stockley doesn't know the answer, he should simply say, "Above my paygrade."

PLAYERS EACH MAKE ROLLS TO ASK STOCKLEY QUESTIONS. Players with + charisma can add that number to their die roll. Stockley will respond to every die roll over 3.

Clues:
- "I heard about that theft. Every jeweler in Hot Springs went on alert after that happened. Old Armando had a major freakout right outside his shop across the street."

- "I went to the exhibit the day of the theft. If I didn't know any better, I'd think Armando's ex-wife might have had a hand in it the way she was drooling over those old jewels. Her face was pressed right up against the glass."

- "I saw the lady who runs the jewelry store, Jewel, there too. Even though they do more modern stuff, I guess she was looking for some inspiration from the classics, right?"

- "You should check out the hotel. In addition to the jewelry, they've got some great art in the exhibit hall from Melania. They were doing some sort of team-up—medieval jewels and modern art."

- "You can probably find out more about the exhibit at the Information Center."

Since Armando's store is right across the street, you decide to go there next.

Armando Alejandro Originals

A bell chimes softly as you walk into the carpeted store. An elegant crystal chandelier illuminates the brocade wallpaper and gold jewelry glittering beneath the glass cases. You're surprised to see you are the only people in the jewelry shop.

As you walk deeper inside, you see a pair of well-shod feet sticking out from behind one of the jewel cases. You rush around the case to find a man lying dead, blood trickling from the wound on his bald head.

PLAYERS EACH ROLL TO SEARCH THE AREA FOR CLUES. Players with + awareness may add that number to their die roll. Any roll over a 3 gets a clue.

Clues:

- The dead man wears a name tag reading ARMANDO ALEJANDRO.

- You see a statuette of a golden Egyptian god lying on the carpet beside its head. The statuette has the head of a jackal. There appears to be blood on the pedestal.

- A business card lies on the glass case nearest the body. The card reads: *Bart Berkeley, Zodiac Boots.*

- It is now eleven-fifteen AM. The sign in the shop window says the store opened at eleven AM.

- A breeze stirs your hair. You look down a hallway behind a rear counter. A door at the back of the hallway stands open.

- You walk down the hallway and discover it ends at a parking lot.

A tall, well-built man with a gray buzz cut walks through the front door and stops short. "Where's the owner?" he asks sharply.

HANK HUNTER

If a player asks you a question and you know the answer (i.e. it's below), you must answer the question honestly (unless they ask if you're the killer. You can lie about that). Make the players work for it and have fun with the character. Ham it up!

Mood: You are the killer!

Objective: Don't get caught.

If Hank doesn't know the answer, he should simply say, "That's confidential," or "I can't reveal discuss ongoing investigation."

PLAYERS EACH MAKE ROLLS TO ASK HANK QUESTIONS. Players with + charisma can add that number to their die roll. Hank will respond to every die roll over 3.

Clues:

- "I'm Special Agent Hank Hunter, FBI." He shows you his badge.

- "I had some questions for Mr. Alejandro. It looks like I won't be able to ask them now."

- "No, he wasn't a suspect in the jewel theft at the Hot Springs Hotel. I just had some questions."

- "We don't have any leads we can share on the jewel theft."

The agent calls the police, and you're interviewed and then released. You decide to check out nearby Zodiac Boots.

Zodiac Boots

You walk into a sleek store with boots displayed on elegant wooden tables and stands. You notice a hallway at the back of the store. Since Zodiac Boots is only a few shops down and on the same side of the street as Armando Alejando Originals, you deduce that it too leads to the parking lot.

    A smiling silver-haired man in a cowboy hat approaches you. "Howdy. How can I help you today?" He's wearing a nametag that reads BART BERKELEY. You tell him about the shocking death at Armando's.

BART BERKELEY

If a player asks you a question and you know the answer (i.e. it's below), you must answer the question honestly. Make the players work for it and have fun with the character. Ham it up!

Mood: Bart is horrified when he learns about the murder. He just talked to Armando yesterday!

Objective: Learn more about the murder.

If Bart doesn't know the answer, he should simply act shocked and say he has no idea.

PLAYERS EACH MAKE ROLLS TO ASK BART QUESTIONS. Players with + charisma can add that number to their die roll. Bart will respond to every die roll over 3.

Clues:
- "I saw Armando yesterday afternoon outside on the sidewalk. He seemed fine. Well, maybe a little preoccupied. But I didn't think anything of it. We're all small businessowners. There are a lot of things to think about when you own your own business."

- "What with the robbery at the Historic Hotel, I wasn't too surprised to see Armando wearing a gun on his hip, though he didn't normally, not that I can remember."

- "I didn't know him too well. We saw each other at chamber of commerce meetings and such. His wife, Adoracion, was usually there with him, until the divorce last year."

- "Adoracion works as a waitress at the Treeline. It's a great restaurant. You should try it."

- "I went to his shop to special order earrings for my wife. It's our gold anniversary. Last year we went to Spain, and she saw these old earrings dating all the way back to 700 AD. I thought I'd surprise her and have Armando make replicas of them for her as a memory."

- "I left my business card with him last week. He was going to call me when the earrings were done. It was really delicate work, but Armando was a master."

- I opened my boot shop at nine AM this morning and have been here ever since.

You walk outside and hear a gunshot. People scream and run past you. You race in the opposite direction of the crowd and across the street. A man lies in a narrow alley decorated with a Trompe-l'œil scene of a Swiss chateau's garden. Blood stains the front of his white shirt. The man is the waiter you talked to earlier, Stockley. You rush to help him, but he is obviously dead.

The FBI agent races around the corner of the alley, gun raised. "Halt!"

Alarmed, you raise your hands. Local police arrive with robo-dogs. They shoo you away from the body. This time, the questioning takes place at the Hot Springs Police Station. After two hours of grueling interrogation, they let you go.

Players should consult the Hot Springs brochure. Where do you go next?

Treeline

It's mid-afternoon, and the elegant restaurant with dark-paneled woods, modern, hanging lights, and leather chairs is uncrowded. The hostess seats you at a table. "You can't go wrong with our grass-fed beef," she says cheerfully.

A slim waitress in a little black dress approaches your table. She looks to be in her mid-fifties, and gray streaks her dark hair, bound in a long braid. "Good afternoon," the waitress says. "I am Adoracion, your server for the day. May I start you with something to drink?"

Do you order drinks? [If they do, each player who orders a drink gets +1 charisma for the next round]

ADORACION ALEJANDRO

If a player asks you a question and you know the answer (i.e. it's below), you must answer the question honestly. Make the players work for it and have fun with the character. Ham it up!

Mood: Adoracion is horrified and worried. Word has spread through town about the murders. She went through a bitter divorce and is worried she may be a suspect in her ex-husband's death.

Objective: Don't get arrested and learn what the players know.

If Adoracion doesn't know the answer, she should say, "I don't know," and ask the players the same question they just asked her.

PLAYERS EACH MAKE ROLLS TO ASK ADORACION QUESTIONS. Players with + charisma can add that number to their die roll. She will respond to every die roll over 3.

Clues:

- "I'm not surprised someone killed him. My ex-husband was an arrogant man. He would never even let me inside his workshop when he was making jewelry. And he did not make life easy for that new jeweler who moved onto the street last year. Jewel was so angry when she learned he was telling customers her designs were uninspired, post-modernist trash."

- "Our divorce was difficult. How could it have been easy? I used to work there, selling the jewelry he made, and now... here I am." [She motions around the restaurant] "But as you see, I am a survivor."

- "Once I stopped working at Armando's, I'm afraid he had to work late managing both the front of the shop and designing jewelry."

- "My husband went to the Sky High Café every weekday for coffee. It was right across the street from his jewelry store, after all. But I do not know of any connection between him and that poor waiter, Stockley. I can't believe someone would kill that waiter. Perhaps Stockley saw something he should not have, and the man who killed my ex-husband killed him?"

- "I knew Stockley from the Sky High Café. He was always pleasant and polite. But I didn't know him well."

- "The last time I saw my husband was yesterday afternoon. He was leaving the Snowbird. Such a vain man. As if a man his age needs designer clothes."

- "I got to work this morning at ten-thirty AM. I came straight from home."

- "Yes, I was at the Hot Springs Hotel the day of the theft, but I left well before the crime occurred. What a shocking crime."

Players should consult the brochure and decide where to go next.

Historic Hot Springs Hotel

As you approach the three-story stone building that is the Historic Hot Springs Hotel, an elaborate wall clock chimes the hour. A little wooden man wheels from the tiny doors in the clock and blows a trumpet. The little man vanishes behind the closing doors, and you walk inside the hotel.

A massive antler chandelier hangs from the ceiling. You make your way to the front desk, of polished wood. A bearded man in a forest-green vest smiles politely. His nametag reads: IAN WALKEN, MANAGER. "How can I help you?" he asks.

You ask to see the jewels. He explains you're in luck. The jewelry exhibit has just reopened. He offers to take you there, and you accept.

He takes you to a high-ceilinged room with dark-paned walls. Gold jewelry glitters beneath glass-encased pedestals on the crimson carpet. Above the modern paintings on the walls, security cameras scan the room.

IAN WALKEN

If a player asks you a question and you know the answer (i.e. it's below), you must answer the question honestly. Make the players work for it and have fun with the character. Ham it up!

Mood: The recovery of the stolen jewels was initially a cause for celebration. But the hotel owners are now looking very carefully at Ian's security precautions and asking how it could have been stolen in the first place. Ian's initial relief has now morphed into a low, persistent anxiety. And he doesn't want to talk to reporters.

Objective: Don't get fired, and don't talk to reporters.

If Ian doesn't know the answer, he should ask, "Are you reporters? I don't want to talk to reporters." Or: "Are you *sure* you're not reporters?"

PLAYERS EACH MAKE ROLLS TO ASK IAN QUESTIONS. Players with + charisma can add that number to their die roll. Ian will respond to every die roll over 3.

Clues:
- "It was an inside job. Someone turned the security system off remotely when the theft occurred. It would have taken someone very knowledgeable about computers or who knew the security system well to do it. All our security staff were interviewed by the FBI."

- "I assure you, Agent Hunter is taking this very seriously. He was afraid this would happen and advised our team, helping us increase security. I think he feels this was a personal failure."

- "Apparently, there've been a string of similar thefts at private museums around the country. Agent Hunter is part of the FBI's task force investigating the crimes. I don't know why he thought something might happen here. But he was right."

- "I'm afraid I can't tell you all the people who came to view the jewels. I just don't know, and Agent Hunter has all the security video now, for what that's worth."

- "Melania was here thirty minutes after the theft, demanding her paintings be removed from the walls. Of course we couldn't then, it was a crime scene. But after the theft, so many tourists came to view the crime scene, the paintings stayed. Everyone thinks they're a detective."

- "I got to the hotel today about thirty minutes before you arrived here. I came straight from home after sleeping in. It's been a stressful few weeks."

- "The FBI agent authenticated the jewels upon their recovery. He's a specialist."

A customer approaches him, and Jan turns from you to help the newcomer.

Players should consult the brochure and decide where to go next.

Information Center

The Information Center is in an old-west brick building just off the main shopping street. Inside, you walk past neat racks filled with brochures and thin travel magazines. A gray-haired woman in an old-west costume smiles. "Howdy! I'm Clementine Colorado. How can I help you today?"

How do you respond?

CLEMENTINE COLORADO

If a player asks you a question and you know the answer (i.e. it's below), you must answer the question honestly. Make the players work for it and have fun with the character. Ham it up!

Mood: Cheerful. You love your job sharing information about The Town of Hot Springs. And you will remind any tourist who makes the mistake that it's THE TOWN OF Hot Springs, and not just Hot Springs.

Objective: Be as helpful as possible.

If Clementine doesn't know the answer, she should tell the players she doesn't know but will be happy to look it up and get to them later.

PLAYERS EACH MAKE ROLLS TO ASK CLEMENTINE QUESTIONS. Players with + charisma can add that number to their die roll. Clementine will respond to every die roll over 3.

Clues:
- "Armando Alejandro Originals has been making and selling fine jewelry in The Town of Hot Springs for nearly thirty years. I can't believe he's gone."

- "Poor Stockley. We tried so hard, but he never had a chance. You do know that the Sky High Café hires the formerly incarcerated? It's wonderful of them. We in The Town of Hot Springs believe it's important to give back, and to support our most challenged community members."

- "Such a nice young man. I believe Stockley was arrested for... Oh, my. He was a jewel thief. You don't think he had anything to do with the theft at the Hot Springs Historical Hotel, do you? I'm sure that nice FBI agent will figure it out."

- "Melania has The Town of Hot Springs's premier collection of modern art. I'm *sure* the rumors that her gallery is in financial trouble aren't true."

- "Have you been to Treeline yet? Its Michelin rated! And their waitstaff is the best in Nevada. They depend on tips, you know, so be sure to be generous. Poor Adoracion. That's Armando's ex-wife. She works there, you know. If you ask me, she had a terrible divorce lawyer... forced to work as a waitress when Armando was making all that money... Well. I shouldn't gossip. Try the Treeline!"

- "If you're not staying at the Historic Hot Springs Hotel, be sure to try the hot springs at Pur Mineral. The manager there, Krystal, is... Oh, dear. Poor thing. She was dating young Stockley. She must be devastated."

- "You can find the finest fashions at Snowbird. Snowbird is the designer, and she's often right there in the shop modeling her latest designs... Oh, dear. Poor thing. She was dating Armando. I don't know how she'll go on."

- "If you're looking for original jewelry, try Jewel. It's more modern than Armando's, but some people like that. Now she'll be the only jeweler on our main shopping street."

- "The medieval jewelry exhibit started four weeks ago and was scheduled to end next week. You're in luck. They returned the jewelry to the exhibit just yesterday. That FBI agent must be closing in on the thief."

- "I got to work today at eleven AM. I was doing some shopping before then. I wish I had seen something so I could help the police."

Players should consult the brochure and decide where to go next.

Melania Gallery

A modern metal sculpture of a horse stands outside the picture windows of the art gallery. You stroll inside a well-lit, wide open space. Splashes of modern art hang upon the blond-wood walls. A tall, elegant blonde approaches you. "Welcome," she says. "I am Melania. If you'd like any information about the art, please don't hesitate to ask."

MELANIA MEZZES

If a player asks you a question and you know the answer (i.e. it's below), you must answer the question honestly. Make the players work for it and have fun with the character. Ham it up!

Mood: She's heard about the murders and is shocked and saddened, but still relieved none of her art was stolen at the jewelry exhibit.

Objective: Sell art.

If Melania doesn't know the answer, she should tell the players she has no idea. It's all so shocking!

PLAYERS EACH MAKE ROLLS TO ASK MELANIA QUESTIONS. Players with + charisma can add that number to their die roll. Melania will respond to every die roll over 3.

Clues:

- "I still can't believe Armando is dead. He was a major talent in the field of applied arts, by which I mean jewelry, of course."

- "I don't know anything about the theft at the hotel. Of course I hurried over there as soon as I heard about it to see if any of the paintings had been stolen or damaged. Fortunately, they had not been."

- "I usually went to the exhibit at the hotel every morning before opening to ensure all was well with our part of the exhibit. The paintings are remarkable works of modern art."

- "I'm shocked the theft happened at all. That FBI agent was there from the planning stages, ensuring everything was secure. I believe he appreciated fine jewelry as well. I saw him at Armando's shop several times before the theft."

- "We'd been planning the joint exhibit for months—the juxtaposition of modern and medieval. It was a triumph. I'm relieved of course that they were able to retrieve the jewels, even if the joint exhibit has effectively ended."

- "I opened the gallery at ten o'clock this morning and came straight from home. I ate lunch here."

A customer wanders into the gallery, and Melania turns her attention to the newcomer. Where would you like to go next?
Players should consult the brochure and decide where to go next.

Pur Mineral

You enter a reception area with a curving wooden desk, gray stone walls, and slate flooring. A woman in a charcoal-colored smock looks up from her computer. Her eyes are bloodshot, and her cheeks splotchy. The tag on her smock reads: MANAGER, KRYSTAL DEVONS. "Hello," she says. "Do you have a reservation?"

KRYSTAL DEVONS

If a player asks you a question and you know the answer (i.e. it's below), you must answer the question honestly. Make the players work for it and have fun with the character. Ham it up!

Mood: She's heard about the murders and is hurting over the loss of her boyfriend, Stockley.

Objective: Stay outwardly calm.

If Krystal doesn't know the answer, she should tell the players she doesn't know.

PLAYERS EACH MAKE ROLLS TO ASK KRYSTAL QUESTIONS. Players with + charisma can add that number to their die roll. Krystal will respond to every die roll over 3.

Clues:

- "Stockley was an amazing man, a reformed jewel thief. I know what people are saying around town about him, but he wasn't involved in the theft at the hotel."

- "I've been working here since nine AM this morning." A woman wearing the Pur Mineral charcoal smock walks into the room and smiles. "Krystal was here with me the whole time. We haven't even had a chance to take a lunch break."

- "Stockley was acting differently the last few weeks. He was tense and unhappy, like he had something on his mind. I thought he was planning to break up with me, but he told me he just didn't like seeing that FBI agent again."

- "Agent Hunter was the one who arrested Stockley five years ago in Vegas. Stockley told me the agent wasn't happy Stockley had gotten out early on good behavior."

- "After the jewel theft at the Historic Hot Springs Hotel, Stockley seemed more relaxed. Lighter. Like he didn't have a care in the world. I thought everything was okay with him, with us, and then someone killed him. I can't believe he's gone."

Players should consult the brochure and decide where to go next.

Snowbird Boutique

You walk inside an elegant clothing boutique that smells like vanilla and pine. Candles flicker on the marble counter. A tall, silver-haired woman in a little black dress walks silently toward you across the wood floor and smiles somberly. "Welcome. I'm Snowbird. How may I help you?"

SNOWBIRD

If a player asks you a question and you know the answer (i.e. it's below), you must answer the question honestly. Make the players work for it and have fun with the character. Ham it up!

Mood: She's heard about the murders and is mourning the loss of her boyfriend, Armando.

Objective:

If Snowbird doesn't know the answer, she should say she doesn't know, she just can't think of anything now that Armando's gone.

PLAYERS EACH MAKE ROLLS TO ASK SNOWBIRD QUESTIONS. Players with + charisma can add that number to their die roll. Snowbird will respond to every die roll over 3.

Clues:
- "I have no idea who would have wanted Armando dead. Though his ex-wife really hated him. She thought he cheated her in the divorce."

- "I've been working here at the boutique since nine o'clock this morning." Another woman wearing a little black dress enters from a back room. "Amber was working here with me the whole time," she finishes.

- "Armando was a huge fan of spy thrillers and always wanted to be in a caper. The fact that he was killed, murdered…" [She shakes her head and sniffs]. "I don't know if he would have been thrilled or horrified."

- "Armando was in a good mood the last several months—excited even. He wouldn't tell me why, but I got the feeling he was excited about a project. But something changed yesterday. I don't know what it was. He wouldn't tell me."

- "Armando left this briefcase with me, but I can't figure out the combination lock."

PLAYERS ROLL TO GUESS THE COMBINATION. A ROLL OF A 5 OR 6 WILL GET THEM THE CODE: 3-2-1.

Inside the briefcase you find jewelry designs and a business card for FBI agent Hank Hunter. One of the designs catches your eye.

The FBI agent, Hank Hunter, strides into the boutique and sees you going through the briefcase. "Is that Armando Alejandro's briefcase. That's evidence!" He takes the briefcase and its contents. "You're lucky I don't arrest all of you for interfering in an investigation." You sputter an apology and hurry away before he does decide to arrest you.

Players should consult the brochure and decide where to go next.

Jewel

You enter a jewelry store. Chunky modern jewelry is displayed behind glass on river rocks and decorates tall stone statues that look like those on Easter Island. A woman in white silk stands behind the counter talking to a slender young man in all black. She tosses her long brown hair and smiles. "I'm Jewel Jones. What are you looking for today?"

JEWEL JONES

If a player asks you a question and you know the answer (i.e. it's below), you must answer the question honestly. Make the players work for it and have fun with the character. Ham it up!

Mood: She's heard about the murders and is shocked something like this could happen in a place like The Town of Hot Springs. But she was no fan of Armando, who was constantly denigrating her modern designs.

Objective: Sell jewelry.

If Jewel doesn't know the answer, she should tell the players he doesn't know

PLAYERS EACH MAKE ROLLS TO ASK JEWEL QUESTIONS. Players with + charisma can add that number to their die roll. Jewel will respond to every die roll over 3.

Clues:

- "Armando might not have been the easiest person to get along with, but I can't believe anyone wanted Armando dead, and I most certainly did not."

- "He was a jewelry snob. He hated modern designs. Granted not everything modern is good, but neither is everything old. He was obsessed with medieval jewelry. So obsessed I saw him at that jewelry exhibit again yesterday. He was there for the exhibit's opening too. I don't know what he expected to see the second time around."

- "Personally, I think original jewelry is better than copies. Armando made copies. Period."

- "Tom and I opened my store at ten o'clock this morning, and I've been here ever since." She motions to the young man in black. "We ordered lunch in, like we do every day." The young man nods glumly. "So I'm afraid we didn't see anything," she continues. "Though we did hear the gunshots. Terrible. Just terrible."

- "I barely knew that poor waiter. He sold me coffee on occasion, but that was all."

Players should consult the brochure and decide where to go next.

Whodunit?

You go to the Historic Doyle Hotel. In a private part of the garden beside a healing spring, you discuss what you've learned. You decide you've gathered enough information. It's time to go to the Hot Springs police with what you know.
Whodunit?
The players should vote now on who killed Armando Alejandro and Stockley Stanton.

Concluding the Mystery

Agent Hank Hunter emerges from behind a tree. He aims a gun at you. "It looks like a falling out among thieves. Or it will look like one when I've finished, and you're all dead."
PLAYERS ROLL TO STALL BY ASKING QUESTIONS. EACH ROLL OVER THREE GETS AN ANSWER. Players with +charisma may add that number to their roll.
- "I got the idea when I was working a museum robbery. The thieves had stolen fake jewels, and I realized I had the perfect opportunity to do my own substitutions under cover of assisting with museum security."
- "When I discovered Stockley, an ex-jewel thief living

right here in Hot Springs, I knew I had the perfect patsy."

- "I told that fool Armando that I needed replicas of the jewelry at the exhibit to catch a thief with. He assumed it was the replicas that were stolen. But I forced Stockley to steal the real gems, and then I pretended to find the replicas in order to put a lid on the investigation and take credit for my genius detective work. I replaced the real ones with the replicas. I've got a buyer in Hong Kong waiting to take the real pieces off my hands."

- "But Armando had to go back to look at the jewels after the theft. He discovered his fakes were there and called to ask. I told him we'd decided to keep the fakes out for the rest of the exhibit. But I couldn't risk him blabbing."

- "I was waiting for Armando in the back parking lot to his shop when he arrived. I went inside with him and waited until he unlocked the front door. Then I killed him and left out the rear."

- "I saw you bunch go in the front of Armando's shop and decided to let you discover the body for me."

- "Once I killed Armando, it was only a matter of time before that weasel Stockley panicked. I told him to meet me in the alley so we could figure things out, and I shot him."

You rush the FBI agent.

PLAYERS GET THREE ROLLS EACH TO AVOID GETTING SHOT. Anything totaling over six is a success. Players with + strength may add that number to their roll. If the players roll a number under three, they deduct that number from their Life Points. If Life Points reach zero, the PLAYER dies.

You disable the FBI agent. Hotel guards, alerted by the gunshots, race into the garden.

"They assaulted me," Agent Hunter shouts. "Grab them."

ONE PLAYER GETS TWO ROLLS TO CONVINCE THE GUARDS THAT THE AGENT IS THE KILLER. Anything totaling over six is a success. Players with + charisma may add that number to their roll (so choose your rolling player wisely).

You explain what happened. The police take you to the station to make a statement. Embarrassed, the FBI hushes the whole thing up, but you know you are heroes.

More Kirsten Weiss

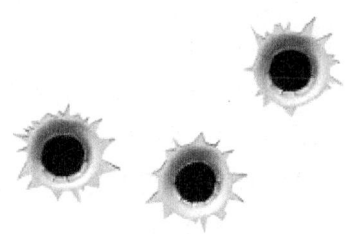

THE PERFECTLY PROPER PARANORMAL Museum Mysteries

When highflying Maddie Kosloski is railroaded into managing her small-town's paranormal museum, she tells herself it's only temporary... until a corpse in the museum embroils her in murders past and present.

If you love quirky characters and cats with attitude, you'll love this laugh-out-loud cozy mystery series with a light paranormal twist. It's perfect for fans of Jana DeLeon, Laura Childs, and Juliet Blackwell. Start with book 1, *The Perfectly Proper Paranormal Museum*, and experience these charming wine-country whodunits today.

The Tea & Tarot Cozy Mysteries

Welcome to Beanblossom's Tea and Tarot, where each and every cozy mystery brews up hilarious trouble.

Abigail Beanblossom's dream of owning a tearoom is about to come true. She's got the lease, the start-up funds, and the recipes. But Abigail's out of a tearoom and into hot water when her realtor turns out to be a conman... and then turns up dead.

Take a whimsical journey with Abigail and her partner Hyperion through the seaside town of San Borromeo (patron saint of heartburn sufferers). And be sure to check out the easy tearoom recipes in the back of each book! Start the adventure with book 1, *Steeped in Murder*.

The Wits' End Cozy Mysteries

Cozy mysteries that are out of this world...

Running the best little UFO-themed B&B in the Sierras takes organization, breakfasting chops, and a talent for turning up trouble.

The truth is out there... Way out there in these hilarious whodunits. Start the series and beam up book 1, *At Wits' End*, today!

Pie Town Cozy Mysteries

When Val followed her fiancé to coastal San Nicholas, she had ambitions of starting a new life and a pie shop. One broken engagement later, at least her dream of opening a pie shop has come true.... Until one of her regulars keels over at the counter.

Welcome to Pie Town, where Val and pie-crust specialist Charlene are baking up hilarious trouble. Start this laugh-out-loud cozy mystery series with book 1, *The Quiche and the Dead*.

A Big Murder Mystery Series

Small Town. Big Murder.

The number one secret to my success as a bodyguard? Staying under the radar. But when a wildly public disaster blew up my career and reputation, it turned my perfect, solitary life upside down.

I thought my tiny hometown of Nowhere would be the ideal out-of-the-way refuge to wait out the media storm.

It wasn't.

My little brother had moved into a treehouse. The obscure mountain town had decided to attract tourists with the world's largest collection of big things... Yes, Nowhere now has the world's largest pizza cutter. And lawn flamingo. And ball of yarn...

And then I stumbled over a dead body.

All the evidence points to my brother being the bad guy. I may have been out of his life for a while—okay, five years—but I know he's no killer. Can I clear my brother before he becomes Nowhere's next Big Fatality?

A fast-paced and funny cozy mystery series, start with Big Shot.

The Doyle Witch Mysteries

In a mountain town where magic lies hidden in its foundations and forests, three witchy sisters must master their powers and shatter a curse before it destroys them and the home they love.

This thrilling witch mystery series is perfect for fans of Annabel Chase, Adele Abbot, and Amanda Lee. If you love stories rich with packed with magic, mystery, and murder, you'll love the Witches of Doyle. Follow the magic with the Doyle Witch trilogy, starting with book 1, *Bound*.

The Riga Hayworth Paranormal Mysteries

Her gargoyle's got an attitude.

Her magic's on the blink.

Alchemy might be the cure... if Riga can survive long enough to puzzle out its mysteries.

All Riga wants is to solve her own personal mystery—how to rebuild her magical life. But her new talent for unearthing murder keeps getting in the way...

If you're looking for a magical page-turner with a complicated, 40-something heroine, read the paranormal mystery series that fans of Patricia Briggs and Ilona Andrews call AMAZING! Start your next adventure with book 1, *The Alchemical Detective*.

Sensibility Grey Steampunk Suspense

California Territory, 1848.

Steam-powered technology is still in its infancy.

Gold has been discovered, emptying the village of San Francisco of its male population.

And newly arrived immigrant, Englishwoman Sensibility Grey, is alone.

The territory may hold more dangers than Sensibility can manage. Pursued by government agents and a secret society, Sensibility must decipher her father's clockwork secrets, before time runs out.

If you love over-the-top characters, twisty mysteries, and complicated heroines, you'll love the Sensibility Grey series of steampunk suspense. Start this steampunk adventure with book 1, *Steam and Sensibility*.

Get Kirsten's Mobile App

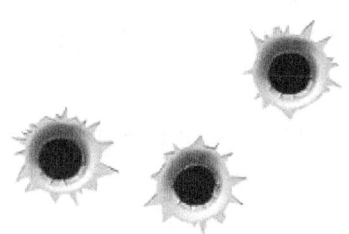

Keep up with the latest book news, and get free short stories, scone recipes and more by downloading Kirsten's mobile app.
Just click HERE to get started or use the QR code below. Or make sure you're on Kirsten's email list to get your free copy of the Tea & Tarot mystery, *Fortune Favors the Grave*. You can do that here: KirstenWeiss.com or use the QR code below:

About the Author

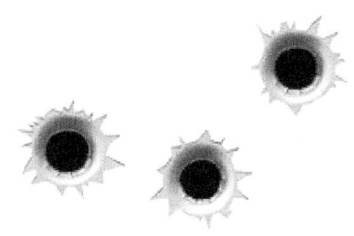

I write laugh-out-loud, page-turning mysteries for people who want to escape with real, complex, and flawed but likable characters. If there's magic in the story, it must work consistently within the world's rules and be based in history or the reality of current magical practices.

I'm best known for my cozy mystery and witch mystery novels, though I've written some steampunk mystery as well. So if you like funny, action-packed mysteries with complicated heroines, just turn the page...

Learn more, grab my **free app**, or sign up for my **newsletter** for exclusive stories and book updates. I also have a read-and-review tea via **Booksprout** and is looking for honest and thoughtful reviews! If you're interested, download the **Booksprout app**, follow me on Booksprout, and opt-in for email notifications.

Connect with Kirsten

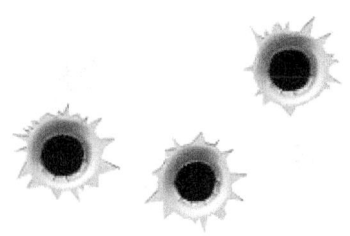

You can download my free app here:
https://kirstenweissbooks.beezer.com
Or sign up for my newsletter and get a special digital prize pack for joining, including an exclusive Tea & Tarot novella, *Fortune Favors the Grave.*
https://kirstenweiss.com
Or maybe you'd like to chat with other whimsical mystery fans? Come join Kirsten's reader page on Facebook:
https://www.facebook.com/kirsten.weiss
Or... sign up for my read and review team on Booksprout:
https://booksprout.co/author/8142/kirsten-weiss

Made in the USA
Middletown, DE
27 April 2023